Watch out for that Boomer Generation ...

No telling what they will get up to!

Samantha, the new Mrs. Jordan Campbell is taking her best friend, Rhonda Sayles—femme fatale—to the Annual Arts Festival to help her with promoting her charity. She should have known that when she asked her pal to "Man the booth" she would take it much too literally!

There must be something in the festival air, or the charming, waterfront town that has couples thinking of romance—but surely there is another term to describe what Rhonda has a case of...?

But trouble is brewing under all the gaiety, events, and charming seaside scenery that has Sam's prosecutor husband extremely distracted and uneasy.

What are the odds that a guy named Peter Potter would actually become a ... Potter?

Rhonda plans to do a thorough, in depth, and very personal investigation to check him out.

If that "Call me Jake" guy will get out of her face.

Beware of Boomer Romances

Guilty Plot: A Beware of Boomer Romance (1)

An Arts and Crafts AfFair: A Beware of Boomer Romance (2)

I Do Knot: A Beware of Boomer Romance (3)* future

National Park Road Series

Buffalo Road: A Yellowstone Park Love Story (1)

Going to the Sun Road: A Glacier Park Love Story (2)

Road to Ancient Mazama: A Crater Lake Park Love Story (3)* future

An Arts and Crafts AffAIR

An Arts and Crafts AFFAIR

a Beware of Boomer Romance

Bett Bone

b.c.
edmonds, washington

Bett Bone

Copyright

Published in the U.S. by Bettina Carter, Edmonds, WA 98026 BettinaCarter.com

ISBN 13:978-0-9983576-8-3 (trade paperback)

ISBN 13:978-0-9983576-9-0 (eBook-Kindle)

Library of Congress Control Number: 2019901759

Product of the United States of America

dedication

For my parents who brought us
to Western Washington
and showed us its wonders,
from the sea stacks off the
Pacific Coast near Taholah, to the crisp
alpine streams & huckleberry picking in the
Cascade Mountains,
on numerous ferry rides, hikes, picnics,
camping trips and the Sunday scenic drives
where we would harmonize, singing in the car
all the way home
— to Edmonds.

Prologue—fall of prior year

Outside of the large number of law enforcers—and even a few enforcees (the formerly detained)—attending the event, it shared a rather common element with most weddings: invitations and guest gifts, lovely dresses and tuxes for attendants, cloth-draped tables and hors d'oeuvres, flowers fragrant and champagne bubbly, topped off with an artful wedding cake. All were present, but they were not *the key* common element.

What was most un-unique about this wedding was that it started out with a small intimate guest list, then grew, and grew, seemingly beyond the control, or initial desire, of the bride and groom.

Particularly the groom, a well-known and respected professional man. He had no relatives and his former friends and peers, of his younger years, had stabbed him in the back, through the heart ... with a wife. His! A poorly chosen first, and now longtime ex-wife. So he expected and wanted to keep this love true, this ceremony special ... and, naturally, all to himself!

His lovely and deeply loved new bride had a close and sizeable network of parents, grown children, their loves, and numerous and fiercely loyal friends. The groom could hardly wait to be adopted into this magic caring circle. They were the family and friends he had always wanted. He welcomed them.

But it turned out his bride had an even larger caring and sharing heart than even he had expected.

While he never thought (or wished) to invite his professional acquaintances to this special private event, his bride feared they'd feel hurt and left out.

"They just want to share our happiness, sweetheart."

That, of course, is what he didn't want this time—to share.

But while the groom cringed each time a colleague asked expectantly on what day, did he say, the wedding was? (He hadn't) Next thing he knew, his sweet Samantha, his tender hearted bride, was thoughtfully adding yet another name to the damn list.

So when the groom stood at the end to toast the woman he had found, treasuring the feel of calling her "wife" for the very first time, only those in the small original circle of desired guests would know, with depth, what was meant when he said the words...

"To my beautiful, most deeply loved, to my darling wife..."

Jordan Campbell tipped his champagne glass and adoring silver eyes toward her.

"Who freed me from prison and released my chains. I owe you, I give you, I pledge you, all my love, and all my life."

"What did he just say?" Asked the common element, that friendly crowd, barely welcome and befuddled.

"That makes no sense!" they exclaimed. Others tittered behind their hands and laughed.

"He must have had too much champagne!" They gasped.

The groom *was* The Prosecutor, after all!

It was the bride that had been freed from jail.

Wasn't it?

Yes, agreed the law enforcees, adding that was where they had met the lovely bride. Much to their dismay, most owed those extended vacations to the groom. They had met him much earlier —in the courtroom!

The bride's best friend and attendant was another mature and beautiful woman, but that was where the similarity between the blushing bride and her bold, never-known-to-blush-in-her-life friend ended. Ms. Rhonda Sayles wore a high necked satin sheath which, from the front, seemed eminently appropriate and modest for the occasion. But for the men that stared at her back throughout the ceremony, well ... they could not focus on a word, though visions of post-ceremony evening activities may have danced through their heads.

The reaction was ageless. Married male or not, young man or

old, they twitched, pulled at suddenly too tight collars, and shifted about in chairs trying to keep their minds, eyes, and etc., from reacting to that still lush hourglass form in a back bared-to-the-waist almost meeting the slit up the seam of her narrow, shimmering dress. A slit that seemed to rise much higher than a woman's long shapely legs could possibly rise, surely!

All in all, the Campbell's wedding turned out to be a most uncommon event after all—at least for some of the spectators.

Chapter one

" **A** aargh!"

The harsh sound could hardly seem to have come from the petite blonde, but she was of the boomer generation, raised by that famous cartoon puppy that knew how to properly express extreme anguish. So Samantha Campbell howled when her computer hung for the third time that morning.

Stabbing fruitlessly at keys, Sam muttered madly to herself.

It would have been one thing if her computer had locked her out months ago. *But, no!* The miserable hi-tech box waited for her to put in a few thousand woman-hours of labor, feeding it all her inspirations *first*, before stealing and scrambling it all, and not letting her have it back!

Ever? Sam scowled. Then panic began to vie with anger. *Never?* That better not be. Or she was going to hurt … *something!*

Tipping back in her home office chair, she sucked in a huge, hopefully calming, breath, then blew it out in a gust. Rumpling both hands through long silvered-gold tresses, she leaned forward and flexed her fingers. A difficult trick when she preferred to keep her fingers crossed.

Slowly, fearfully, she tried to recover her novel, step by careful step. She made it past the initial icons, all opening now as they should, found her folder, highlighted the file she needed ... and it opened!

Yes! She rushed to hit print to get a hard copy quickly while she had the chance. Wait. No! What was this?

Instead of the box asking how many and which pages to print, she got one that stated in no uncertain terms:

"You Have Performed An ILLEGAL OPERATION and Will Be Shut Down Now. Data Will Be Lost."

"Well, ex-c-uuse me ...," Sam started to snarl when, poof! Past tense. Screen black. Data gone!

Sam blinked, stared at the blankness, blinked again, blank again. A queasy panic lurched in her throat. Shoving the laptop back, she buried her head in her arms on the desk and begged.

"Please, benevolent Computer God, just give me one hard copy of all my work. That's all I ask. Beg! I'll retype it all. Really, I won't mind. Just give it back. Please...pretty please? It can't be gone forever?"

Getting no reply, she peeked an eye up over her arm. The screen just sat there, cold and unforgiving and blank.

Crap! Sam sat up abruptly.

Sad at first, now she was mad.

"ILLEGAL OPERATION? I could have used that a year ago!"

If she had only known it was this simple, when seeking a harmless crime to get in jail. Glaring at the laptop, she shook an accusing finger at it.

"Well! That really tops it. First you steal my work, then you mock me! You miserable m-m-m-machine!"

And with that tongue lashing, Sam stalked out of the room.

Wait until my husband gets home, she silently threatened. He would know what to do. He would have a thing or two to say to that ...that...THIEF!

Muttering every vile curse that she knew, repeating herself, frustrated she only knew two, Sam headed to the kitchen to check the fridge to see what she had to prepare for dinner tonight. She was ready to deal with some lower-tech appliances. Ones that did not have the ability to talk back to her, yet. She ignored the microwave, still annoyed at the way it started dinging at her again that morning just because she hadn't run to grab her reheated coffee.

One more sassy machine today, and she might just commit serial machine murders. Most likely another illegal operation.

Maybe Jordan would get home before she went on a rampage.

She hoped he would know how to fix things, or where to take it to get all her months of creative work back from that...robber machine!

He'd do it for her if he could, and he wouldn't even tell her it was her own fault for not having saved multiple backups. Sam sighed, he was such a sweetie!

If she hadn't been on such a creative roll the last few months, she would have printed and backed up her work. Maybe. The irony was that when she sat for hours uninspired, with little to write, she saved and printed out every single paragraph or sentence she was able to squeeze out, filling time while she sat staring with reluctant brain cells.

Sam decided right then that she would go back to her old methods. She preferred to write with a good old pen and notepads anyway, before she had gotten out of jail to find Jordan had a brand new laptop waiting for her.

So thoughtful. What a guy she had gotten in that bargain!

And he thought he was the lucky one.

Sam was crazy about her husband and not shy about telling him, or the world, so. This fall would be their first wedding anniversary! She sighed at the sentimental thought.

Well, lucky in love ... so what if the computer was a thief? Couldn't have it all. Just the best part of it Sam decided with a smile, feeling better.

Deciding not to try using Jordan's home computer for work, afraid her touch might kill it also, she planned to use her unexpected spare time to fix something really yummy for his dinner. Let the guy know he was appreciated.

Before she whined for his computer help.

Besides, Sam would be busy the end of this week with a booth at the Art's Festival, so she better spoil her man now.

Jordan Campbell was a revered and distinguished prosecutor. He was dedicated. He was also so handsome that woman unashamedly chased after him and fell at his feet.

You can imagine how he reacted to that!

He hated it!

He was also the man that used to hate to come home to his cold, empty kitchen. But when he stepped in from the garage that night, the first sight he saw was a very womanly and shapely derriere bent over his kitchen sink. He just couldn't keep himself from lighting up with a grin at the sight of his sweet Sam.

Though ..., was that growling he heard?

"Hey, doll, how was your day?" Jordan set his briefcase on the counter and leaned over the sink to give Sam a big smooch on the check.

"Great!" The dazzling smile she flashed over her shoulder made him want to turn the water and stove off and drag her to the couch to play.

Then her smile shut off suddenly, and a frown creased her forehead, as she remembered something.

"Well, ah...actually, my computer crashed earlier and ate two months of work I didn't have printed out, but...," the smile came back, "I'm glad you're home! I made pot roast and brownies for dessert!" She bragged, grinning at him.

"I can smell them. It smells terrific in here, but," he gave her a teasing smile and wiggled his eyebrows, adding, "I do still get my usual dessert, don't I?"

Sam felt warmth flow into her from all directions. A blush stole up her fair cheeks at the playful innuendo, along with a pleasurable tingle. Her heart expanded, and her brown eyes glowed for sheer love of this man. Amazed anew at the total happiness she had found so unexpectedly at this late time in her life, when she hadn't even been seeking it.

In her late fifties, (okay, she'd been fifty-nine for several years) with two wonderful grown children, it amazed her to think she had someone who made her feel like this. As giddy as a teen sometimes, like a lushly desirable woman at others, and always warmed, surrounded, and filled with the deep, steady heat of his love.

Setting down the pot that she was rinsing, she turned to Jordan and just quietly wrapped her arms around his waist, nuzzling her face into his throat, breathing in his scent and feeling his heart pound against her breast. She just held him, and he hugged her, reconnecting to heaven after the day.

Leaning back to look up at him, Sam whispered, "I'm so lucky. I love you so much. How did I ever find you?"

Smiling tenderly down at her with those soft sea gray eyes of his, Jordan kissed the tip of her nose, before lifting his head and breaking out in a grin.

"I found you, remember?"

Sam laughed at their running joke.

"Yes, you did, handsome. You found me in jail, after you put me there, Mr. Prosecutor."

"No, I found you there and got you sprung after you put *yourself* there. All to write that novel, which, did you just say you lost half of?"

"Oh god, I hope not," she groaned, turning back to start dishing up dinner. "Let's eat first, relax on the deck, smell a few roses, then I'll tell you all about it."

"Sounds like a plan. Let me wash up and I'll be right back."

After Sam had filled her husband in on all her trials with 'The Thief', as she now referred to her laptop, she laughed at the irony of it all.

"Wait until I tell Ronnie that I have been performing illegal operations! Now! When I don't even need to. She will die when I tell her how easy it is… Jordan? Is something wrong?" Sam's dark eyes were troubled when he glanced up at her, surprised.

"No. Nothing to worry about. To my knowledge, performing illegal operations on or near a personal computer, that is not connected to the internet, doesn't even rate a misdemeanor. Especially if there are mitigating circumstances. And you mentioned a theft against your person? In this case I can't see that there would be any sentence you would need to worry about at all, not even community service."

Unable to hold the charade any longer, his deep chuckles joined Sam's light, musical laughter, floating out to join the last twittering of birds bedding down for the night in the dusky, lushly landscaped yard.

But his wife only let him divert her for a while, then the concern resettled on her face.

"You've got that double crease between your eyebrows, honey. It showed up when I mentioned Ronnie. Has she done something? Is … ?"

"Oh, no. Nothing like that at all, Sam. It was just that when you mentioned your friend it reminded me of something. I saw an old friend of Rhonda's today. A Detective Mallory."

It was her turn for a creased forehead. She could not think of anyone by that name that Ronnie had mentioned. But Ronnie did have a lot of *'friends'*. And, thank goodness, Sam had not had to meet most of them.

"He isn't married, is he?" She visibly winced.

Jordan snorted out a laugh. "Yes, *very* married. But it wasn't that kind of old friend I meant this time. No, he just tried to pin a bank robbery on her."

"Oh." Her voice was so quiet he could barely hear it, but her blush spoke loudly enough.

He grinned. "Yes. Oh. *that* bank robbery. Anyway, the detective came by my office today is all."

She seemed to wait for more while Jordan grabbed another roll and buttered it. Her eyes flicked to his forehead; he tried to ease the tension there, and failed. His sweet wife reached across the table to lay her fingers on his free arm, asking softly, "So tell me, what happened with this Detective Mallory to put that crease in your forehead?"

Jordan had been a bachelor for most of his adult life after a very brief and very disastrous first marriage that left him *very* bitter toward females. He wasn't used to having anyone at home to ask him about his day, or a crease on his forehead. It was nice to be cared about. More than nice. But strange, very foreign to him.

It was so incredibly rich to live with and be loved by *this* woman. But sharing himself, the inside of himself, thoughts, feelings, even everyday work issues, was something he was having to learn slowly. And thank god, she was patient with him.

"If it's confidential, please, you don't need to say anything. I understand." She had misinterpreted his look, and the long pause without an answer.

"No, sweetheart, it's not. I just got a little lost in your eyes there for a moment. By the way, thanks for dinner, everything is delicious. And thanks for worrying about my creases." His voice was as deeply soft and sincere as his words, before he continued, briskly.

"Detective Mallory came by to tell me there has been an uptick in drug arrests since last year. Mostly since the start of the summer. Nothing too serious yet, but definitely an increase since we rolled up Damon's group and put them away last year."

After many determined attempts by Jordan over the years to pin down the slippery "model citizen" that headed an operation that corrupted the youth into not only running his drugs, but auto, mail, and credit card theft, there had been a large and blessed drop in all crimes in the area after that supply and distribution network was rolled up. But a few months back, the detective saw things start to pick up again.

Nothing at all like it had been, but a new spotty supply line was coming in again from somewhere. He'd alerted Jordan so they could work together to try to identify and stop the main source before it grew and got its hooks in where the prior group had left a vacuum.

A vacuum Jordan had hoped to see filled by increased community youth programs and legitimate job opportunities, not by a different predator. Some good things had gotten started, including a new Youth shelter run by a guy that knew what he was doing, but it wasn't enough yet.

It was never enough when there were hungry adult sharks circling, looking for a weakness to get into a fresh pool of vulnerable victims.

Seeing his wife staring at his forehead, Jordan shook off the depressing thoughts, reminding himself that one very good thing had come from all the trials of last year – the lovely, sexy, blonde sitting across from him. The wife he never would have met if Sam and her friend Rhonda hadn't gotten all tangled up with himself and Detective Mallory in their investigation of those crimes. And that had turned out to have benefits well beyond his imagination!

His mood greatly improved, Jordan grinned at his wife, saying, "Anyway, the good detective always asks me how the 'delightful Ms. Sayles' is doing whenever I see him. He seems to have forgiven her for lying to him so skillfully, since it all turned out for such a good cause in the end." Jordan's eyes twinkled with a mischievous glint in their silvery depths as he added, "I told him she was just as wicked as ever."

"Jordan!"

"Delightfully wicked," he amended with a laugh.

Sam smiled fondly at him. "That's better." She nudged a plate of his favorite brownies closer to him as she asked, "So?"

"So? Oh, no thanks, sweetheart. They look delicious, but I'm stuffed with all your other goodies right now. I'll raid them later tonight to restore my energy after I ravish you a few times."

Sam smiled and nodded. "Save some for the ravished. So what else did Detective Mallory have to say?"

"Nothing much else work related, but," leaning his dark head closer he confided, "there was an intriguing bit of office talk, not about me for once," he smiled wryly, "but definitely in your area of interest. You remember Kevin MacClarty? The youth shelter guy? Well Mallory went by there to see him the other day, but mostly to volunteer a few hours, and Kevin and Shelley were just coming back from an outing with Timmy…"

"Oh, I think it's wonderful the way she is helping young Timmy out," Sam interjected quickly.

"Yeah," her husband agreed, "She is the best," he paused to make sure his wife caught the qualifier, "… professional decision I've made. She has turned into a great assistant prosecutor. Better than when she was a public defender—"

"Objection!" Sam laughed. "Bias."

"Okay, sustained. Shelley was a great public defender, but she was the enemy then. Anyway, what I wanted to say is that she is pure gold the way she has taken that boy to heart and helped him. So, of course, after all that help she has given him, the little twerp ratted her out." Laughter nearly barked out of him, he was so amused. He liked the little rascal.

"Ratted her out how?" Sam leaned in, propping an elbow on the table, chin in palm, impatient for the *low down*, which was guy talk for gossip.

"Timmy sidled up to the Detective where he was serving up sandwiches and whispered in that deep voice he uses to be cool, says, "Hey, I think my man, Shel, is getting gushy on old Kev. She was doing that red faced thing all day!' Which Mallory finally figured out meant that she must have been blushing."

"You are kidding!" Sam's honey brown eyes danced with laughter and fascination. "Oh, and isn't that sweet?" She said in that way woman did.

"Romance in the Youth Shelter, I can see the title of your next book now, or maybe Passion on an old Army Surplus Cot?" He grinned at her.

"Oh, you are being foolish!" She waved her hand at him. "Besides, when I said it was so sweet, I meant Timmy. That he calls Shelley his man, or 'my man', I guess. Though Shel and Kevin? Hmm."

"It's just rumor from a kid. Probably isn't true, so I won't tease her about it."

"Jordan! Don't you dare!"

"Oh, come on Sam. I just want to see her do that red face thing. Okay, Okay. Unscrunch that pretty face of yours. I promise I won't say a word to Shelley. I'll just pass the rumor on to Todd and Elsa." Seeing her scowl, he quickly went on the attack, "Sooo, speaking of Rhonda…"

"We aren't speaking of Ronnie, we …"

"We were speaking of Rhonda earlier," he inserted deftly.

Then leaning back in his chair with his arms folded across his chest, he questioned her with a sly smile.

"So what *is* your partner in crime up to lately?" He ribbed her.

Friends forever, Rhonda Sayles and Samantha were opposites in appearance and personality, but loyal unto death to each other —or unto prison, as it turned out.

Sam was a homemaker.

Rhonda was more of the home breaker style, if one wanted to be rude about it.

Bold, brash, brunette, elegantly tall and sensual, that was the woman Sam called Ronnie, her best friend, but admitted privately was a bit of an unmarried female rake. And a very successful one at that!

Sam couldn't count the number of men that Rhonda had left with broken hearts. Or used and abused bodies. But just that last thought had the basically shy and inherently prim Samantha blushing. A tendency her best friend loved to take advantage of, saving all her most bawdy exploits to "share with Sam to put a little color in her cheeks".

Who needed makeup when you had a pal like that?

But when Sam had turned the tables on Rhonda, and told her she was planning to get arrested so she could go to jail and write her long dreamt of novel, Rhonda gave her the support and help she needed. *After* many stern lectures, arguments, and alternative suggestions, of course.

But when it came down to it, Ronnie helped and kept her mouth shut. She helped Sam *appear* to commit a crime so she could get into that free hotel otherwise known as prison. When the prosecutor, Sam's current husband, started questioning Rhonda about a major crime that had happened at the same time and location, Ronnie had a big problem on her hands trying to protect Sam from being proven innocent of her non-crime, without getting herself arrested for bank robbery!

Ever since that time, Jordan had laughingly called her Sam's partner in crime.

"She is going to help me with my booth at the Annual Arts & Crafts Festival," Sam answered, delighted.

Jordan smiled back, hiding his skepticism. He knew better than most that Rhonda would do anything for her friend, but somehow he couldn't picture that bold, sultry brunette doing anything as tame as tending a fair booth for three days. He better keep a close eye on the ladies. No telling *what* Ronnie might decide to auction off if she got bored or she thought Sam's charity wasn't getting enough funding!

Ms. Rhonda Sayles, the subject of so many other people's conversations, had also been on the computer that afternoon, in her sleek office that she kept as firmly controlled as her string of unloved lovers.

Her monitor was concealed beneath a glass window under the sleek mahogany surface of her desk, the keyboard in a recessed drawer, so the surface of her work area remained hard, smooth, and uncluttered. The only family photographs in this office were of two children, Sam's children, and the picture the kids had taken once long ago of their mother with her arm around the shoulder of her best pal, mugging for the camera. "Aunt Ronnie" the kids had always called her, though it was only an honorary, if much cherished, title. Rhonda didn't have any children of her own, so she had borrowed Sam's ever since they were youngsters. Now full grown adults, with lives of their own, she was still their Aunt Ronnie, and her pride in them showed in the exquisite professional photographs that lined the walls in her office. Not portraits, but professional landscapes shot by Samantha's son, Paul.

Rhonda had no children of her own because they required a father, and she had never found a man that she had enough patience or respect for to honor with the title of husband, much less father.

She liked men. Thoroughly enjoyed playing with them, exploring their prowess at what they did best and most often, on a short term basis. But while men had always fallen easily and quickly for her tall, slender, sultry body, and salty sophistication, they never quite understood how she could toy with them, instead of being the one toyed with.

Rhonda was on her computer now disposing of her latest lover —by email. It was most annoying as he was also one of her buyers. She would have to replace him as one of her purchasing agents, a much more difficult task than finding another lover. She was too discrete to have a waiting list for *that* on her computer, though she had a mental catalog of potential applicants.

But no more employees, she decided, no matter how much they begged and insisted it wouldn't affect their output—except, of course, to make them much more productive. She did *not* sexually harass her employees. She thought it so tiring and unfair the way male executives did, but when she felt harassed herself, she had handed out the occasional... bonus, so to speak ... but she vowed never more to anyone that worked directly for her. But handsome consultants? Hmm, now she would have to consider that possibility.

She had had a most handsome and virile specimen to install the computerized system in her office years ago. If she had known Samantha was having computer problems, she might have recommended him. But only because he was as safely and happily married now as her best friend was. And few men could compete with Sam's husband Jordan, though her prim friend would never even consider the possibility.

They were such a strange combination to become best friends. Herself, tall, dark, and very naughty, and Samantha, petite and as sweet and prim as her name, but they had been best friends for decades. She was looking forward to helping Sam out at the upcoming Art's Festival. And maybe she would find some interesting pieces for her shops at the same time, since she would have to do some of her own buying for a while until the agency could send her some new candidates.

"And lose my email address and private phone numbers if you want a decent severance package." Rhonda typed on the end of her email to her latest ex-lover, before hitting the send button.

chapter two

An Island Archipelago in the Northern Straits

"**G**osh, are you going to be in that Art Fair on the Mainland?"

Pete startled, then casually, carefully, finished packing the bulky items, covering them with a final layer of bubble wrap. He fit the lid of the fish box in place and snapped it down so that it was flush in the bottom of the boat deck before rising and turning to the unwelcome visitor on the dock. He hadn't expected anyone about at this hour—especially in this weather.

Dawn had broken an hour ago overhead, but had not yet been able to edge its way down to the waters of the cove. Its presence announced only in the way it illuminated and backlit the morning fog, making it even more ghostly as it draped itself in slumber around the archipelago sandwiched in the watery boundary between the U.S. and Canada.

From the air above, the rounded humps of over a hundred islands rising up in the mist would have looked like pods of the local orcas breaching, rounded greenish black backs rolling in the straits, sounding in a misty white spray of spume. But below in the mist it was thick, quiet, and concealing, visibility under ten feet. It must have muffled the sound of the teen's sneakers as she came out to the end of the dock where he had been working in what he had assumed was complete privacy.

He wondered how long she'd lurked silently behind his back before working up the courage to speak to him? This girl-woman whose eye, and apparently heart, he had unwittingly caught.

Bett Bone

At first it had been amusing, even flattering, to see her blush to her toes and stutter every time he accidentally ran across her in town with her friends or family. He remembered when his sister was that age, just starting high school, starting to lose her gangly youth and bud into a young female. She had crush after crush on older men, blushed every time one spoke to her. She breathlessly told her girlfriends about each inconsequential time she was in the same room, or on the same street as her current heartthrob. How without any encouragement or likely even acknowledgment, had covered her school notebooks with hearts entwining their names.

After a while his amusement had worn off when he began to realize he was accidentally running into this teen much too frequently to be coincidence. He shuddered to think some of those hearts and flowers in this young girls diary might encircle the name Mrs. Peter James Potter. The damn little chit was following him around like an overeager puppy. It was starting to become more than a nuisance, developing into a distinct problem. But he could hardly complain to the parents that supported his work in their gallery in the resort town, an old, influential island family, that their underage daughter was stalking him.

He did not need that kind of grief or scrutiny.

He had come to these remote islands because there were other artists and eccentrics that had landed here and been welcomed. After the first novelty wore off, they had usually been left to pursue their work in relative privacy, if they wished.

And he did.

He let it be known around the island that unlike the artists that had opened their studios to the public, he required seclusion for his creative process. When that request was too subtle to warn off a local cub reporter that came to inquire about "his muse"—of all stupid interruptions—he realized he needed to display his "arrogant, artistic temper", as was later reported.

> *"During an abbreviated interview with this reporter, Mr. Potter stated he was reclusive, his pieces were unique, his prices exorbitant, and as he sold his work primarily on the mainland, he didn't want anyone dropping by his private studio, claiming he lived in mortal fear that someone would steal his exclusive high-end designs."*

Message delivered. In print. The only nice thing the reporter was left to say about the new resident artist was that he was ruggedly lean and handsome, and his few less exalted pieces that the island gallery showed were said to be selling well. It was no coincidence that after the article appeared, Peter arranged his trips to town for groceries *after* returning from fishing or crabbing trips in his sailboat, *before* changing out of his smelly bait-cutting clothes.

"So, do you need some help loading?" chirped his current nemesis.

"No, thanks. I've got it."

"Gosh it must be fun to be in one of those festivals. I've never been to one."

Peter checked a line on his rigging, pretending not to hear the hopeful pause before she added, "Must be exciting, huh?"

"Just a job," he replied in his most boring tone, stepping into his boat to check a sail cover on the far side, trying to brush off the over eager teen. Luckily he was loaded and could shove off as soon as the mist lifted and the tide turned, meanwhile he could hide in his cabin.

"Well, see ya," he muttered, distracted, not looking her direction as he slid inside, pulling the curtain across the door as he closed it.

With any luck she would have found a new target for her affections by next week, or he would have to find a way to deal with this problem when he returned from his trip. Maybe he should bring some hot bombshell babe back with him, that should cool her little jets, though it wouldn't do much for his privacy. Hell!

Edmonds on the Sound

Driving into Edmonds on 7th Avenue to set up for the Fair, Sam glanced over to her right at the Civic Center Playfield. Once the football stadium for the old high school, the open playfields stretched for three city blocks and offered ball fields, tennis courts and a charming 1920s era false fronted red clapboard field house, now the Boys & Girls Club. Yet it was the large area that held the quarter-mile track that captured her eye. Sporting walkers and joggers normally, today the track held a modern day version of circling the wagons. An RV, Camper, and U-Haul Artist's encampment circled the track in the days leading up to the opening of the festival.

"I'm sure glad we live close so we don't have to stay cooped up in a trailer like the other fair vendors," Sam commented, watching for pedestrians as she drove. It would be chaos by tomorrow afternoon, with as many people in the middle of the road as cars, plus all the parked cars coating every available inch of curb in front of the older garage-less residences in this historic part of town.

"Oh, I don't know," Rhonda commented languidly, rolling the window down to let the summer wind toss and tangle her long, dark hair. "I think it might be kind of fun. Maybe a *lot* of fun," she said in that low smoky tone that said she was thinking her usual naughty thoughts. "Just think Sam, it would be like a gypsy camp with creative artists moving from one fair to the next, and one big party at the campsite every night."

"Well, *you* are certainly dressed for it," Sam laughed, tossing a quick glance at the collection of gold bangles dangling from Ronnie's wrist, and her multi-colored flirty peasant skirt and bright crimson blouse. "Should I just drop you off here?" She asked wryly.

"Not today," Rhonda replied, reluctantly. "I promised to help you set up. And I will," she sighed.

As they went uphill and turned at the Frances Anderson Center, to jockey for a place by the events field to park and unload, Sam suddenly blurted, "I'm going to do it! I requested a brochure."

"Do what?" Ronnie asked absently, her thoughts somewhere else that Sam didn't dare locate, probably at some steamy bed in a camper at her imagined artistic gypsy camp

"The annual writer's conference. They hold it here, that's what reminded me. I'm kinda scared about it, but I decided I'm going to go to that conference this year."

"Sam, that's great!" She had her friend's full attention and support now. "But why be scared? It will be a marvelous experience for you."

"I know, I know, that's why I'm going. I've told Jordan and my kids, and now you, because I know you guys will keep me from chickening out when the sign-up form comes. It's just, well… it feels strange going to it when I'm not really a writer …"

"What do you mean, not a writer?" Ronnie jumped in indignant. "You have an almost completed manuscript, don't you?"

"Well, yeah," Sam shrugged, "but it's not a book yet, so I'm not really a writer yet."

"Bull! You're not a published *author* yet—you have to be rejected a few hundred times first for that. But you definitely *are* a writer. You have been writing for decades, you even write funny stories for me every time I need cheering up. And you write birthday cards for all of us every year, that capture a special memory, or write us a poem, with hand drawn pictures … actually, that is what you aren't, Sam. An illustrator. I don't mean to hurt your feelings, but girl, you can't draw worth a damn. But a writer you are. Besides, isn't the deal to have workshops to help you learn how to write and publish? You think bestselling authors take those classes? NOT. It's for people like you who are just unfinished authors."

"Unfinished authors, huh? Okay, I like that way of thinking about it. But I'm still nervous." And she still had to finish, or rewrite her whole darn book, Sam grumbled to herself, recalling she still had a computer thief to be dealt with. Shaking off that worry, she focused on the present event, skillfully snagging a just vacated parking spot.

"This is going to be so much fun, don't you think, Ronnie? I can hardly wait to see all the wares on display this year!"

Distracted by some of the male wares on display, muscles straining lifting heavy boxes and shifting displays, Rhonda answered vaguely, "I think I just might find something interesting to buy myself this year."

Since Sam had taken space at the annual arts and crafts fair to promote a worthy charity instead of her artistic works—which were non-existent, especially now with her vanishing book issue—she and Ronnie did not have a great deal to haul in and set-up. Especially since her friend selected a cadre of muscular male artists she enticed to carry the few boxes, table and chairs that *did* need hauling. Once Rhonda managed to graciously disperse her admirer-laborers, Sam and Rhonda had plenty of time to just sit and chat while they unloaded and stacked brochures and informational documentation on their tabletop, and enjoy the bustle and building excitement all around them.

Many of the exhibitors were long time veterans, but for others—

especially local artists—this was their first festival. First public showing, the first time they tried to earn money by following their passion—possibly the most terrifying, nerve racking moment of their lives, as they laid themselves bare through their work—hoping at least for approval even if that was a voice saying "how lovely!", instead of cold hard cash. So emotions ran high, today, whether in excited anticipation, the joy of reconnecting with peers, or the fear and nerves of taking an important life step, dreading potential humiliation. But at least today it was all tempered with the hard work of getting set-up and being part of a prestigious art fair that had passed its sixtieth year.

In her brief stint as a guest of the Women's Correctional Center, Sam had become aware of an amazing rehabilitation program and service run by the institution. At the time she had been unable to get involved, but had wanted to find a way to support such a worthy program. The Service Dog Inmate Program allowed qualified inmates to work with carefully selected animals and train them to assist the blind and handicapped, or to just be gentle, well-trained visitors to nursing homes and children's hospitals. In addition to being invaluable to people with disabilities, man's best friend could soothe, calm, lighten and brighten the day for those facing illness, stress, and loneliness.

Not only the patients benefited. In addition to work training and college credits, inmates also benefited from receiving a friend that loved without judging, listened without arguing, and healed self-esteem by giving a sense of purpose. The recidivism rate of inmates involved in the program was almost halved, so society as a whole benefited

But like most such programs across the country, demand outstripped supply and budgets were always strained, so Sam had come to take advantage of the crowds of art and culture lovers that would attend the fair. She didn't plan on twisting any arms – though Rhonda seemed a little too eager in that regard. Yet Sam was not beyond applying a dose of guilt, intending to remind people how lucky they were that, unlike the blind, *they* could actually *see* all the beautiful works that would be on display at the festival.

When she made her proposal to the Correction Center, many of the women from the prison program had not been comfortable appearing in person, and being publicly identified and judged. But when Candy heard about Sam's plans, she had volunteered cheerfully. Eager to describe her life, be open about her past and mistakes, and proud of the changes she was making in her life now, Candy was enthusiastic about being the youngest trainer. She regularly volunteered at youth centers spreading the word about her life as a street kid. Boldly challenging her peers that not only *could* they, but they *must* take action *now*, take the rare chance to get a better life while they had the support and help of the shelter.

"I am an example of stubborn pride, proving I can take the world on alone...and becoming a loser, big time. Now," Candy grinned, "I am still stubborn, determined, and wise enough to grab help. And I have *real* pride in myself. I can do this."

Candy was bringing her seeing-eye dog, Bernie, to the fair to demonstrate how a trained service dog could guide people even through the chaos, crowds, and booths at the fair.

"Candy is coming?" Rhonda asked with a laugh. "Oh, little Timmy has a huge crush on her!"

"What?" Sam spun to stare at Rhonda, to see if she was teasing. "I thought it was Shelley he hero-worshipped!"

"That was six months ago. Besides the kid is smart. He is not about to step in that hunky youth center director's turf."

"Kevin?"

"Right. Besides, lawyers make him edgy, especially with half his family doing hard time."

"No. He calls Shelley 'his man', Ronnie. He isn't edgy around her."

"Not as a pal, or Big Sister, or whatever she is, but as his true love? He seems to identify more with Candy."

"He's ten! Or I guess eleven now. Isn't that a little young for her?" Sam was shocked.

"That's just what I hear she told her young Romeo and you know what he told her? 'You'll appreciate a handsome young stud like me that can still get it up when you're older'."

Sam gasped and turned bright red from her ears to her neck, scolding, "Ronnie!"

"Hey, he's the one that said it, don't blame me. Besides, I thought it was kind of cute. Sounds like he has already picked out his blushing bride. And blushing was the only response she gave him."

"Good Lord!" was all Sam could manage.

Neither Sam nor Ronnie mentioned the incongruity of a former prostitute blushing at such a comment. Candy looked like any late-teen girl next door, and her sunny, sweet attitude now was a blessing. She had been a street kid, abandoned very young, and turned out on the street by one of her pals. She'd had no choice if she had wanted to survive. and had finally learned to forgive herself for what she was blameless for, tossing the ugliness of a past behind her where it belonged. She had become, again, the sweet kid she had once been, before life had punched her in the face. Sam was proud of her.

Turning to Ronnie she asked, "How is it that you know all this stuff? I see Shelley and Kevin all the time, and I hadn't heard ... Well ... about this."

"Oh," Rhonda turned her head away, watching the activity in another space being prepped, "I stop by on occasion. Drop ... things off."

From her evasiveness, Sam suspected that what she dropped off were huge anonymous donation checks for the Youth Center. That was Ronnie, tough on the outside, but a crème puff pastry inside. Even Sam, her best friend for years didn't know all the generous things Ronnie did so casually.

Even when Sam had found out Ronnie was a big secret donor to a local charity once, she had been hushed up.

"Don't ruin my image, Sam. Besides, I only did it because I was trying to get a handsome stud on the committee in bed."

There were, of course, no handsome men on that committee. Ronnie didn't know Sam had checked and never mentioned it to her buddy, the fake, the big marshmallow, the best, and most generous friend ever. Though Sam reconsidered when Rhonda nudged her in the ribs with a very sharp elbow.

"Well, my oh my," Rhonda's purr almost qualified for a predatory growl. "Who is this deliciously handsome man?" And that *was* the species the purr-growl was reserved for, Sam noted. It seemed highly appropriate as one never knew whether her friend was in cuddle or attack mode. Often, not even Rhonda.

"Hmm, looks like fair game to me," Ronnie mused. "Though you *do* look a bit like my best friend's husband, but *he*, the infamous Jordan Campbell and Mr. Prosecutor Man, would *never* be caught wearing a *pink* oxford shirt like that with those old jeans rubbed white in all the most tantalizing places. I hear he hates pink."

The handsome dark-haired man with silver eyes, and the lean

muscled grace and often manner of a sleek and deadly panther, flushed a shade of color that matched his shirt.

"Ms. Sayles, a pleasure I'm sure," Jordan acknowledged with a wry twist to his lips.

Samantha slapped a hand over her mouth to stifle a giggle, but her big, warm brown eyes danced with delighted mischief. The stern warning glance Jordan aimed at his wife only set her off on another round of laughter.

Rhonda's eyebrows arched as she caught the exchanged look and wondered what little husband and wife secret she was missing. She knew Jordan wasn't blushing from her bawdy, sensual innuendos. He was used to her, and completely immune. His whole heart and soul, not to mention that gorgeous body, belonged to her best friend, and she couldn't help but love him just for loving Sam so deeply.

Which didn't stop Ronnie from relentlessly teasing him, of course.

"Oh my, I sense a deep dark secret story about this pink shirt and the big male blush. Is it a naughty story?"

"Rhonda!" Jordan protested, motioning with his head to the young boy at his side, who just grinned when she winked at him.

"Never mind. I'll just weasel the story out of Sam, later."

Not! Sam thought, shaking her head vigorously and laughing. Though she might sneak the tale into one of her romance stories, someday, Sam decided. It was rather charming, and…

Last Valentine's Day, her outwardly stern and serious husband had treated her with a gift—a very special, very private gift. A gift he gave her in their bedroom that he had romantically filled with flowers and dimmed all the lights except for a few sultry scented candles and a little music. Music with a very distinct beat. The gift of a strip tease dance that he did for her, right down to the glow of a fluorescent red, glow in the dark, male G-string he had found in some back alley shop to delight her. He danced down to it, then beyond. Dancing a love dance intimately with his wife all night long. It was wonderful, and romantic, and so very naughty, and…

After making love all night to his valentine, and a little dazed still from the intense emotions and pleasure, in a further caring gesture, he had done a load of laundry, so his lover could just rest, while he fixed her a morning after breakfast in bed.

The load of laundry he grabbed and tossed in the washer while the bacon was sizzling was from his hamper. It included all his soft white oxford shirts, his athletic socks, his white jockey shorts and the rest of his underwear, including one bright red non-colorfast item he had worn, briefly, the night before.

It was amazing what such a little piece of fabric could do to a whole load of white clothes! Jordan had created for himself a complete wardrobe of his least favorite color in the world—pink. It was most unfortunate, and actually quite hilarious.

Samantha had gone out the next day he worked and bought him a complete replacement set of white everything, and laundered them and put them in his dresser and closet, to ease his embarrassment. After laughing herself silly, of course. But for some reason he kept some of his "pinks" and occasionally wore them.

"Why?" Sam had asked. "Why don't you just give them to Goodwill?"

"I did give them most of it, but saved a few to wear just for you."

"For me?" And she had been treated to a sizzling look from those black rimmed silver eyes of his.

"When I wear them I want to remind you and myself of that night and how they got that way."

Sam found it terribly sweet and romantic that such a serious man on the outside, would wear a color everyone knew he did *not* favor, just for her. She still got a giggle from it, just before a long, dreamy sigh when she remembered *everything!*

"You will tell me what all that smiling and sighing is about someday," Ronnie threatened, nudging her back to the present. She glanced quickly at Jordan and he smiled at her. He knew his pink reminder was working.

The young boy at his side impatiently shoved up to the table.

"Hey, Sam. Rhonda. Have you... Sheesh!" he muttered when Jordan gave him a soft rap on the head. "I mean *Mrs. Jordan, and Ms. Sayles."* Close enough, Mr. Samantha decided not to interrupt the kid again.

Glancing around, little Timmy asked, casually, "Have you seen my girlfriend around?"

Sam choked, but Rhonda just grinned.

"I don't know, what does she look like?" She teased Timmy.

"Well, she has short blond hair, cute cut, she's about six inches taller than me, she has a nice sporty body, you know, nice calf muscles." He paused a moment and smiled. "Real nice! She has eyes the color of those new model pale blue BMWs, and freckles on her nose. She's almost twenty, but she looks closer to my age."

"Your age?" Rhonda goaded.

"Well, she looks about sixteen, okay, wise lady!" The impatient eleven year old huffed. "So have you seen her, or what?"

Sam shoved Ronnie to the side before she could annoy the poor kid anymore and answered. "If you are referring to Candy, we decided it was too crazy here today for her and the dog, so she will be over to Jordan's later to do a practice run-through of her demonstration. You are welcome to join us for dinner."

"Sure, no problem," the cocky kid replied, ducking away from the head scrub Jordan gave him while trying hard not to laugh out loud.

"Where is Shelley, Jordan? Is she here?"

"Naw, she had court today so I'm filling in with the kid. He swears she promised to take him to go-carting today, which I doubt, but hey, why not." Turning to shout, "Wait up, kid!" Then turning back to his wife, added, "But I came by to tell you that Elsa just blurted out that she has a nephew who is a first class nerd."

Sam just blinked, arched her brows at her husband.

"Yeah, surprised me too. She loves her nephew, but apparently that is a compliment. I had mentioned your book thief problem at the office and Elsa explained that she meant he was a big computer geek and really sharp on fixing problems. But, I thought maybe," hesitating, his face tinted the color of his shirt, "I thought maybe someone older, and not a friend might be a better idea?"

Jordan knew he and Sam had "acted out" a number of romantic scenes for her book, but wasn't sure if she had used them in detail. And if a teenager were to read that… nerd, or not, he was *still* a teen age boy.

Glancing from Sam to her pink faced husband, then back to Sam becoming a matching tint, Rhonda read the silent message and laughed out loud.

Rising, still laughing she told them she would leave them to discuss all those "high-tech details" alone for a bit while she checked out the festival venue. "I'd offer you my computer guy Sam, but I just dumped him, so he might do more damage than good. See you. Bye stud," Snickering, Rhonda sauntered off to explore.

After Ronnie was out of earshot, Jordan mentioned that Detective Mallory had given him the name of a consultant his department used for re-constructing hard drive information.

"He is really good, has been background checked and signs a confidentially agreement. So if it's okay with you, Timmy and I will take your computer over to him this afternoon. He has some jobs ahead of it, but said he would get on it as soon as he could."

"Oh, Jordan, that sounds wonderful. Thank you, honey. I take it you have Timmy all day?"

"Yeah, Shel and I thought it was important not to let him down when she had to be in court today."

"Of course, not. He's had enough of that in his short life. I meant what I said about having him to dinner, so if you think of it when you get home, would you pull some hamburger out of the freezer? I'm planning salmon, but if he doesn't like it, maybe I ..."

Jordan interrupted with a bark of laughter.

"Will do, but I suspect that he will choose to eat what his 'girlfriend' does. Even if he hates it."

Rhonda had never paid much attention to the Frances Anderson Center in Edmonds before, though she had driven by it many times. The event venue was an inventive patchwork of old and new that took advantage of the downhill slope to the Sound, and a large block of central land originally set aside for schools in the early township.

It started on the high east side with the immense leveled grass area of the former playgrounds—now covered with a grid of hundreds of canopied artist booths—then dropped down to the recess door in the old school building, tucked in a corner where the old wood floored gymnasium bumped out from the original rectangular school building that still proudly perched on the hill, overseeing the town citizens. Bypassing where the Juried Art Exhibits were being completed in the gym, and down various corridors, Rhonda took a quick peek into the alcove in the entryway to see this year's poster for the prestigious festival, and the other works by the artist that had been selected for the honor. She liked the fresh, brightly colored design of the watercolor that traditionally pictured a local Edmonds scene.

Scampering down a staircase she entered a long, wide, dim corridor lined on either side with classrooms, grade school crayon drawings taped along every wall. It was a journey bound to tweak the memories of any adult. Rhonda could still smell the ghostly trace of chalk, finding herself moving quickly down the glossy linoleum floor, as if afraid of being caught again without her hall pass. Slamming against the push bar at the end, she escaped back into sunshine on the west side of the old school, to face a vast series of modern concrete terraces, lined with deep planters filled with shrubs, trees, tucked around niches of lawn with picnic table, bronze sculpture, or a dedicated black iron bench. Railed and walled concrete footpaths and handicap ramps exited either side down to the roads surrounding the block.

Straight ahead a wide landscaped lined path led to a newer building, with deep windows all around, alongside a vast open terrace, called The Plaza, that extended out above the length of the Sound, suddenly in view just above the low walled railings. As she moved forward she appreciated the clever design that disguised the fact that she was actually walking on an open sky bridge over a parking area below, to the vast view terrace that roofed the Library underneath. Reaching the far western railing, the view filled her senses.

Beneath her the town continued its steps down to the water, full of peaked roofs of historic Victorians with lush picket fenced gardens, intermingled with older flat roofed false fronted businesses and the square blocks of more recent buildings and condominiums. Yet all the roofs were polite enough to duck their heads low and not impede any view of the great expanse of water, so that its power and beauty could be shared by all. The Sound stretched broad and lazy toward Seattle to the south and stretched north up the coast, and out to the Pacific, in straits dividing Washington from not only Canada, but some of its own islands and Peninsula, with salt water stretching between and among dark green forested land for as far as the eye could see.

Directly across the Sound, a line of clouds drifted low in the distance, from some incoming ocean weather system, playing a familiar and well known game, making the far peninsula look like a land of innocent low rolling hills and forests. But the veil of low clouds were just part of a game of peek-a-boo that nature played, probably with tourists, as the locals knew better. Suddenly the clouds would part and a chain of high, steeled-blue ragged mountain spikes, topped with white glacial icing, would pop up from north to south and shout "Fooled you!" in startled, awed, faces, and the beauty of the scenery would go from gorgeous to truly stunning.

Today they were in hiding, unwilling to unveil their splendor just for Rhonda. Though she had seen the Olympic Coastal Range a thousand times, it was never enough. Disappointed, she leaned a hip against the low wall and turned her gaze to the north where sun breaks were turning the vast expanse of waters, their nap ruffled up by the breeze, into a glittering landscape of shattered sparkling diamonds on a background of slate blue velvet.

And there, gliding, flying really, across the shimmer were a trio of sailboats, each gleaming white with colorful slashes of primary colors in blue, red, or yellow splashed across their full bellied white sails. She watched as they speed down the Sound, before tipping out some of their wind and turning in toward the southern end of town. They must be heading in to the Port of Edmonds Marina she thought, though her view was blocked to the south by the only obstruction, a line of deciduous trees that rattled their green leaves so cheerily in the soft breeze that she couldn't resent their temporary claim over the view.

Grasping the railing with both hands, she closed her eyes, tipped her face up to the sun, breathing deeply of the fresh sea air she let the breeze tangle and play with her dark strands of hair, picturing herself flying fast and free across that glittering expanse of water, a colorful sail billowing above.

Maybe she should get one.

A sailboat.

Yes. She could see herself with a chilled glass of champagne in her hand, and a handsome, wind and weather tanned and hardened man at her feet.

Or maybe... she should just get a man with a boat, to handle all the lines – and reef in a few of hers. Hmm. Now there was a plan.

A satisfied grin lingered on her face as she turned to make her way back across the plaza, through the former school, up the back court where food vendors were setting up their equipment, and past the area where the finishing touches were being put on the stage for music groups that would entertain, day and evening. She wandered back to the streets of booths, signposts, and—today—

chaos, as artworks and hand crafted items were being hauled in, set up and prepared for the opening tomorrow, browsing as she went.

Suddenly she spotted a piece of art that she just had to possess. A sculpture. A male sculpture. Clothed.

Damn, thought Rhonda, but truly the garments hid none of the beauty of the male form, but rather enhanced it. Made her wish for a chisel. Ronnie wanted one of those "sold" stickers to plant on that nice tight butt, because this masterpiece was meant for her.

And this masterpiece had another key quality. It breathed.

It breathed in a deep, chest expanding breath and caught her appreciative appraisal with an amused, knowing gaze of gold-rimmed green eyes. A slow grin showed off strong even white teeth and cut deep dimples to frame the ruggedly handsome, weathered and tanned face. His hair had a life of its own. Thick, rich sun-streaked over a deeper bronze, it looked like the wind combed hair of a sailor, or maybe, Rhonda thought, added to that hard athletic body, an adventurer, or even pirate. He certainly had the swagger.

Flicking her glance away from him for a moment, before he became too confident in his ability to trap her with those tawny green eyes, and sculpted torso, she arched an elegant black eyebrow, nodding toward the wares behind him.

"Pottery?"

"Of course." He let his gaze scan quite obviously down her body, pausing to study and appraise points of interest, just as blatantly as she had just surveyed him. A wicked quirk to his mouth, and a voice slow and sensual, he explained.

"I have an irresistible need to work with my hands. To smooth them continuously over wet, slippery, silky curves." Letting his eyes rise directly to hers, he added, "What else could I have chosen to do? Besides, it's my namesake."

Ignoring the obvious hint, Rhonda cast a last dismissive glance at his wares—*and* the pottery in the booth behind him—and turned and slowly sauntered back to Sam's booth which was conveniently located on the opposite corner.

She didn't look back. Rhonda didn't need to.

She knew his eyes were locked on her gently swaying ass. Seating herself languidly, facing Sam, the rest of her curves in profile, she let him look his fill and realize she was convenient to chase in the coming days of the fair.

And he was convenient to her for scenery.

Leaning forward, Sam whispered, "There is a man over there staring at you, Ronnie."

"Ignore him."

"He is really good looking, maybe…"

"And he knows it. I'll deal with him. Later. Let his irrepressible hands twitch a little while first."

"He has twitchy hands?" Sam frowned.

Ronnie gave her a mysterious smile and changed the subject.

chapter three

B anners had been stretched above all roads leading into the waterfront community for weeks announcing the upcoming Annual Arts & Crafts Festival.

There would be a significant audience.

The unique character and appeal of Edmonds lay deep in its early history. Once, and for a long time after its founding, there *were* no roads to span with banners. There were no roads *at all* to even get to Edmonds. All traffic in and out was by small boats or steamers. The small community growing just north of the King County line, had more in common with its neighbor to the south, Seattle, than with Snohomish, which was then the inland seat of their county, bearing the same name. Edmonds was remote and isolated from the rest of Snohomish County not only by lack of roads and great distances, but through lack of support or interest from the agricultural and mining interests that ruled the county to the inland north. Failing in its attempts to get itself annexed to its King County neighbors, Edmonds found itself alone and cut off.

So the town set out to move forward and create its own destiny, suited to its own needs and interests, and used its profitable timber and shingle mills to create a place it called "The Gem of the Puget Sound". And a shining gem it became, especially due to its deep and early support and commitment to the arts.

Early records show funds assigned for bands, improvement committees, schools, theaters, and about as many clubs and lodges as it had streets. One of these early clubs was the Coterie Club, which would eventually create the first annual arts festival in 1957.

It was a community known for this past support of the arts, and in recent decades had significantly increased that patronage. A new library was built and the old Carnegie Library became the town museum. An old high school had been converted to a Performing Arts Center. Brick walled downtown alleys sported murals created by carefully selected artists, and a map for a walking tour of their works. There were annual jazz festivals, and summer Sunday musicians at the Port. There were waterfront festivals, farmers markets, writer's conferences, and the town had long had its own live theater and small movie house, even when it seemed much too small to support them. But support of the arts was what Edmonds was about, with bronze seals along the shore to welcome their live friends, an amazed sculpted tourist family huddled by the pier gazing out across the sound in awe, and a school of metal salmon leaped from the water and froze for photos, to name a few. And in 1979, a center block of prime land was turned, not into developments, but into a venue for events, and named the Frances Anderson Center. Miss Anderson was the first president of the Edmonds Improvement Club formed in 1910, a decade after the town's incorporation as a "Village-4th Class", and the same year that the Interurban Road was completed between Seattle and Everett— but without a spur down to isolated Edmonds. The determination of Miss Anderson, and that of other Edmonds pioneers, was honored now by this center that hosted the annual writer's conference, and the annual arts festival.

There are—now—a number of different routes into Edmonds, favored depending on weather, time of year, and ultimate destination.

The Edmonds ferry crossing Puget Sound was one of the main funnels of traffic to the exquisite rainforests of the Olympic Peninsula and the rugged Pacific Coast beaches that extended to California and points south. From the peninsula, ferries plowed north across the Strait of Juan de Fuca to Whidbey Island or to Canada's Vancouver Island with the charming British Columbia capitol of Victoria, and its English flavored gardens and high tea at the Empress. And back to Edmonds for the Festival.

By land, the choices were now numerous, with a feeder highway connecting with Interstate 5 freeway, south to Seattle and beyond, or north to Canada, bringing ferry traffic in to toll booths on the south end of town. The rest of the routes feed into the main parts of downtown. One was a winding road through the trees that was a lush green tunnel in spring and summer and a gold and russet wonderland in late fall. It had long had the unofficial name of "Snake Road" by the locals, as it twisted down from the north.

Another main route cuts straight from Interstate-5 west through Lynnwood on 196th, then curves downhill at Maplewood through a short steep wooded ravine. This stretch can be a little unnerving with its trees clearly struggling to stay upright on a slope that has a tendency to get saturated in the rainy season—essentially all but July, August and just enough of September to make returning schoolkids long to stay outdoors. The road on the side of this ravine, is as much bridge as road and tends to be a little crumbly on the downhill slope, before swooping into the open with a great sound view. Joining up with the snaky road, they sweep majestically down past the bowl of old residences into the north end of town.

The final main approach leaves the old north- south Highway 99, (unromantically renamed "State Route # something or other") and heads past the High School, then bends just enough at Five Corners to change its name so that when it emerges shortly after at the top of a steep, *very steep* hill, it dives right down the center of Edmonds as Main Street.

Steep and curving only up and down like a rollercoaster, rather than writhing side to side, this very businesslike, no nonsense approach headed straight west into the water. As the Northwest is always damp, overnight moisture in winter tends to freeze to black ice (that looks like just another wet road) and makes this route a little too exciting at times—or really anytime you can't quite recall the last time you had a brake job. But barring pedestrians and other cars you could essentially roar right down and fly right onto a ferry —and possibly right off the other end for a swim in Puget Sound!

However, the scenario above could rarely happen now. Not because the ferry traffic is first diverted to holding lanes, but because there is a fountain right smack in the middle of Main Street in the heart of downtown—an occasionally working fountain, depending on the last time it was used for emergency brakes. You can't miss it—literally! And if you did, it should be noted that big solid trains run across the whole waterfront of Edmonds.

But the heart of downtown Edmonds is really worth stopping to see—one way or the other. And braking just a few blocks above the fountain on Main will place you conveniently—and safely—

beside the Festival Center.

But fairgoers have another option, rather than just relying on roads entering, ferries unloading visitors, and the passenger train depot. More significantly, it has a port and marina focused on its most long standing attraction—boating. And specifically now, pleasure boating.

Uniquely located across from where the Pacific Ocean found its way into Puget Sound through the Strait, not only salty waters but winds arriving from across the ocean run through this channel to get around the high Olympic Mountains, to range south or north, creating a paradise for sailboats. The same features brought in the salmon for the sport fishermen in their powerboats, and created the stunning scenery that brought the yachts from near and far to an award winning Port.

So there is no problem reaching the formerly isolated town today. A huge audience was expected for the opening of the Arts Festival that Edmonds had been proudly hosting for over a half century.

Every year it took over four hundred volunteers alone, just to produce the three day event. And every year hundreds of thousands of people answered the call to attend the festival, along with the hundreds of artists, musicians, and vendors of both old favorites and exotic new foods for the patrons.

Each year a juried art contest gave serious weight to the artworks that would be on view, along with a separate contest held to select the work, and artist, that would evoke the character of the town in the annual festival poster.

People from all over flooded, converged, and flocked to the event each year during its three day run, whether to purchase arts and crafts or just to take advantage of such a massive gallery of works all in one place. Local artists from Northwest Washington predominated, but artists brought their wares from Montana and surrounding states as well, due to the prestige of this long standing fair. Even those who just came to browse and enjoy the food and the music found it difficult to leave without some token item as a gift or special memory, especially knowing that a percentage of all purchases at the fair went to provide local art scholarships.

With just an hour to go before the excitement began, every curbside parking space for blocks and blocks around was lined with cars. Sidewalks filled with people walking from cars, boats, buses, trains, and ferries, all headed in one direction.

Inside the fenced playfield, a city within the heart of the city waited. Paralleling Main Street, the inner boulevards ran east to west: O'Keefe, Monet, Dali, Picasso, and Renoir Boulevards. The avenues ran north and south: Rembrandt, Gauguin, Degas, and Van Gogh. With a Food Terrace framing the upper east side, and the Food Court and Music Amphitheater on the lower west end. In the twenty some spaces that lined each side of each boulevard, one might find: hand blown glass, hand crafted furnishings and fixtures in wood or metal, ceramics, original jewelry made from everything including sea glass, leather tooled goods, textile art, and wearable fiber originals, garden art, paintings in oil, pastels, watercolors, acrylics, and mixed media pieces, photography, sculpture, in addition to scented soaps, candles, and traditional crafts. And this was just the fair market, the juried artwork galleries were indoors.

Artwork registered to be juried by the Festival Panel was exhibited indoors, along with the winners of First through Third, and Honorable Mention award winners in each of the categories, for original: Painting, Artisan Works, Sculpture, Prints, Drawings, Miniatures, and Photography. Future artists were honored in a student art exhibit, with a juried top twenty that covered works from kindergarten to very professional looking high school works.

And there was even more, much more, and the constant revelation that each of these pieces, from the hand carved wooden bowl, to the exquisite needlework, or original oil painting, was made by hands, carefully and thoughtfully. These were not mass factory goods made in a far off land, but a bonanza of items lovingly crafted one at a time, far from the goods found in any chain or box store. With the artisan standing by to share the tale of inspiration and the crafting of each individual piece.

And because the people who poured into the show were people who cared about individuals and their labors of love, appreciating their artistry, dreams, and causes, there were a few informational and charitable spaces like Samantha's.

Waiting for the crowds to enter opening day, Sam and Rhonda sat with coffees, relaxed and chatting, reminiscing about old times, full of hope for success for the charity, but free of the nerves of their artist neighbors in this lull before the event opening.

Sam was telling Ronnie how clumsy she felt trying to navigate her computer without getting herself in trouble.

"I remember when the kids were in grade school and they first brought computers in. It's second nature to them, so it's hard for them to understand how intimidating it is for me. When I went to high school and took a typing class, we thought the new electric typewriters were cool. We could type an A without breaking off our little finger!"

"Oh, my god, I'd forgotten that!" Rhonda laughed, flexing her long, slender, manicured ones.

"I finally went back and took a course at the community college, to keep from getting too far behind my kids. Remember that?" Sam asked. " My semester of Computer Science-101 when I was in my thirties?"

"I remember you got an A+ as usual," Rhonda commented.

"Yup. I mastered all that stuff. Letter, colon, backslash, run, file name, dot, b-a-t or e-x-e, then in the blink of an eye, it all changed and changed again. I was obsolete before I even turned around! One step forward, two steps back. I like to use computers to store my work, but they're sneaky and mysterious, and I get the sense that my computer is using me, more than the reverse!"

"Especially now, I bet!"

"Oh yes," Sam laughed ruefully. "Jordan has it handled, though."

Sipping their hot brew carefully they watched a young girl walk by, heavily pierced, wearing what looked like just her bra and a canvas skirt, dragging along a boy stumbling in jeans overlong, because he wore the waist belted somewhere between his butt and his knees, jockeys on display, with one hand permanently clutched on his belt buckle.

Almost in unison, the two old friends seemed to sigh, shake their heads, and murmur that times sure *had* changed since their youth.

Sam and Rhonda were from a generation of women that took pains to *hide* their bra straps—though Ronnie claimed to have burned one of her bras in college during a women's liberation rally. Their generation had had to wear dresses or skirts to school, then kneel to have them measured to make sure their hems weren't shorter than regulation length.

Parents in those days shook their heads and said the high school girls were 'just asking to be raped with those mini-skirts'. That was before the laws understood that no woman ever *asked* for that, and these girls were way too innocent back then to even understand the comment.

Rhonda nodded, a distant glaze in her normal cobalt eyes turning them a glacial blue hue. Pushing a brunette hair off her face, she sighed, "I forget sometimes how much has changed in our lives, how much has happened. I heard something on the news the other night that reminded me of when I was a kid. One time my dad took me with him to the lumberyards. He was pricing concrete blocks and looking at plans to build a backyard bomb shelter, in case of nuclear war with Russia. He never built it, figuring the basement would do instead. We had an old-fashioned basement, not the daylight kind common now. But I remember how it was, and the very real fear with all the duck and cover drills at grade school. Especially during the Cuban missile crisis. I can't remember the outside world ever penetrating my kid world before that."

"Same for me. We had one of those basements, also. We also had a garden where we grew strawberries and corn, carrots, lettuce, and lots of cucumbers. My mom use to home can pickles, and pears and peaches that the whole family went out to grower's fields to pick ourselves. We had a pantry in that basement, larger than the bedrooms in most new tract homes, with shelves all around where mom stocked up for the winter. That pantry was going to be our shelter in case a bomb went off in an attack on the airbase nearby. No one realized back then how unrealistic it was to think we could just hide a few days, then come back out to normal." Sam mused, then remembered something else she'd almost forgotten from her long distant childhood fears.

"And the Cuban thing, that really scared me. Our grade school had us do those duck and cover drills every day and even sent everyone home several times, to turn around and come back, so they could time how long it took to evacuate us safely. Most moms were home all day, so it made sense back then. Oh, and I remember at night, after they blocked a Russian ship, all the adults seemed so worried. I was afraid a bomber would come that night and be able to see me in bed through my window, and drop a bomb on me. So all night I tried to keep myself squished up against the wall, right under the window, laying on my side. That way I was in the shadow, and they wouldn't be able to get me. I was terrified! I'd always felt so safe, but how could my parents fight a bomber with a nuclear missile and protect me?

"God, that decades old memory is so intense still, it makes me wonder what scars children in real worn torn countries have?"

The somber mood blanketed the women in silence for a while, before Rhonda added, "Then there were all the horrible assassinations here. JFK, Martin Luther King, Jr., and Bobby Kennedy. And the terrorists at the Munich Olympics, then all the plane hijackings around the world, all the American hostages in Iran—

"You know, Sam, it's hard for the younger generation to understand that our generation went through a period of so many PLO hijackings, when Arafat seemed to be just a major terrorist, that we had an ingrained understanding of them. We knew that scenario—or *thought* we did. They hijacked a plane, had the pilots fly it to a different airport, which usually turned out to be anywhere they would let it land before they ran out of gas. Then they made demands, but rarely killed their hostages before being tricked and captured, or negotiated down first. Though now I think back, one or two poor souls usually paid the ultimate sacrifice, to show the hijackers were serious.

"But to all of us, to our generation, we knew what a hijacked plane meant. Or thought we knew. It meant: don't panic, wait for it to land, then negotiate. I think that training of our psyches, of generations of our nation's leaders in government, at the airlines, in security, was what made us so paralyzed responding to what was happening on that day, that horrid 9/11. Until it was too late for all those poor people." Rhonda shuddered, her voice having trailed off softer than Sam had ever heard it.

They both sat silently, staring off into the bustle around them, not seeing it, not feeling the life around them, and just remembering. Remembering all the lives lost that day. When it never should have happened that way—or at all.

Ten minutes later, a passerby glanced into the booth and asked, "Hey, what's made you ladies look so sad? We're supposed to be getting ready for a festival!"

They didn't know how to answer. Life, some lives, just went on anyway.

Pushing up from their chairs, they tried to give him weak smiles.

Their job as survivors was to live it. To make the best of it, while never forgetting a silent moment for those who could not.

Time to get to it.

There were people that *could* be helped right *now,* with the Service Dog Program. Sam and Rhonda stood in front of the booth with brochures in hand, and began to smile and cajole for donations as the crowds began to filter down the grass-lined streets of the fairground.

And soon the crowds, the noise, the laughter, loud excited chatter, and wonderful happy chaos of a festival market engulfed them.

"Time for a break, ladies. I brought Shelley to mind the booth while I take you both to lunch. But first, I thought…," with a quick glance at Ronnie, Jordan turned back to his lovely bride with a grin. "Have you had a chance to see any of the Juried Art Exhibits yet?"

"Why no," Rhonda replied on cue. "How delightful! Come on Sam, let's go be fairgoers for a while. We must check out the awards and then your handsome man can buy us something sinfully greasy and fattening from the food carts." She was already heaving Sam up to make room for Shelley, who plunked down before Sam could object. Though she could hardly object to letting anyone else gather money for her charity when that someone was not only a trusted friend, but a member of the law courts.

"Okay, well," a little flustered with Ronnie still tugging on one arm, Sam scooped up her purse, and managed to hand Shelley a key before she was dragged off. "This is to the lock box under the table, the receipt book is under there also, and…"

"Got it," Shelley grinned, "Go have some fun."

They, meaning her best friend and her husband, decided to start first with the juried exhibits, though Sam's tummy growled loudly as they passed a B-B-Q Ribs food truck. And continued to growl to her great embarrassment as they quietly worked their way around the art exhibit gallery with other patrons, before moving into the juried photography exhibit.

Ronnie seemed to almost gallop past each photograph, while Sam took her time to study and appreciate each, Jordan waiting patiently at her side. Photography was a favorite hobby of her son's, and she couldn't resist studying each picture carefully, without bias, she told herself, before deciding her own son's were just as good. She thought he could make a career of his hobby. If that is what he wanted.

Moving on with subtle nudges from her husband, they finally caught up to Ronnie.

"I like this one best," she declared over her shoulder when they came up behind her. Then stepped to the side to make room for Sam with Jordan on her other side.

"Oh, that's exquisite, isn't it?" Sam agreed. "And look it won a prize. Honorable Mention." She studied the ribbon and descriptive card, and suddenly let out an excited shriek.

"OH! Oh my god, it is Paul's. Look Ronnie! It's Paul's! And it has a ribbon! Honey look!" She turned to her husband, beaming, pointing, excited.

Jordan looked down into those glowing honey brown eyes, filled with a mother's joy and pride, draping an arm around her shoulder to give her a little squeeze of understanding—and to hold her steady as she literally bounced with happiness.

Turning back to study the photo again, then the ribbon, then the photo, then the card, her smile suddenly turned off, and a disappointed "Oh, no" left her lips, before she forced her smile back. "It's sold already! See the sticker. How nice for Paul." And she was happy, she just ... Sam felt that tug, as a mom that had saved all her children's accomplishments over the years, from the indecipherable crayon scribbles that she first hung on the fridge, to their later efforts as they advanced through grade school and beyond. She now had several of Paul's photographs. Not stuck to the fridge with a magnet, but beautifully framed on her walls. She was so happy for her son that someone had purchased his work, especially so early in the show. But ... someone *else* had bought it.

Unaware she had whispered those last words forlornly, Jordan felt a sharp tug on his heart, followed by a sharp pointy elbow in his side from Rhonda. He had meant to hold the surprise and bring the painting home at the end of the fair, but the look of mixed emotions clouding his wife's eyes, made him realize he had better speak up now. But he apparently hesitated too long for her impatient friend.

"It's for *you*, Sam. The photograph and the card that notes his award. The ribbon of course will go to Paul. Thank god you haven't had time to read the list of awards in the festival brochure, or it would have ruined the surprise."

"For me? OH! Oh." Again that mother's mix of joy and concern. "But he shouldn't give it to me. Of course I would *love* to have it, but he should sell it, make a profit, and make his name as an artist." She turned to Jordan seeking agreement, only to register the smug smile on his face, at the same time she heard her friend's hoot of laughter.

"Oh hon, don't worry about that. Your darling son charged your handsome hubby three times what he was going to sell it for. Paul said, "If it is a gift for my mom, she is worth more, a lot more!"

Jordan's grin broadened, rueful, "And I would have paid three times that amount again and still never gotten close to your value to me." He gave her shoulder a squeeze, bending over to look in her face, asking, "Are you happy?" Her speechless nod, and the tears pouring down her cheeks over a shaky smile, was all the answer he needed. Rubbing her shoulder, his voice and hands tender, he murmured in her ear, "And this will make you even happier. Not only was your son such a savvy businessman, but I convinced him to set up a booth at next year's festival."

A hopeful, if watery, "Really?" from his wife.

"Truly. We made a deal and shook on it."

"After," Rhonda added wryly, "Your husband first guilted him with how much it would mean to you. Then he bribed him shamelessly by promising to pay all the fees for the festival space and fees to submit more art to be juried."

"Jordan!" Sam gasped, then laughed. "Oh, you are devious. And so wonderful. I love you!"

"Anything for you, my love, and yours, who, by the way, I now consider mine also." He brushed the moisture from her cheek with a gentle finger.

"Yours also," she sighed, "that is one of the sweetest things I have ever heard you say, Jordan."

"O - kay!" Rhonda interrupted. "As much as I am enjoying this little mutual appreciation scene, it is getting a bit too mushy for me. I see a very interesting, shapely piece of pottery in the next juried exhibit. I think I'll check it out and leave you two to it. Don't wait lunch for me."

Rhonda deserted them to go check out her shapely piece of pottery—or maybe it was the shape of the potter she went to check out, Sam noted wryly before turning back to her husband, recognizing the added subtle sway to Rhonda's saunter, as she bore down on her prey.

Worried that she had left Shel covering the booth too long, Sam and Jordan worked quickly through the rest of the photography exhibit—Sam determined first to see *who* had deserved higher ribbons than *her* son!

They gathered up B-B-Q, gyros, piroshkies, and crepes from the food court, along with Italian sodas, before Sam felt like she had enough food to carry back to the booth to quiet her noisy, if now excited, tummy.

Returning with extra food to relieve Shelley, they found she had already had private catering by the guy who ran the Youth Shelter, Kevin MacClarty.

"Hey, Kev," Jordan greeted a friend with a rough handshake, before the men stepped aside to talk business, while Shelley filled Sam in on everything that had happened in her absence. When Sam started to tell about Paul's award and her husband's gift, Shelley just smiled.

Of course! That was why she had come! So her boss could take his wife to see her gift! They were all in on it probably. Jordan's office was a tight knit group of friends as well as colleagues. Turning to tease her husband about being the last to know, she waited patiently for her husband to finish what he was quietly telling Kevin.

"...so the Coast Guard asked the DEA to activate an undercover agent they have set up in this region."

"Good. Every eye helps. I'll keep that to myself." MacClarty responded quietly before turning back to the ladies. Smiling at Shelley, he reached out a hand, asking courteously, "May I have the honor of a stroll through the Festival with you? I like to have a pretty girl on my arm at these events." Grinning at Shelley's frown. "No offense. Compliment," he laughed, pulling her up and keeping hold of her hand.

"Kevin, wait," Jordan called. "What about Timmy?"

Kevin just snorted. "Timmy is *assisting* his lady love, Candy. Walking around with his eyes closed while Bernie guides him, so he is currently too busy floating in heaven to get into any mischief."

"I guess," Jordan laughed with him, then took a seat beside his wife when she tugged him down to whisper in his ear. She told him she had accidentally heard his confidence to Kevin, and assured him she wouldn't tell a soul, even Rhonda.

"I know, sweetheart. I trust you completely," he replied, surprised she didn't yet realize his total faith in her. But then again, they were still newlyweds.

Shelley sighed inwardly, as she strolled away with Kevin, their hand holding contact already broken by a patron shoving through the crowds. She was thinking about what a happy, besotted man her boss was with his new wife. What a change!

"You know he has a romance book club secretly shipping him monthly novels at the office?" She blurted the thought out loud, slapped a hand over her mouth, and then relaxed. Kevin was a safe confidant.

"Jordan?" Kevin's thoroughly shocked voice rose comically along with his dark auburn eyebrows. "You have got to be kidding me, Shel."

"Nope." She gave a smug little smile leaning in against his shoulder confidingly, "When I first started working for him, I swear he was a total misogynist. Well, not total, I guess. Actually, that is not fair at all, he did give *me* a chance. Though he used to call me Ms. Airhead, instead of Airton, as if he thought that was my last name." Laughing she strolled besides him through the crowds, filling him in on the story.

So far their relationship had grown mostly around their mutual commitment to mentoring Timmy. Making plans for doing things together with Timmy had been an excuse for going on outings that might otherwise be considered dates.

Like their visit to the art festival today, after she'd finished in the courtroom for the day.

The boy was off exploring, absorbing sights he never had as a youth, and probably driving the girl, many years his senior, crazy. Just innocent puppy love, and probably a lot of actual puppy love also, as the girl was a dog handler, and he always begged to help her. Timmy would check back in with them about a dozen times, cadging money to try out the spiral fries at one booth, then the gyros at another, and by the end of the day would probably have sampled from every single stall at the international food court, checked out all the bands and musicians scheduled for the day, and hopefully, actually look at some of the art, and the awards earned by students from grade through high school. Timmy was just a normal, happy, hungry, healthy whirlwind of a young boy growing up – now. And that was just what he needed. Exactly what they wanted for him to experience. It gave the couple a lot of time alone, to talk and get to know each other better, while they keep an eye out on Tim.

Shelley and Kevin had started out with an immediate connection and closeness that felt like they had been friends forever, but that initial spark of heat had not fizzled – at least for Shelley. She felt it shimmering beneath the fun and chaos of the fair, and experiencing it, with him.

"Frowning?" The brunette arched questing dark brows at the man staring at a rather dubious clay toned sculpture on a pedestal. No ribbon graced this work.

"Venus X?" She queried, after a look at the card, pulling the man from his funk.

"Yes!" In true earnest artist fashion, he explained, "It is supposed to be a modern day representation of an ancient Venus W. A progression you know, Venus W, now X? But..." he scraped a hand through the thatch of already rumpled bronzed hair, green eyes troubled, "But it doesn't look the same here as it seemed in my studio."

"Ah, well no need to pout, many a man has seen beauty in a dim room late at night, that doesn't look quite as good to him in the bright lights, but . .," with a careless wave of her hand, the sultry brunette cautioned, "Men *do* have their expectations, usually blinded by a *certain* anticipation, but ... I'm sure your model looked better in tight jeans and push-up bra. Quite voluptuous clothed I'm sure."

Her tone was cool, dismissive, as she had been the day before, right after giving him a twice over scan with those eyes that had nearly set his bones on fire. Off balance, he defended himself. "What? No, it's not based on a real model, but an ancient fertility goddess. The Venus ..."

"W. Fertility goddess. The Venus of Willendorf," Rhonda finished for him.

"You recognized her?" Surprised and pleased, his smile faded when she took another look at the rather lumpy sculpture and slowly shook her head.

"Let's just say I followed the word clues, but I suppose...," she studied the piece again, "Ah... no. I would never have guessed, though I suppose that adding red painted nipples on her was the modern "progression" of the art? I'm afraid styles have changed quite a bit more than that. While I'm sure the men that carried her around in their sweaty palms thirty thousand years ago thought she was a goddess, I doubt she would be instantly recognizable in today's world."

Especially as you have made her! Rhonda thought to herself. But she had seen his pottery, and it was lovely. No need to crush him by telling him he stunk as a sculptor. Besides, *his* body was the piece of work, the sculpture, she most appreciated. And women did have their expectations...

"I think it's the hips," the artist murmured, chin thoughtfully braced in a bronzed, long-fingered hand.

Smoothing her hand down one of her own well balanced hips Rhonda glanced at his hands, her amazing cobalt eyes sheathed beneath dark lashes, her voice naturally dropped to a huskier timbre.

"I think you might need a new model."

With an appreciative but wary smile he turned his full focus on her, assessing, agreeing.

"Maybe I do. I wonder if I could entice a woman that had," he paused to run his eyes over her, "a most perfect form to model for me? Do you think I could bribe one with a sunset sail in the Sound in my sailboat?"

Watching her study him silently, dark winged brows slightly raised, full luscious lips pursed as she considered him, he quickly added, "Of course, I *could* just snap a few photographs, work from pictures, on a perfect form and a lovely muse framed against the setting sun...?"

"How quaint."

"Pardon?" Still, unsure, after her prior dismissal of him yesterday.

"Working from photos," she clarified, a mischievous gleam dancing in those bluer than blue eyes.

"I would think an artist such as yourself would want to work from a live model. Fill your hands with wet clay and smooth and slick it over the form you wished to create first, create a muscle memory so to speak, before transferring it to the vase, but, then ...," she paused, a taunting smile on her face as she watched his Adams apple dance on his strong tanned throat as he tried to recall how to speak, knowing what was going through his mind.

Was this another trick? He asked himself. Another set down? This woman had gobbled him with her eyes then dismissed him with a cool flick of her wrist the day before, then ignored him though they had faced each other across just twenty feet for the last day and a half. Was she testing, teasing, just basically cruel? Did he dare hope? Or speak? Lest this all disappeared in smoke?

"So it's a date?" She spoke for him, more statement than question, watching his speechless nod. "Tonight, then. I'll model for you on your sailboat. At sunset. Come get me at the booth, and...," turning away to head back to her friends, she warned over her shoulder, "Do not be late. The offer will not be repeated."

"And," pausing momentarily to turn back toward the still wary, mildly stunned man, Rhonda added, "Do not forget to bring some wine." Then she gave him a wicked wink.

"And a *lot* of clay."

chapter four

"Hey, Airhead! Over here." Kevin loved to tease.
Shelley would regret telling him her current boss used to refer to her as 'Mzz Airhead'. But Shelley Airton was no piece of fluff. Kevin knew it—though she did look the part. Slim but very well curved, the delicate bones of her face were framed in a soft cloud of honey-blond hair that curled around wide-eyed blues that seemed innocent and unwary. Yet that was a mere physical illusion, not a reality; a trait they shared.

Kevin MacClarty knew that at first glance his red hair, green eyes, and freckles might convey a youthful look, while a closer look revealed the hard life etched into his features. As a boy, he had been a big-city gang banger, on drugs, booze, his heart encased in a bitter steel wall, his young muscles wiry, tense, tattooed, resentful, and explosive. All that when he was barely older than young Timmy.

Years later, someone had stepped in for him. Someone had yanked him out of that life; and fought for his heart and soul. While he was never able to live the life of just a normal young boy after that experience, he had become a man. A man committed to making sure that endangered youth could do just that—be young, be just boys having fun. Healthy fun.

Running his Youth Shelter was not just a job for Kevin. It was a commitment, a mission, a whole heart dream he was determined to make a reality for *his* boys. They were a tough bunch; it could be a tough job. He had to defend them from budget cuts and the drug dealers that constantly tried to prey on the weak and isolated, in addition to finding a way past their hardened shells to make them listen and see that there was another way. The first thing he let them

see was that he *had* known the street and now lived a better life—
though he never lied to them that it was easy.

When he first met Shelley, Kevin thought she looked like a do-
gooder piece of fluff. She even sounded like one with that soft,
sweet voice, when she had first asked him to help rescue young ten
year old Timmy. The boy's father and elder brother had just gone to
jail; the mother had long past given up. Shelley said she was
Timmy's new Big Sister and she needed Kevin's help. He had
snorted to himself, thinking she was in for a rude shock.

But he was.

Scooting between people Shelley joined him at the booth, with
a soft laugh.

"Airhead now, huh? I think calling me that name embarrasses
Jordan now more than it ever irked me. I still can't believe he hired
me. I thought he hated my guts. I hoped his hostility was just
because I was the enemy, and not personal. I knew it was *not*
because he hated *any* attractive woman back then, as I was
certainly no femme-fatale!' She laughed, shaking her head at the
memory.

Kevin was shaking his head also, but he wasn't laughing.

"You might just be more of an airhead than I thought," he said,
pursing his lips. "Either that or you don't have any mirrors in your
house." He watched her eyes widen for a moment, then narrow.
Either she didn't believe, or didn't trust his compliment.

"I can pretty much guarantee Jordan probably hired you in spite
of your beauty," he added, watching her closely. "He told me once
you had a brilliant mind and talent and that you two were 'kindred
spirits'."

"Ah," she nodded her head, face sober, then turned to gaze off
into the distance, remaining silent.

Kevin broke the puzzling silence. Something more there than
he had realized.

"I'm thinking I might be just a wee bit jealous?" Kevin spoke in
a slow, lilting, brogue that he'd never had, but developed for effect.
He waited to see how it worked on Shelley.

And waited in vain. Whatever her thoughts, she didn't share
them. He watched her closely in fascination as her saw that
deceptive softness glow across her features for a moment before
shifting in a kaleidoscope of emotions, flickering with that steely
determination at her core that had been such a shock to him, then

back to a soft, thoughtful frown. He would give anything to be able to read her mind right now.

"Maybe we should track down Timmy," she said. And he knew that had not been the focus of those elusive thoughts, but as a way to divert him.

Shelley's illusions were more than physical once.

Illusions were something the young Shelley had aplenty setting out on her chosen career path—crusade, might be more accurate. Charging forward with her law degree like Lady Justice with her torch raised high to wave in the face of the old dragons guarding an unbalanced system, unfair to the poor innocent masses.

She joined the fray immediately in the Public Defender's Office. The scales needed to be balanced and she was eager to start her mission. Client after client gazed into those wide, soft and sympathetic innocent blue eyes and let her see what she wanted to see. Their words told her what she wanted to hear. They were all innocent, just as she had thought, all these poor maligned people that couldn't even afford an attorney to defend themselves from a cruelly unbalanced system. Accepting, trusting, yet diligent and capable, Shelley put her research skills to work to find the facts, the evidence, to prove the charges false.

And all that sweet, crusading innocence of her own was in for a terribly rude shock.

So many had lied to her! Looked her in the eye and lied to her face! She must have misheard, or maybe they misunderstood her questions, or maybe … Maybe she was a naïve little fool?

The sound of her illusions being crushed nearly echoed in a breaking heart. But she had rallied. Some of her clients *were* innocent, and for them alone her work was worth the effort. And when it got right down to it, it was not her job to believe in the liars. It *was* her job to believe that, regardless, they deserved the best possible defense, because every man and woman was innocent until the state could provide convincing evidence otherwise.

So she did her job, and gloried in the rightful successes, and toughened up and pursued every motion she could press for the clients that needed all the help they could get.

But over time, when she saw the same clients repeating again and again, her smile of victory became more and more grim. A new crack grew in her heart as she saw her wide-eyed jurors pronounce "not guilty" when she knew it was only a result of all the repeat offenses being successfully withheld from the testimony—by her skills. They were guilty as hell. She had cheated, legally. But *that* was her job—as a public defender. She began to feel her 'innocent masses' were the people outside the courtroom, unaware of what she might release on them with her victories. The weight of her personal guilt became too heavy to bear.

Then her greatest enemy, the Prosecutor, Mr. Jordan Campbell, who used to mock and torment her, calling her Mzzz Airhead, when he knew very well her name was Ms. Airton, stepped in and saved her.

He hired her.

He had hired her because though she may look like fluff, and dressed her hair and clothes much too fluffy for him back then, he admired and respected her skills, her drive to do what was right, and wanted to give her an opportunity to crusade on his team. He had started much as she had, seen his illusions crash, and switched sides. He had spotted a kindred spirit and given her a new opportunity to help, and make more of a difference now that her eyes were not glazed with naivety. If her experiences had toughened her mind, and bruised her soul, they had not left her with a hardened heart. It was still vulnerable, just much better defended.

When it came to justice, anyway.

But love? Personal relationships? That was a game Shelley had never had the time or energy to play. There her heart lay naked and vulnerable, shy and terrified of trusting. But not closed. She had more guts than that. And maybe she even had a man that was just a tiny bit jealous strolling about the fair at her side. Or was that just wishful thinking?

Shelley had been a little—okay, a lot—awed by Kevin at first. And still. Despite all her early tingles of awareness, she hadn't expected or imagined that he would feel any interest in her as a female. As a professional colleague, sure, that had brought them together. But was that all?

Kevin was so handsome, self-confident, and worldly. He had become a man the hard way. Solidly muscled, strong, honest, and fair, he was a leader to respect physically and someone that wasn't about to fall for any bullshit from the boys at his shelter. And because of his past life, what they probably feared most—those tough boys trying to be men—was when Kev pinned them with those green eyes and demanded, "Can I count on you, man?" And they dared to hope.

Timmy thought Kevin hung the moon.

Shelley thought so too. And her attraction was much more than just professional respect. Her nerves seem to vibrate whenever she was near this particular male. And *very* male he was. She hadn't realized how empty the three-piece-suits she used to date were until she was exposed to Kevin. He was so solid, inside and out, that he seemed to project a magnetic force field.

And Shelley seemed to have become a magnet.

It terrified her almost as much as it thrilled her. Because she didn't know if it was one sided. Was he truly jealous?

"Timmy will find us. Come see this, beautiful." Kevin recaptured her hand and turned, pulling her through the crowds in his wake. Shelley nearly stumbled, at the offhand compliment. Had he really said she was beautiful? She tried to catch her breath when Kevin pulled her over to a booth that had handmade jewelry. She studied his profile, while he seemed to be intently studying trays of earrings.

More dark auburn than red, his hair was cut fairly short to control its tendency to curl. His jaw was firm and square, his cheekbones firm but high enough to hint that he had probably looked like a cherub as a child. Now his strong neck, jaw and shoulders denied the faint sprinkle of innocent freckles just noticeable on a tanned face that made his green eyes glitter like gemstones, between lashes darker, and longer than a man deserved. Standing so close beside him, her hand still trapped in his strong clasp, Shelley could smell his scent—woodsy, with a touch of male and spice. She was trying not to breathe it in too obviously when he spoke. "Is this pretty?"

"What? Oh yes, lovely," she answered, barely glancing at what he showed her, but smiling up at the artist.

"We'll take this one." Kevin passed his credit card to the lady.

We? Shell thought. Are we a *we?* She wondered.

Then Kevin turned and clasped the exquisitely simple bracelet around her wrist, telling the artist, in a matter of fact tone, "It matches her eyes."

Shelley just stood there dumbly, staring at her outstretched arm. The blue eyes the bracelet matched, going soft, even a little damp. She still had not recovered from him saying she was beautiful, if she had heard him right. And now this? The ground seemed to roll under her feet like it had in the last earthquake. When she looked up into his smiling eyes, her heart seemed to roll up against her ribs and bounce back. She opened her mouth to say....

"Hey, Kev, Shel, what's up? Can I have a gyro? I'm about starved," Timmy shoved between them. "Let's go check the food out."

"Sure kid, "Kevin agreed, ruffling Timmy's hair, because it made the kid crazy. "Shel?" he turned to her, but Timmy had already placed himself between them and was tugging them both to the closest food stand.

The wide grass lane of Rembrandt Avenue was filled with the ebb and flow of energetic fairgoers dressed casually in slacks and jeans, shorts and sandals, sweatpants and jogging suits, with the occasional flowered shirt or skirt, all jostled between the banks of the tented booths like a river in constant motion. In its midst was a couple that looked as if they had been joined together forever, all the rest parted to flow around this solid structure, like waters around a boulder. Slowly they worked their way downstream, his footed cane solidly planted then followed by the age-shortened couple with slow careful steps. Her hand was tucked under his arm and held gallantly against his side, whether for support or long time habit, or both, they were one unit. Their eyes were bright and flickered with interest among the artworks and young folks, and between each other with simple pleasure in the day's outing.

She wore a matching jacket, shell, and below the knee length skirt of a particular tint of mint green with white trimmed lapels and buttons that had surely been created by the first designers of polyester fashions in the '70s. He wore a tan polyester 'leisure suit' of the same vintage with its snap front closure and distinctive shiny weave. Purchased back when they were the newest fashion and fabric, these were their Sunday best clothes and had been carefully cherished and protected over the years. She wore pearls and a tiny hat on her white curls. He wore a starched white shirt, its collar now too loose for his neck, but secured with a string tie. Her shoes were white shiny low heeled patent leather and the purse dangling from her arm matched, of course. At a guess, white cotton gloves and an embroidered handkerchief nestled inside; his hidden cloth handkerchief was most likely monogrammed, despite their 'mod' attire. And surely she would have always signed her name with his full name with a 'Mrs.' in front. Everyone parted respectfully for them, even young Timmy, though he did turn his head back to stare wistfully at them a moment, seeing someone's great-or-more grandparents, and wishing . . .

They were long past him when they spoke, so he wasn't shocked (or delighted).

They were nearing the grassy intersection when the lady did a double take and peered hard into a corner booth. "Why for heaven's sake I do believe…," she muttered to herself, then turned to shout into her husband's ear.

"LOOK OVER THERE! IT'S THAT JAILBIRD! I DO DECLARE!" Getting her hearing-impaired husband's attention, she pointed as accurately as she could with an arthritically curved finger. "SEE HER RIGHT THERE?"

He stuttered to a halt and turned to peer. As did everyone in shouting distance.

"YOU MEAN THAT WENCH THAT LOOKS LIKE SHE CHEWS RAKES FOR BREAKFAST?" He yelled back in a quavering, faintly British accent. And he was not referring to the garden variety rake, either. He might yell because he couldn't hear himself, or others, and his shoulders might be stooped, and his legs frail, but there was nothing wrong with his high-powered eyeglasses—except that the longer he focused on the brunette babe, the more they seemed to fog.

"NOT HER. THE LITTLE BLONDE BESIDE HER. I AM SURE SHE IS THAT JAILBIRD THAT WAS IN THE NEWSPAPERS!" Yelled back his sweet white-haired and rouged cheeked wife.

If there was anyone in the crowd that didn't swing around to stare at Samantha, well, they must have been stone deaf!

Rhonda gave the gent an appreciative smile and seductive wink acknowledging the compliment. He may have had three or four decades on her, but he was still male—her very favorite type of species. Meanwhile Sam shrunk down in her chair wishing she could slide down right underneath the cloth draped table and hide there—may be forever! Would she ever live her foolishness down?

"SHE MARRIED THE MAN THAT TOSSED HER IN JAIL. THAT PROSECUTOR," the lady screamed above the excited murmurs of the crowd.

Oh, poor Jordan, Sam thought, her guilt increasing.

"SUCH A HANDSOME LAD! DON'T BLAME THE LASS FOR GRABBING ONTO HIM. HANDY TO HAVE AROUND, TOO, I IMAGINE, WHEN YOU ARE THE JAILBIRD TYPE. GOOD CONNECTIONS HE HAS, THAT BOY." The hollered private conversation continued endlessly.

And Ronnie, her dear friend—the traitor—was near hysterical with laughter.

Yet the incident didn't turn out to be a disaster after all. Sam was even able to have a good laugh over it herself. Much, much later.

When the ancient elders finally moved off, the fascinated staring crowd remained behind. It wasn't that Sam had ever meant to keep her past hidden; it was part of her story of how she got involved in the charity. She just wished her husband's reputation hadn't had to take a bruising. And, to be honest, she had really planned to present her story with a bit more … subtlety. A lot more, actually.

But she had come to the fair to get attention for her program, and now she had a captivated audience. She would have to be a cowardly fool not to take advantage of the opportunity. And Sam was no fool—at least so far this year. But cowardly was feeling pretty darn comfortable.

Blowing out a deep breath, Samantha started wiggling herself out from beneath the table, trying to pretend she didn't know her face was fire engine red. Scooting up straight in her chair, she folded her hands primly on the tabletop, straightening her shoulders. Everyone still seemed to loom accusingly above her.

So she stood up. Abruptly.

The crowd jumped back a step. Ronnie snorted.

"Try to look less threatening," she softly advised her petite friend with a suspicious sounding cough.

Pasting a wide smile on her face, spreading her open palms wide, Sam started speaking in a calm but carrying voice, trying to cajole her audience

"Yes, I'm afraid I do have a rather unique story. And it *is* a long and foolish tale, but I would be more than happy to share it with you..."

The crowd now took a step closer, the most curious took two. As Sam continued to speak with passion they edged near.

"... and tell you how I became involved in this project. It's something that should be especially near and dear to the hearts of everyone who has come here today to see and appreciate all these fine visual artworks. Why? Because you *can* see their beauty, see the way they speak and share sights and emotions, and you of all people can realize what an incredible gift and joy that is. You recognize what a tragedy a life without that vision would be . . ."

They had to send to the printers for more information sheets on the seeing-eye dog training program within an hour. Candy and her canine pal found themselves guiding not just individuals but groups around the fair all afternoon. And artists started filtering over to talk about ways they could get involved, not only with auctioning a piece for the charity, but about how their own eyes had been opened to trying out some new textural techniques with their oils and acrylics to add vision for the fingertips to their works.

As they packed up that night, Ronnie leaned over and rubbed her hand over Sam's back, murmuring, "Way to go, Jailbird."

chapter five

The Northern Straits

The Puget Sound trough was part of a series of lowland valleys that stretched from British Columbia down through the Willamette Valley in Oregon, between the western Coastal Mountain Ranges and the parallel volcanic Cascade Mountain Range. Like the valley of the Willamette today, these were once river valleys that drained the mountains and flowed north, with a river branching and draining west between a gap in the coastal range between the Olympics and Vancouver Island. Then the Ice Ages came and mountain glaciers poured into the valleys and ice sheets advanced down from the north. The former rivers were blocked and their valleys gouged out by great fingerlike lobes of ice sheets less than twenty thousand years ago.

As the great ice sheets began to retreat, the gouged out and blocked valleys were filled with melt waters, creating first Puget Sound to the south, then finally backing up past the western ice plow, filling and flooding what is now the Strait of Juan de Fuca to the west, and freeing it to the Pacific. Then the ice sheet lingered for a while, still blockading the trough to the north between the south end of Vancouver Island and the Washington Coast, calving off icebergs to float in the sound and strait as they do in Alaska today.

Finally, the ice sheet made its final retreat north into Canada, backfilling with melt water the rest of the trough with permanent waterways, and uncovering some of the high spots in the middle that it had been crushing and grinding into low rounded humps—

the San Juan and Gulf Islands.

Depending on how many rocks and reefs are counted, there are potentially up to seven hundred islands in the San Juan Island Archipelago in the waters between the coast of Washington and the Canadian shores of Vancouver Island to the west, along with a dizzying number of channels, straits, sounds, bays, and inlets.

From a low spit of land west of Anacortes, the Washington State Ferry dock loaded passengers heading to any one of the four main San Juan Islands, and international passengers continuing west to the Canadian island. The last U.S. docking was at Friday Harbor, on San Juan Island. Beyond that U.S. and Canadian waters began to dance a watery boundary line between the Canadian Gulf and Vancouver Islands, and the scattered San Juan grouping of Washington State.

He had debated taking the ferry direct to Friday Harbor, just over an hour cruise, but had decided he'd rather scope out as many of the one hundred seventy-two named islands as he could see from the multi-stop almost two hour ferry ride. Before reaching the larger islands, the ferry first threaded a path between the islands of Guemes, Cypress, and Blakely to the north, with views of James and Decatur to the south before making its first stop at a Lopez Island headland. From there it would go on to Shaw, Orcas, and then San Juan Island docks.

He spent most of his trip at the railings with his camera's telescopic lens to his face, fighting for balance with the plunging of the ferry in the waves, and the sharp winds carrying a mist of sea spray. But it gave him a chance to study the scenery in privacy— almost.

"You must be a first timer, young fella." He pretended he hadn't heard.

"Yep, usually first-timers are the only ones standing at the front rail, parting the wind, trying to take pictures instead of staying warm and cozy in the lounge to see the view."

"Got me there," he muttered, still shielding his face behind the camera, but he was no match for the persistently friendly rotund man.

"My name is Bud." An outstretched hand was shoved in his

ribcage. He finally lowered his camera and turned to face the man, giving his hand a quick shake.

"Hell," a jovial Bud said, "I've lived on Orcas for years. Ever since I retired. Love the place. Just love it. You're going to love it too, I bet. Seen any whales out there yet? Usually don't see them much through here, but we have pods of resident killer whales. Bet you didn't know that, did you? But no need to worry, they mostly just chew on salmon. Heh, heh."

Finally registering the patient but blank expression on the stranger's face, Bud seemed to decide the fella wasn't too interested in a welcome wagon, offering his hand a final time, a question in his voice, "Well, it was nice meeting you…"

"Just call me Jake." He shook, thanked Bud, then waited with a polite smile on his face for him to go back into the passenger lounge and let him get on with logging photos of the islands and navigable inlets they were passing.

'Jake' analyzed Lopez, Shaw, and Orcas as the ferry docked at each and decided the final large island, San Juan Island, with the dock and marina at Friday Harbor, was where he would create a temporary base, easily arranging for a rental with such a large itinerate artist community. He would bring his own boat to thoroughly explore the maze of surrounding islands.

Edmonds by the Sound

"What is *that* skinny ass doing over there?"

Rhonda clapped a hand over her lips, then mouthed a silent apology for her indignant blurt to the far side of the booth, where Sam had turned from patrons she was working with this morning. Then Rhonda turned irritated eyes back to the space across the way, hoping she had been mistaken.

She had glanced over to catch a little view of the delicious potter, to enjoy like a pastry with her morning sip of coffee, and caught him just as she had hoped—bending over. But the wrong butt was filling, or unfortunately, not filling out, the back of those jeans. Instead she had seen a skinny, scrawny ass that matched the long-haired man now standing among the pots in Potter's space.

Peter Potter was nowhere to be seen.

Where the hell was he? Taking a break? Or, her lips curled in a smug smile, maybe the poor boy was running errands, trying to find clay? Ignoring the disappointing view, the increasing morning crowds, and the quiet conversation across their booth, Rhonda settled back in her chair, enjoying her latte, and let herself sort through her impressions of last evening.

It had started out unpleasantly.

Rhonda had sent Sam off with the bank bag to drop the day's donations off at the bank for credit to the charity, promising to finish tucking things away for the night. She took her time, lingered, then left.

She had drifted over to hear the new ensemble setting up for the evening, when musical artistry took center stage. All day music had swirled around the fairgoers. A mariachi band had been a favorite earlier today, followed by blues, then a folk singer with a guitar. And jazz, country, and rock bands were on the agenda for tonight. Standing behind the people seated in a semicircular amphitheater, to listen to the jazz saxophone for a moment before heading home, she tensed when hands came to rest lightly on her waist.

"Are you going to tell me your name, or should I just call you Beautiful? Oomph!"

"Well, if it isn't the delinquent potter," she turned to him, eyes frosty. "Oh dear, I didn't hurt you did I?" She asked, sweetly insincere.

Rubbing his ribs, he frowned muttering, "You must sharpen those elbows. What was that for? I thought we had a date?"

She ignored the second question. "That? That was what men get that sneak up behind me and have the gall to touch me without permission. And for ones that have pathetic, practiced lines," she added with a scornful look.

"But we had a date!"

"We *had* a date. You're late. You missed it."

"But I got tied up with a client, I couldn't help it ..."

She raised an eyebrow, pursed her lips, and studied him, arms folded at her waist. His space had been empty and closed, though he might have been meeting with a client elsewhere . . .

"Please have mercy, woman." Then he grinned—he had a hell of a dimpled grin. Without shame, hand on heart, adding, "Then you can be named both Beautiful and Merciful."

"Enough. You are making me nauseous. I suppose I could grant you a second chance, just this once," she relented.

"Great!' Grasping her hand firmly in his, before she could change her mind, he had towed Rhonda away to walk her down to the center of town. "You won't regret this."

But had she?

Jubilant, receipt book in hand, Samantha waved to her new acquaintances—and generous donors—then danced over to join Ronnie at the table.

"Oh, you got me a latte, too! You are a life savior, I had to rush out without my coffee this morning. Thank you," Sam's exuberance was running at full speed. "I wish you could have made it to our barbeque last night. We had so much fun, and it was crazy with the kids there. Candy and Timmy blindfolded Jordan, then she had her guide dog, Bernie, lead him all around the house and yard. Of course, Timmy rearranged all my chairs, and set up all kinds of traps in the house, just so Jordan couldn't cheat in familiar territory. He was so impressed."

"Young Timmy?"

"No. Well, yes, of course. Timmy thinks Candy walks on water. But I meant my husband was very impressed. So, naturally," with a giggle, "I hit him up for a big donation to the cause."

"What are husbands for?" Rhonda asked and watched Sam's eyes glow even brighter, pink tinting her cheeks, "Besides that." Rhonda laughed as Sam turned even redder.

"It, ah, was a monetary donation," Sam insisted.

"I'm sure the first donation to the cause was," her friend teased.

Hoping to change the subject of the conversation—at least from her private life, to her friend's—Sam took a big swallow of her lukewarm coffee and went on the offensive.

Leaning forward, eager, she asked, "And how was your date?"

"It was more like a half of a date," Ronnie replied wryly.

"Half a date?"

"Maybe a third, on consideration."

"Oh. Dear." Wary, and unsure what to say, Sam patted her friend's hand, knowing better than to ask Ronnie a leading question by asking which third; this could be one of her teasing traps, after all. But Ronnie didn't have her mischievous face on. She looked very sober. "Were you very disappointed?" Sam asked softly.

"I haven't decided yet. But it looks like you have some more people interested in a guide-dog tour. Why don't you go help them while I think it over?"

He had held Rhonda's hand as they walked, stroking her palm with his thumb, sliding his long fingers against hers, then tangling and weaving them together. It had been rather sweet, really, she admitted.

Though a bit of a novelty for her. She generally tended to get directly to the entangling things part of a date, and skipped all that romance stuff.

But it seemed to fit as they strolled downhill on Main to the central core of town around the fountain. Small trees planted along the curb rustled their leaves as they walked through the dappled light beneath them, adding to the lazy ambiance of a summer evening. Birds hidden in a thick bush near the library seemed to be carrying on a muted conversation.

It was the dinner hour, the earlier heavy traffic on the sidewalks and roads had mostly gone home or found somewhere to sit, dine, linger, and restore energies spent, and now savored. The early evening was still bright on summertime hours, but the sun's position to the west cast its light at an angle that seemed to gild even the most ordinary objects, and give them a slow, soft magic.

It painted the old store fronts along Main in a sepia tint, making them look like old-fashioned photographs of themselves in an older Edmonds. At the fountain intersection on Main the cars moved in a round-a-bout circle, but there were no painted markings or stripes for crosswalks. Instead wide cobbled, herringbone pavers were set in the pavement, and the light lovingly etched and enhanced each stone in the artistry set in the road. Brass glimmered beneath their feet, where a sculpted salmon was embedded in the sidewalk. The gold tinted light fell on the shoulders of the diners, warming, stroking, where a large outdoor terrace held etched wrought iron tables for the row of restaurants on 5th Avenue. The outdoor café tables were filled, as they had been all day, but rather than raucous, the laughter was light, voices were hushed, charmed by the light, and smiles replaced chatter.

As charming as it looked, after being outside all day, Rhonda opted for the upscale Mexican Restaurant that bordered one side of the open table terrace. Choosing the more intimate indoors, she was content to separate herself from people and watch them out the window for a while like a silent movie of a café scene. And, of course, she had the handsome potter as scenery, also.

"They have the best corn-husk wrapped tamales here. You will want to try them." She informed her silent companion, sipping wine, not bothering to glance at the menu.

"And did you notice the murals painted on the brick sides of the buildings as we passed?" Rhonda added, "It was a fabulous idea; I love this town's devotion to art. We should stroll around the Mural Walking Tour after dinner, there are about 14 large murals in all so far, I believe. They are primarily focused here in the downtown core and down Main Street to the ferry. It should stay light until ten, we should have plenty of time." Rhonda was used to defining the terms of how she expected a date to go. Her men were usually eager to do anything she suggested, for a chance to…

"Umm, that sounds lovely however I'm afraid I have a little problem. You said you would only give one second chance, but I am hoping that you could reconsider, give me a little extra leeway." Potter saw her arched brows but tried to cajole her. "You see, I didn't know I would have an opportunity to meet someone special like you, and I'm not quite prepared. I mean I had another business appointment later this evening and in the rush today, I haven't had an opportunity to even restock my supply of clay, and I didn't want to disappoint you—or myself, of course. So I was hoping to treat you to a quick dinner and explain and beg another day to get organized and clean up my boat. Have our *real* date tomorrow evening. Doesn't that sound better? "

"Better for whom?" Her words sounded bitten.

"Ah, the lady I would like to warm with a slick coating of clay?" He attempted another charming smile to soften her.

"So, you are breaking our date." Rhonda's voice was cool, as were those blue eyes over her wine glass.

"No, not really. We are together now, aren't we?" He reached for her hand; she moved it out of his reach. "The rest is just a slight delay." As if gently scolding, he added, "I already had an appointment lined up with a buyer in Seattle this evening before I came to the fair. You didn't really give me a chance to confirm the timing today, you know."

True, she hadn't. But she felt he had taken advantage of maneuvering her here, before explaining they didn't really have a date. She would have preferred to go to Sam's barbeque if she had known. If he'd had the courtesy to step across the way, at any time earlier today, and make other arrangements...

She would have probably have said ... 'no', and not listened to an explanation. Rhonda was only listening now because she was famished and wanted her damn dinner.

"You are buying dinner," she told him as their plates arrived. "And don't think you are getting any quickies except for dinner, sweet buns." Then she smiled widely up at the waiter, who was pretending to be deaf.

Potter looked relieved until he seemed to realize she had not agreed to another date, yet—if ever.

Peter Potter the potter did *not* get his answer from Rhonda before she left the restaurant—alone—either. She left him to wait and wonder overnight—and regret his error.

Getting down into the harbor area by vehicle was restricted to two access points, both across the railroad tracks on either end of a busy railroad station. Both had railroad crossing bars with flashing lights that blocked traffic every time a commuter shuttle, Amtrak passenger, or freight train passed—which was often.

The northern crossing was primarily the ferry loading access, and under the constant and watchful eye and control of either ferry security, or police, or both.

The southern crossing gave access to the Port, Marina, beaches. Little commercial traffic had a need to cross as the port was for boaters, not cargo handling. And about the only commercial traffic wanted there were the trailers hauling new yachts.

There were, however, two major restaurants, a beach café, and a Yacht Club all down in the restricted marina area, so no special notice was paid to the panel van that crossed the tracks and pulled into the parking lot of one of the restaurants. It had the name of a restaurant supply company clearly and boldly painted on both sides and the back. After stopping a while near a restaurant, it slowly made its way over to a parking area for over-length vehicles close to the southern marina slip access gates.

The driver got out, locked his van and putting his hands in his pockets, set off for a stroll along the waterfront. Just like anyone else taking time out on a break to get in a little exercise while breathing the fresh sea air and enjoying the sights. He smiled and nodded at the people he passed when he got out of the van, heading north along the boardwalk beside the boat slips at a brisk pace.

He made it very easy to identify him as the driver of the van. His shirt and navy ball cap both carried embroidered logos with the name of the restaurant supply company. His shirt also announced his name in a friendly cursive red thread that said 'John' on a crisp white field bordered in red and sewn above his pocket. It was one of four similar names patches: John, Tom, George, and Harry. All had been made at the same time as the embroidered patches announcing the name of the restaurant supply company that did not exist—except in red thread and paint.

While he had made it easy to recognize him as the driver of the van, he made it difficult to track him down. Moving quickly north skirting the marina and harbor, he headed out the broad concrete fishing pier jutting into the waters north of the boat slips. Beyond the harbor seawall it took a left turn and widened to accommodate not only strollers, but fishermen and crabbers, with cleaning sinks and shaded seating where one could watch their pole tip, or the mountains across the sound and passing ferries. Anyone seated would be extremely difficult to see from shore.

When port security finally did track him down out there, he apologized, said 'aw shucks' a lot, grinned, and confessed he was just enjoying a break and the view and had no *idea* his vehicle was not authorized to park where it was. 'So sorry, no idea, never happen again, I'll get it right out of your way' was his general refrain as he was escorted, grinning, to do just that.

When he reached his van he noticed the pickup he had parked

beside had an empty bed, no longer filled to the brim with all those canvas bags that looked like they were filled with sails being taken out to mend. He unlocked his door, hopped right in the driver's seat without checking the back cargo area, and waved to his escort and drove off smiling, clearly relaxed and refreshed from his scenic break. After he crossed the railroad tracks, he turned south to catch the road that would connect him to the I-5 interstate heading south to Seattle, along with heavy ferry traffic that had just unloaded.

Rhonda was still wondering what her decision would be today; unsure if she regretted giving Potter that second chance last evening. But she had been tired, and hungry, her resistance down, and she hadn't known the full story when she had agreed to dinner with him.

She could always, she supposed, just play with him over the weekend and dump him after the fair. And after a nice long sail on that boat of his.

That plan brought a wicked smile to her face.

But looking across the way again, she saw he was still missing from his booth. Just the skinny substitute was there. And he was just no fun at all to gaze at.

So where was that missing man?

chapter six

"Well, if you are just going to sit there all morning staring into space—the pottery space to be specific—I have plenty for you to do with your hands while you are in la-la land."

Sam's teasing voice brought Rhonda abruptly back to the cheerful noise and busy chaos of the second day of the arts festival. "Sorry."

"Not a problem, I've been enjoying steady interest all morning so it looks like it will be a promising day for us."

"Lots of people stopping by to see the infamous jailbird?" Ronnie couldn't resist payback for the 'la-la land' comment—even if it *was* true.

"That too!" Sam's laugh was relaxed and happy. "But they are paying for the privilege in donations this morning. So maybe you could get these handouts stuffed and ready for today." Sam tapped the carton sitting on the table in front of Rhonda.

Blinking, she stared at the printer's box right beneath her nose. "How did that get here?"

The guy just came and delivered it to you. You looked right through him. But don't worry, he was just a gawky kid, so you didn't miss any prime males, though," Sam saw someone enter their space and headed over, tossing a taunt over her shoulder with the words, "*that* might have snapped you back from la-la-la-la...."

"Enough! Go see to your fans, I will get these ready." Lifting off the top of the carton Rhonda started folding the brochures and flyers together that explained the blind-guide-dog prison program. In addition to the rushed flyers they had gotten last night, Sam had created a more professional 3-fold piece on Jordan's computer and had him email it to the printer along with a single sheet donation voucher and receipt. It looked good, she thought, as she folded the sheets into triple fold brochures and tucked a donation sheet into each one, starting to create a stack of handouts in the basket Sam had provided. But it was mindless work and Rhonda's mind soon drifted back to the prior evening and the question of whether the potter deserved another date.

It was not his well-rounded rear that finally decided Rhonda, by the time she finished folding, nor his practiced lines. And it was certainly not his name!

While they had waited for their tamale specials, the conversation had been in that strange territory of trying to get to know a stranger on a first date. Usually Rhonda didn't bother, preferring to get on with the sex and skipping all that verbal intimacy. But the potter only had time for chatty foreplay while they had dinner.

"I've never heard such a convenient name. Tell me, which came first, the man Potter or the potter, Potter?" She had teased, plucking the olive from her drink and slowly removing it from the toothpick with her teeth, amused at how his gaze was riveted on her lips. "Is it one of those Old English things where they gave people the last name of their craft, and your family has carried on the tradition all down the centuries?"

"Actually," he had paused to watch her lips as she dealt with a second olive, "you're not far off. There have been a few double Potters since the first Englishman. My great-grandfather was the last before me. But I like art, have the talent, hate business suits, and it was a built-in marketing benefit. I don't even need business cards; no one forgets Potter the potter, and my web address is just that. No fuss life and marketing, all in one!" He leaned closer over the table, placing his hand over Rhonda's. "And it gives me all the more time to enjoy life's other exquisite pleasures ... sailing, for instance."

His unusual gold trimmed green eyes had been intimate, his hand caressing hers during his significant pause to ensure she understood she was the most exquisite pleasure he wished to enjoy. His voice had deepened and softened into a low growl.

"You're a very desirable woman, Rhonda. I think you'd enjoy my sailboat, too. The captain is at your command."

Very sexy, Rhonda had thought, and very fast. She liked fast. Especially in this package, but she wanted him to understand she was a player also. And he needed to understand which game they were playing, and more to the point, that she wouldn't play his slave, despite his pretty, false words. Not that she didn't mind a little sensual dress up and role playing. As long as it was clear, in reality, who held the cutlass.

Narrowing her blue eyes, she shifted the conversation, and control, from his scripted lines.

"Did you know that in 1992 I was told unequivocally that I was undesirable?" She told him laughing.

"I did not take it to heart." Rhonda gave him a smug grin. "I can't count the number of men that have disproved that theory!"

"I can imagine," he smiled back a little dryly. Not especially liking the competitive numbers more than any man would, "but I can't fathom the idiot that would say that you were undesirable. Were you on your death-bed at the time?"

"No, I was dressed to kill at the time," Rhonda replied, delighted he had scored fairly well in that test, so far.

"Not possible. Who's the blind man?" he asked, stroking lightly down her fingers.

"A border guard."

His eyebrows raised. "Really?" he drawled. "You should stay away from men in uniform you know." He leaned back, draping one arm over the back of his chair, raising his drink with the other. His eyes remained on Rhonda, fascinated, listening with the intensity a woman appreciates.

"Apparently there was some computer mix up that flagged my car when I tried to cross the border. He told me I would not be allowed to enter. Not only he, but his whole country, considered me an undesirable! I had never even heard that word in my life before that!"

"No doubt! Or since, I'm sure!" He humorously soothed her mock indignation.

"So I had my attorney contact their government and straighten it all out. In fact, he also sent them a letter, which he copied to the border guard, informing them that I was the most desirable woman that he had ever slept with, and he would gladly attest to that, and so could all the partners in his firm!" She finished with a flourish, and raised her glass to drink.

Potter the potter, the handsome hunk, raised his also, in toast to her. His curiosity now satisfied, beyond his need to know, but he leaned forward again, his eyes intimate. "I like to check things out for myself. How would you like a nice, slow, thorough reappraisal ... or two, on my boat tomorrow night?" When she didn't respond right away, he lowered his eyes and voice, adding, "With some soft, slick clay?"

"Maybe." Rhonda seemed to consider.

He had smiled.

"And maybe not." His smile collapsed.

"I'll let you know when I decide."

No, it was not the nice butt, or silly name, and it was definitely not his arrogance that made him think he could be late, or delay, and still have her come when he beckoned, which had decided her today.

It was his eyes. Those playful green eyes that danced with laughter even as she tried to glare a hole through him. Eyes that heated, eyes that caressed, eyes that constantly dueled directly with hers, no matter her mood, to tempt and tease her into coming out to play with him.

Rhonda did not like being the one that had to lower her gaze— especially when it landed on those lips, and that damn dimpled smile of his. When he flashed that special smile of his her way she could almost hear the whoosh, she could certainly feel it, of a furnace fired up for the first time since winter. And those long fingered twitchy hands of his. Those hands that couldn't just touch, couldn't just hold hers, but had to pat, and stroke, and twine, and rub, and tingle, and weave, and just would not hold still and just clasp.

Yes, it was that silly hand holding that had finally decided her, concerned her, that she might weaken in her old age due to a silly teen age tender gesture. She knew it was all his act, but dammit, she wouldn't let him get under her skin. She didn't need a man like that. Especially one so obviously flawed.

That did it. Though she would die before admitting the reason. Rhonda would *not* date the potter! He was history.

Relieved she had made a firm decision, she bounced up,

energized.

"Sam, I'm going to go gather us some exotic foods for lunch from all the vendors at the Food Court. Be back as soon as I can. Have your appetite ready." Laughing, she passed the missing potter's space, glad she was ready for his return.

When Ronnie got back to Sam's booth her arms were loaded down with a smorgasbord of wrapped bundles and enticing scents. She tried to shove a brown paper bag aside to make room to drop her burden, but she had to shove hard to nudge it aside to set down the food.

"Oh, that's for you," Sam said with a funny smile.

Pulling back the top of the bag, Rhonda peered down inside and saw a bow-tied round plastic tub.

Of clay.

With a fresh rosebud on top.

She could feel those playful eyes, and that damn smile searing between her shoulder blades. She refused to turn around. He was *not* lighting her furnace.

"Sam, pass me that folding chair and I'll sit on this side facing you. Then we can talk, and maybe people will see we are lunching and will be too polite to interrupt."

The fair had opened just before mid-day on Friday, with the usual amazing crowds for a week day. Waves of retirees showed up along with others in the community that had eagerly anticipated the event since the prior year. Among the art lovers were the proud local grandparents, with their cadres of friends, eager to show off the young prodigies in their families. The lower level of the former school at the arts center was devoted exclusively to the abundant display of all the community's school age budding artists. It was a beloved and inspiring exhibition with the proud ancestors boasting of their soon to be future famous, each crayon drawing, charcoal, watercolor, and ink etching admired, blue ribbons and honorable mentions to be boasted over. Even the most indecipherable works of kindergarteners could be cooed over as latent abstract artists in the making. Even an objective eye could be startled by the skill and imagination evident in the older student works, but every piece and age group had its loyal local fan club.

That exhibition in itself showed another level and layer of the community commitment to not only support the arts as a whole, but to its daily nourishment and development. The sculptures throughout the town, including the brassy seals climbing from the beaches, the permanent family of tourists watching the ferries cross back and forth across the sound, the salmon flying near the pier and embedded in the sidewalks, and the old buildings downtown splashed with colorful murals, spoke of the joy of art, the fair and arts events and centers and numerous galleries registered the town support. But it was the space allotted to the exhibition of the local youths at the prestigious annual event that spoke of the heart of the community, and carried the message that had been unique to the independent settlement from its earliest days as the "gem" of Puget Sound.

By the second day, the only full day into night of the three day event, it seemed as if the whole world had arrived in the small coastal city.

Without Kevin there to help her keep track of Timmy in the Saturday festival chaos, Shelley had asked the eleven year old 'man' to hold her hand.

"So I don't get lost from you in the crowd," she explained, all wide blue-eyed helpless blonde innocence.

Timmy's disgusted "No way!" was a clear indication he wasn't buying her fiction.

Stopping in the middle of the food court, looking at all the different choices, Shelley breathed deeply, visibly appreciating all the tantalizing aromas, "Well, I just hope you can track me down later ..."

That was all it took to remind her reluctant escort that *she* held the generous purse he would benefit from keeping close. She lived —barely—to regret it.

Tim towed her around all day like she was a battered broken down car being dragged on a chain behind a shiny, engine roaring, racing new truck, squealing around corners, skidding across lanes, diving between the crowds barely avoiding collisions, slamming to sudden stops, and darting into illegal U-turns until Shelley feared her wrist might break off before her stumbling feet blew out their rubber.

"Did Kevin happen to mention whether he planned to join us later?" She gasped, hope desperate in her voice, when the young machine paused to decide which exotic food he wanted to gas up on.

"Nah, he's gone. Left before dawn this morning and won't be back today."

"Oh." Too disheartened to ask, she tried to shake some blood back into her mangled wrist, looking for a bench or rock or low wall to sit on—to no avail.

"Don't know where he took off to," Timmy shrugged. "Hey, gyros, cool, and look over there..." Shelley managed to elude his reach for her wounded hand. His grasp clamped her elbow, and with a firm yank they plunged back into the masses surrounding the food carts.

Saturdays at the art's festival always rocked.

At every intersection, from Rembrandt Avenue and Degas, to Picasso and Monet, sound and motion shifted and flowed down lanes lined and blooming with gardens of flowers, looming mountain scenes capped with snow, silvered shimmering lakes reflected cloud cluttered skies, and autumn aspens vied with crimson maples beside wandering streams and tufted fields lined with picturesque broken roofed barns, rusted wheels, wildlife peeking wide-eyed from forests dense with fir, or fluttering leaves, storm tossed seas rose, and wooden boats strained at their ropes, abstract dreams were imagined, and harsh realities slashed in bold colors across canvas, wood, metal, stone, tortured wire, glass hand blown, oils, watercolors, acrylics, pieced wooden bowls, straining statues, dangled jewelry, tightly curved cedar and spruce root baskets, where all that man could see or feel or experience, or hope exploded in the celebration of life that was art. The festival was bursting with its every color and emotion.

As the energy flowed, into the evening, never ebbing, the music rocked, cajoled, jazzed, and flowed out into the star capped night and down over the waterfront where waves lapped and slapped lazily at the massed boats lolling in the port marina.

In one sailboat, at the distant end of a long dock, one artist still plied his craft, with reverent fingers and concentrated focus, late into the night and early into the hours before dawn.

For Ms. Rhonda Sayles, the muse, and artist Potter, it was a raucous, boat rocking night of unbridled sex.

They playfully molded clay busts out of live breasts, and other available male and female body parts, until a frigid midnight dockside dip was needed to cleanse what heat and passion had smeared and melted to discomfort.

Then the playfulness changed to something more intense. Chilled and nude in the moonlight they started all over again, firing and shaping their erotic poses with just raw skin, as if rehearsing for a Roman orgy, resting only briefly before coming together forcefully again just before dawn started to break and the port came alive with the sounds of boats and gulls crying for herring.

Potter, on his back staring at the cabin ceiling, wrapped an arm around Rhonda and pulled her head to his chest, tangling his fingers idly in her hair, like a tamed lover.

His voice casual, but seeming to hold some tension still, maybe unfinished need, asked, "So, how did you become buddies with a jailbird?"

Rhonda's laugh was deep and lazy. "Oh, that. I guess you heard. Who didn't? It's a long story but nothing you need to worry about. My friend is married to the city prosecutor after all, so I *am* on the right side of the law."

Her hand stroked his sweaty chest, his heartbeat still fast beneath her ear, his breath not as calm as hers. She let her fingers trickle down the dampened hair that arrowed down his belly, following the path teasingly until his hand clamped down hard, stopping hers.

"The prosecutor? What are you, some kind of law enforcement groupie?" His laugh sounded forced and false.

"No need to get jealous." She yanked her hand from beneath his and rolled off the bunk. "I don't enjoy jealously and I am no one's groupie, you can be sure." Her voice snapped with warning. "But if you want to be part of *my* fan club," her chin rose arrogantly, blue eyes chilled, "you will show some respect."

Slipping from his grasping hand she slid her sundress over her head, flipped her long dark hair out and quickly spun and tucked it into an elegant bun at her nape, changing from wild lover to elegant cover model in a heartbeat—and just as icily beautiful.

"Get dressed," she ordered, "and I might let you buy me breakfast as you apologize." Gathering her purse and sandals she went out on deck, shutting the cabin door behind her. The boat rocked only moments later as she stepped on the dock, making it clear that she would not wait submissively for any man.

Potter had to scramble for his clothes, and chase half way down the dock before catching up with her. He had never seen a woman that could walk so fast in heeled sandals over uneven surfaces. It must be those firm mile long legs he had been tangling with.

Worth an apology, but for what he wasn't quite sure.

He would need to be more careful around this one.

Bett Bone

.

chapter seven

Shelley had hoped to sleep in longer Sunday. She had turned off the alarm, but her internal clock wasn't giving her much mercy, nagging at her conscience and consciousness as she burrowed in her pillow, fighting to regain sweet oblivion. But she had spent so much time at the Arts Festival on Friday and Saturday she had ignored her chores, and she had to be at work bright, early, and ready for an intensive week tomorrow morning. Playtime was over.

She gave herself a few more moments in the comfort of her bed, justified by working on a mental to do list while she stretched her reluctant body lazily and lingered. She felt the soreness of abused muscles, thinking that Timmy must have dragged her over every single foot of the festival several times over to make sure they didn't miss a single sight, or vendor of food, but mostly "watching" Candy and her guide dog weave people through the crowds. Shelley yawned, trying to remember if she had been that obsessed with her first crush.

Her eyes blinked open as she realized she couldn't even remember who her first crush was. Eyes open or closed, the only face that came to mind was the one of her current crush. With a soft smile she reached out to her nightstand and picked up her new bracelet, clasping it around her wrist then holding her arm up to the light, turning her arm gracefully, admiring the sight. She hopped out of bed and was heading for her mirror so she could hold the bracelet against her cheek to see if her eyes were really that lovely blue color when the phone rang. Despite her excited leap for the phone, it was the other male in her life calling.

"Hey! My man, Shel! What are you up to today?"

"Well, Timmy," she laughed, "I'm up to my neck in chores today."

"Bummer. What kind of chores?"

"Well, let's see: dusting, vacuuming, dishes, laundry, changing sheets, cleaning the bathroom, grocery shopping, and then home to cook meals to eat next week when I won't have time…"

Timmy cut her off. "How about washing windows?"

"Well," she had planned to put that chore off to another time, but…

"Because I am an expert window washer," he boasted, quickly adding, "with a step ladder."

What was this? The scamp was up to something. They hadn't had any plans to get together today.

"See I'm thinking," the youngster wove his spell, "See Candy has worked so hard, I kind of thought she deserved something special, like flowers or something, a bouquet like, to show appreciation, you know? And the fair ends today, so it's the time you do stuff like that. At the end.

"But," the little charmer continued, "Kev's gone somewhere today and I don't have any way to get over there and, umm, well like I have to buy the flowers first to give her, and I'm a little short on funds, but maybe we could work a deal? Like I could do windows and chores for you, huh? But see the fair closes early today, so I'd need to buy the flowers and get a ride like on credit this morning, then this afternoon I could work for you . . . and , um, well, what do you think?"

Shelley thought he would be downright dangerous to women when he got older, but she couldn't bear to crush his hopes. This young boy had never had a childhood. His family had used him, instead of supporting and caring for him. She knew how much courage it took him to hope that there was an adult he could count on, trust, someone who cared about what mattered to his young, bruised heart.

She tried to clear the tightness in her throat. "I think we better step on it then. I'll try and get over there by ten, but we are going to have to hit the grocery store first and come back here and unload before heading over to the fair." She had to be sure she got at least that much done today, especially if she was going to have a young male eating machine here helping her with chores.

"Sure. Hey, that's great! And I can get a bouquet at the store. You can help me pick it out so it isn't something dorky, but smells good. Thanks, Shel, You are the man!"

She heard him whoop in the background as he hung up the phone, and couldn't help but chuckle. Just what she always wanted, to be 'the man'. But she was fond of the little rascal, and she knew that was his boyish way of saying she was special to him too. Without, of course, losing his cool.

Yanking a clean pair of jeans out of her dresser, she saw the bracelet on her wrist, and wondered where Kevin had taken off to now.

Samantha and Candy with her guide dog were already in the space getting ready for the final morning of the fair when Ronnie sauntered up with what looked suspiciously like the swagger of a dangerous female rake. One of her devoted victims trailed behind her as far as the pottery space.

Sam covered a smile with her hand; even Candy giggled before becoming intensely focused on grooming every hair of her shepherd to perfection, as Rhonda pulled up a chair at the table, and passed out pastries and Starbucks coffee.

"Good morning, and thanks!" Sam smiled. "Hey, before we get crazy today, I wanted to tell you both that Jordan wants to have a B-B-Q this afternoon after we get everything all closed up and hauled out to thank you guys for all your help at the fair. I think we'll have a lot to celebrate once we get all the donations tabulated. We will also have a few artists coming who want to work with us on creating heavily textured oils and acrylic paintings that can be read like a Braille book. Isn't that exciting?"

"That's terrific, Sam! Both the fundraising success and the new project. I was more than happy to make myself slightly useful. However I am afraid I'm going to have to take a rain check on the B-B-Q. I promised another grateful person that I would go on a sunset cruise with him on his sailboat after the fair. I'd put him off but he has to return to his island and work tomorrow, and I don't want to miss the opportunity to go sailing. It promises to be a lovely sunset tonight."

No doubt, Sam thought, noting the way Ronnie glowed this

morning as if she had just spend a week at a spa. She wondered if this was just one of Rhonda's short flings, or something more serious, not sure how to ask if this affair would last beyond the Arts & Crafts Fair. Or if she even should ask. But Sam's curiosity got the better of her.

"I'd grab my only chance to go sailing over our dinner, also," Sam said casually, busy setting baskets of handouts out on the table.

"Oh, he'll be back," Ronnie stretched lazy as a cat, rolling her shoulders. "He wants to take me on the Edmonds Gallery walk when he comes back in ten days to deliver some pottery orders, and he plans to stay the weekend then. But, one never knows when the weather might turn stormy."

The way she said that last made Sam wonder which weather Rhonda might be referring to. Her best friend admitted to a short temper and lack of patience with her male friends. The duration of most her relationships was about as changeable and predictable as the Pacific Northwest weather forecast.

"True," Sam agreed, "But sailing sounds like fun and you can come to our place for a B-B-Q anytime. Maybe next time you will want to bring your Pete along?"

Rhonda just smiled a little. She always called the man Peter, not for the formality, of course, but because it seemed to amuse her.

"We'll see," she drawled, "though I think *my* Peter is a little nervous around . . . jailbirds." She ducked the wad of packing material Sam threw at her.

"Yo! Where's Candy?"

"Yo yourself," Sam giggled. "Hi Shelley, Timmy. I'm afraid your favorite girl is out giving a guided tour. But she should be back any minute. Why don't you two come on under the shade and grab a couple of those folding chairs."

Shelley accepted gratefully while the young Lothario just stepped under the awning's shade and stood stiffly, one arm behind his back, glancing out into the crowds eagerly.

Ronnie couldn't resist teasing. Sniffing the air dramatically, she said, "My, something sure smells nice! Is that you Tim? A new aftershave, maybe?" She had never had any trouble making a man, of any age, blush until the tips of his ears turned red. Standing, she stepped closer, sniffing, "Yum, I do believe that is coming from you."

He tried to back into the corner as she came closer. But, just as he feared, she saw over his shoulder.

"Flowers! Oh, you brought flowers. Such a charming gentlemen. Are they for me?"

"Umm, well, ah ...," stepping from foot to foot, still trying to hide his bouquet from the predatory female, "I guess maybe I might have brought *one* for you, and for Mrs. Prosecutor..."

"Ronnie, stop!" Sam laughed. "Poor guy. We know those flowers aren't for us but thanks for offering to share, Timmy. Ms. Sayles is just teasing you. She gets jealous when anyone gets flowers except her—especially when they are for a younger woman."

"Oh, low blow, Sam. But I guess I deserved it." Rhonda laughed. "Candy will love the flowers, Tim, don't break them up for greedy old ladies."

"Shelley isn't old," Tim said in her defense, not realizing the unintended insult that had all three women burst out laughing. He saw Candy weaving toward him and could barely wait for her to step into the booth out of the crowds, before yanking his bouquet out from hiding to shove it toward Candy with an awkward bow.

Stunned, she didn't even reach for them, just stared at the flowers, then at him.

"They are for you, Candy. In, um, 'preciation for how hard you worked for the fair." He shoved them impatiently against her hand, his ears burning red, his smile shy, eyes looking up at the taller girl with hope, and a tinge of fear. When she took them he gave a sigh of relief and looked away to pat her dog on the head.

"Flowers? For me?" She said in a soft voice filled with wonder. "I...No one has ever," she swallowed hard, moisture welling in her eyes, "Timmy, no one has ever given me flowers before. Thank you!" She learned over and gave him a quick kiss on his check, then buried her face in the bouquet to smell deeply of the carnations and to shield her emotions.

Sam, watching, knew what it must mean to the young girl, still in her teens, that had had to go on many 'dates' that had nothing to do with flowers, just to survive on the streets. To see her so strong and capable in her new life, and enjoy the joy a normal girl took in her first flowers, had Sam's eyes watering with happiness. This was the other part of her commitment to her project, the second chance it gave for a new, different life. Clearing her throat, Sam broke the tension in the small space,

"I have an announcement to make, an invitation, really. You are all invited to our "appreciation" BBQ this afternoon. And that includes you Shelley, for helping out in the space."

"Oh, Sam I'd loved to, but I have avoided all the chores I need to get done before work...," seeing the crestfallen look on Timmy's face, "but, maybe Tim and I could stop by later."

The words were barely out of her mouth before her bruised wrist was snagged and Tim was bouncing off grinning and shouting "Great! We'll be there! Come on Shel, hurry, we have chores."

They had stopped first by the shelter. Shelley waited in the car while Tim dashed in for extra clean clothes.

"A guy doesn't want to stink up a party after working all day," he informed her. "Doesn't need to smell like a flower, though," he had grumbled under his breath. She suspected the carnation flavored guy had taken a ribbing inside.

It had been impressive how hard and fast a motivated eleven year old could work, though the freshly cleaned bathroom looked like it had tornado damage after the youth washed up and changed for the party. Even the tow headed tangle of hair had been flattened into temporary submission. Shelley smiled to see his scrubbed face still had one patch on his cheek with the sheen of a lip glossed kiss. The poor lad had quite the crush on Candy.

She tried to deny she might be a 'poor' lass with a crush of her own.

"Did you happen to see Kevin when you were at the shelter?" She kept her focus on the road as she drove them over to the Campbell's house for the barbeque.

"Nah, no one's seen him since Friday night. He's still gone somewhere," Timmy shrugged. "Too bad. He's missing all the fun we're having."

She couldn't help but laugh. "Those chores were fun?"

He didn't answer for a minute, looking off out his window at the residential neighborhood they were passing through before saying softly, "Sure, you want a nice home."

"Well, um, I guess Kevin deserves a little time off, huh? He works pretty hard for all you boys." She was glad to see him perk up and turn to watch the road in front, eager to get to the party.

"Yeah, he's probably just out chasing some babes."

Shelley noticed the bracelet on her arm as she turned the wheel to steer into their hosts' driveway. It wasn't sparkling quite as brightly in the sunshine.

This close to the summer solstice, daylight lingered like a lover that couldn't bear to depart, as if one more moment of joy, one more longed for endearment might be missed and lost forever if held to await another day. With so many hours stretching ahead before sunset, there was plenty of time for the excellent early dinner seafood and steak special at four at a local restaurant at the port.

Though she had offered to assist Peter with the packaging and transfer of his unsold pottery pieces, he had refused her assistance, suggesting that she secure a prime outdoor table at the restaurant, instead. If she had known, Rhonda might have gone to the Campbell barbeque, *instead*. But she did find it restoring after the busy weekend to have a quiet, private drink sitting outside over the boat docks, with a view of all the coastal water traffic, and the soft scent and touch of gentle sea breezes that flirted with her hair.

All the fairgoers and weekend tourists that arrived by boat were heading home. They were jockeying for position to squeeze out between the rock wall framed entrance to the port, escaping into the sound, heading to all compass points—except east, where she sat watching enviously still ashore and alone. The yachts and sailboats of every size and color streaming out of the port below added their color and motion to the busy waterway. The white and green state ferries made their steady and stately crossings; a faster hydrofoil ferry out of Seattle rose up on its stilts to skim north to Victoria in British Columbia; container ships made their slow slog making their way into or out of the Straits of Juan de Fuca; and dodging it all was a colorful dipping and diving sailboat race.

Rhonda was eager to be out there playing on those crisp looking, sparkling and dancing waters, feeling the wind and salt spray on her face. Sighing she glanced around but saw no sign of the potter. Patience was not her strong suit, especially when it came to men. She was beginning to reconsider heading over to Sam and Jordan's, but ordered one more drink and some appetizers instead, as the view truly was dazzling. And she *was* determined to get her promised sailboat ride. So far the only sailboat she had ridden had been tied to the dock—though she had to admit they had been most enjoyable rides. But it was only the promise of a sunset spent sailing that kept her waiting around for the damn man now.

A flash of sunlight glinting red captured and turned Shelley's head out toward the lawn as soon as they arrived on Sam and Jordan's deck. Kevin's dark mahogany hair gleamed near the garden shrubbery, bent in conversation with another redhead, this one a perky copper color on a female with a knockout figure, undisguised by her long, flowing, gauzy dress. Her face was turned up to his, eyes locked on him with that rapt attention meant to flatter a man. Her fingertips frequently touching his arm, she leaned closer each time she spoke in return, or laughed lightly at his words.

Timmy's casual comment rang in Shelley's head. *Probably just chasing babes.*

She turned away, trying to slide behind Jordan at the barbeque, before she was noticed, but Timmy with a happy shout, grabbed her wrist and drug her across the lawn.

"Hey, Kev, my man! We've been wondering where you were."

Shelley flushed, not knowing how to free herself or deny his claim gracefully.

"Busy." Kevin turned and thumped Timmy on the shoulder. "Right now I'm trying to charm this lovely lady with a proposition."

Shelley wanted to disappear, sink into the grass, turn into a bee and fly away—after stinging the two redheads. She almost didn't hear his next words.

"I'm trying to use all my charm to convince her to set up an art clinic for you guys at the shelter."

All his charms? Shelley managed to free her wrist from Timmy only to have Kevin capture it and pull her close to his side.

"Shel, this is Maire McKindrick, one of the artists from the festival that has agreed to work with Sam on textured acrylic paintings for the blind. I've told her the boys would do a great job of globing on the paint to make stick figures and mountains and sun rays with just some artistic guidance—well, a lot of artistic guidance," he grinned. "Maire, this is Timmy the rascal, and my cohort, Shelley Airton, with the prosecutor's office, that I've been telling you about."

"I've heard so much about you both," Maire gushed.

Shelley pasted a smile on her face, hoping it looked polite. "It's nice to meet you Miss McKindrick, maybe we can chat later. I promised to help Sam with the food, though, so if you'll excuse me—" Kevin would not release her arm.

"Yes, we should all go and help." He steered his group toward the party on the deck, leaning close to her ear, he murmured, "I see you are wearing my bracelet."

"It matched my sundress." Did the man just charm any female in sight? "So, I guess you had a busy weekend, also."

"I did."

chapter eight

"**S**orry I made you wait so long."

His arrogant confidence that she *would* wait, annoyed her. She shouldn't have gotten so caught up in the view.

Noting the irritated lines between her brows and the frosted cobalt color of Rhonda's eyes, Potter changed tactics and set out to charm and placate the sultry brunette. The empty appetizer plate on the table warned him to order their dinners right away. He needed to get her fed and stowed away on his boat before she rebelled and escaped. When he told the waiter to bring her favorite wine, he managed not to wince when she deliberately *favored* one of the most expensive ones on the wine list.

This was a woman that knew how to make a man pay for his transgressions and his pleasures. But if he could handle her, it would be well worth the danger.

Over brimming wineglasses, and succulent seafood, he confided that while sales had been excellent during the art's fair, at least half of his sales had been for customized pottery pieces.

"I had arranged with a local gallery here in town to take some left over pieces on consignment, so we just had to move those across town. But," he gave her a slow smile, "I didn't want to crowd the boat with all the other boxes of unsold works. We will want plenty of room on the boat to enjoy our sail," and other activities his tone and frisky green eyes added silently. "So I'm afraid I took a little extra time to arrange a storage unit for those pieces to remain on the mainland until I need them." Potter did not, however, get the forgiveness for his tardiness he was angling for.

Eyes still cool and voice skeptical, Rhonda asked, "I thought you had already arranged shipping your pieces to a Seattle gallery?"

He blinked. "Oh, no, that shipment was from a previous order. I just brought it over to deliver at the same time since I was coming for the show anyway."

"I see. Which gallery in Seattle is your work at?"

"The one in Seattle?" He looked up and smiled at her, placing his hand over hers on the table. "It's a relatively small one, but quite upscale, and I will be a featured exhibit. You'll love it. Sometime I want to take you down there and personally show off my works displayed there. Can I pour you more wine?" Already refilling her glass while he launched into a description of all the custom pottery he had on order and had to create that summer.

"I hope to be able to get a lot of work done in the coming week or so. When I come back to take you to the Gallery Walk I will bring and deliver what I have finished while I'm here that weekend. I easily have enough orders to be shuttling over here all summer."

"Wouldn't it be more efficient to stay and complete all your custom orders and deliver them in one load?"

"Ah, but then I wouldn't have a good excuse."

"Excuse for what?"

"To see my beautiful muse regularly for motivation and inspiration, of course." He raised his wineglass and proposed a toast, giving her his most winning grin, and silkiest voice. "Here's to a long, hot summer of sunset sailing with a beautiful and passionate lady."

Rhonda hesitated, then raised her glass to touch his, with a wry smile, voice low, she added, "Here is to getting on with the first one, anyway."

Motioning for the check, he rose, then apologized to the dark haired man sitting behind him that he bumped in his rush to reach and pull out Rhonda's chair.

He didn't like the way the handsome dark haired stranger scanned Rhonda's figure as she rose, before turning back to his own solitary dinner. He especially didn't care for the way his brunette slowly scanned the man right back.

At least once they sailed off, Potter would have her undivided attention.

Except for the pair of leaping, weaving dolphins that delighted Rhonda. And later the seal pup that circled them in the deserted cove where they anchored. That adorable one she said had the most beautiful brown eyes she had ever seen. And the stunning sunset that she couldn't bear to miss a moment of . . . But with the sails down and the boat riding at anchor, Potter finally had both hands free to grab the attention he needed.

If Shelley had felt abandoned all weekend, she couldn't complain now. She had Kevin's undivided attention. He followed in her every footstep with the puppy like devotion that Timmy followed after Candy at the barbeque. If she wasn't careful, or stopped or turned too suddenly, she had a large male body bumping into her. It wasn't wise to try to walk around with a plate of food, or a full drink; her clothes were already decorated with iced tea and pork & beans. Not that in a different situation she would mind the feel of a nice, lean muscled chest against her back, or the scent of crisp spicy male fragrance drifting over her shoulder, though the ready handkerchief dabbing the sauce off her chest before it could stain was a little embarrassing in public.

But the damn man didn't have one more word to say about where he had been or what he had been doing all weekend.

The third time he stepped on the back of her sandal, bringing her to a painful halt, Shelley exploded. Twisting she drove a hard elbow into his stomach.

"What the hell are you doing?" she snarled.

His ego was apparently as hard as his stomach. Smiling at her, curling an arm around her waist and rubbing her sore elbow with his other hand, "I missed you. Did you know you smell delicious today?"

"Have a hamburger!" Sliding her shoe away and twisting out of his grip she stomped away.

He followed.

Heading for Sam, she hoped to engage in some girl talk about shopping and fashion, hoping that would drive him off. He just stood behind her patiently waiting. When Ms. McKindrick strolled over and joined the discussion, he edged closer until Shelley's elbow was brushing against him. Finally she excused herself and headed for the house, when he again followed in her wake, she spun and ordered, "Stay right there!" Planting a hand in his chest, "I'm going to the bathroom. Alone!"

She took her time in the bathroom, safely locked away, then

she heard Sam's voice in the hallway.

"Oh Kevin, there you are. Jordan asked me to find you, he needs your help with the picnic table." Moments later, Shelley heard a knock on the door, and Sam's giggled, "It's safe to come out now."

Throwing open the door, yanking Sam inside and relocking it, she asked, "What is wrong with Kevin? Did you see him?"

Sam was bent over laughing and nodding her head. Finally she gasped out, "That has got to be the funniest thing I ever saw!" Taking a calming breath before continuing, "The three of you have been circling the yard, like a broken train."

"Three of us? All I know is Kevin is tail-gaiting me to a point where he is walking on my shoes."

"The poor man is desperate, Shel, have a heart. If I had known, I never would have invited her, but from the moment I introduced that artist to Kevin and he showed the slightest interest and courtesy, she has been after him like crazy. She keeps grabbing onto his arm. I heard him tell her several times he needed to talk to his date, when he was trying to shake her off. Then he made a beeline for you and glued himself, but she is right behind him like a caboose."

Breaking out in gleeful laughter again until her eyes watered, Sam confessed, "Oh my god, all of us have been trying so hard to keep a straight face watching the three of you trail through the party. Jordan said it reminded him of that dance where everyone puts their hands on the waist of the person in front, and snakes around, kicking their feet. What was that called? Well, never mind, I told him I was sure we didn't have the music to go with it and it would be rude anyway to play it . . .

"Oh! I'm sorry," Sam said, finally taking in the horrified look and deep red blush on Shelley's face. "I guess this isn't very funny for you, is it?

"Well," Sam patted her arm, "you will probably be glad to hear that Timmy just told Maire off. She made the mistake of asking him if Kevin was married or had a steady girlfriend and he told her that you were Kevin's 'main man' and to 'just keep her grabby hands off of him or Shelley will have her thrown in jail'!"

Sam folded her lips tight, but couldn't hold in the giggles. "Okay, I'm done laughing now. And you can come out. She left. I guess it took an eleven year old to get her to understand *'No'*."

After Sam left, Shelley just stood there looking at her blank face in the mirror, unsure if she wanted to laugh, die of embarrassment, or hope that Tim was right.

Or bolt home, Shelley considered, noticing the stained mess on the front of her sundress.

What she really wanted was for Kevin to volunteer information about where he had been all weekend.

Pinching the bridge of her nose, Shelley rubbed trying to ease the tension centered in her brow before it grew into a headache. She hadn't slept well the prior night.

It had not helped that when she arrived at work this morning, her boss had barely been able to choke out a hello before laughing all the way into his office. She was *so* pleased to have been able to offer the entertainment yesterday for Jordan's barbeque.

She blew out a huff of air, blowing blonde strands of hair away from her face, knowing she would probably also find it all very funny, also, some day in the future. The far distant future.

After the 'grabby hands lady', as Timmy named her, had left last night, the party had been quite enjoyable. Yet, while Kevin had remained attentive for the rest of the evening, from a comfortable distance, he had never shared his secrets. Even when she had tried to tease them out of him.

"Don't you want to hear what all I did over the weekend?"

"Nah," a mischievous green-eyed grin, "Timmy already told me."

"Ah. And you were . . .?"

"Busy."

Obviously he did not understand 'main man' sharing rules.

Or it was none of her business.

Or she wasn't really his main anything, just a shield or distraction, or... She shook her head, refusing to go back to that loop of conflicting thoughts and emotions that had kept her awake all night. Shelley did not need her sleep, or her head, or her feelings all messed up. She was never comfortable feeling so insecure. And she couldn't waste energy letting a guy get to her like this, needing her focus back now.

Grabbing her pen and legal pad, rising from her chair to go to the meeting Jordan had called, her strained calf muscles and tender feet reminded her that she had two guys to blame for her emotionally and physically exhausting weekend.

When she learned in her meeting that a major flood of new drugs had infiltrated the region, Shelley's own minor personal issues where washed aside. They had major concerns to deal with. Over the weekend while she had been playing, area hospital emergency rooms had reported numerous overdoses, even some fatalities, from a new pure uncut drug hitting the streets.

San Juan Island

The young teen had been disappointed early that morning when she checked the docks below Friday Harbor and saw that his sailboat had still not returned to its berth. So she was happy to spot him across the street on the sidewalk, as she walked home after school. She waved at him, but he just turned away, pushed the door open at the bank, and disappeared inside.

"He must not have seen me," she murmured to herself.

"Who was that guy you were waving at?" asked her classmate, as they walked home.

"Oh, don't you know of him? That's Peter Potter, he's a famous artist in pottery. He even had his works displayed at that big Art's Festival over on the mainland last weekend. He..."

"Yeah?" Her classmate cut into her burst of devotion. "My parents drug us over to that art fair. It was cool, I guess. I thought that guy looked familiar."

"You saw him there?"

"Well, not at the fair. At a restaurant. He came in holding hands with a gorgeous dark-haired lady. Old, like him, but tall like she was a former model or something. They were holding hands. My mom pointed them out, reminding my dad that he used to hold her hand that way. But the tamales were great, all wrapped in corn husks." She raved on about the food, unaware she had crushed the bright hopes of her companion.

"Listen, I just remembered I have stuff to do. I'll catch you later."

"Sure you don't want to come to my place? We have new DVDs."

"Thanks, not today. I'll text you later."

The young teen headed off down to another part of town, her steps had lost their bounce. She pushed into a small gift shop and gallery, trying not to jar the bell attached to the door too loudly. But when the sales clerk looked up and recognized her, she just ignored her and went back to working with a tourist couple.

Working her way over to a back corner where local artists' work was displayed, she ran her fingers slowly over the pottery pieces. She noticed her fingers were leaving trails in the dusty surface. These were some of his older works. She dug in her purse and pulled out some tissues, and cleared off the evidence she had ignored the 'do not touch, please' sign.

She had seen his newer, more vibrantly shaped and colored pieces on his web site, but these were old familiar friends. They all looked much nicer now that she had shined them up, but she almost hoped they didn't sell too soon.

Leaving the gift shop she went a few doors down to a used book store, seeking the comfort of possibly finding some old classics to fill in the gaps of her favorite series.

Across the Sound, the tall dark-haired woman had her gorgeous model-like legs stretched out from her leather office chair, high heels crossed on her desk.

Rhonda was studying her new pottery vase on the steel credenza across her office.

The bold colors and rounded curves and textures of the piece seemed almost startling in the otherwise sterile severe environment. She thought the tall stalks of pure white calla lilies that she had selected for the vase were perfect. She would have her receptionist put in a standing order to refresh them with the same, every Monday, or more often if needed.

Tipping her head back further, resting it on the chair back, she closed her eyes and let her mind go sailing again.

"That is definitely my sport!" She claimed out loud. Yes, sailing, lazing around on the deck in the sun, the salty breeze and spray, the sights, trailing her hands in the crisp waters, with a handsome half-naked man doing all the work and providing eye candy—and more. That was her sport, for sure. Maybe she should just buy her own sailboat, and hire a man to, well, man it.

She smiled at the thought, thinking how she would word an ad to offer *that* job description. It was something she would have to think about. But no rush. Rhonda had it covered for now with the potter.

In fact, her willingness to see Peter again—okay, maybe the term looking forward to was more accurate—made her wonder if she might even be in the early stages of falling in... Lust?

Surely not.

Though . . . maybe.

She would have a much better read on her feelings in a week or so when she saw him again after some distance. *If* she even still remembered in a week or so that she had a date with him for the Gallery Walk—without looking at her appointment book—which should be a sure sign she was interested.

Somewhat.

"Why am I even spending so much time thinking like this?"

It was out of character for her, she knew, not comfortable with even the thought of anything to do with *needing* to see any particular man more than a few times. He spoke of dating all summer.

That sounded so... permanent!

How long was a 'summer', three months?

Though it almost seemed a bit relaxing in a way to not have to change men for such a long time.

And that thought really made Rhonda wonder what was wrong with her.

Was it just because she was getting old? Actually, the term aging sounded better, even when she was just talking in her own head. She always hated it when someone had the nerve to offer her a senior discount. It didn't happen often, thank god.

Was she just bored?

Something was messing with her head lately, it didn't seem to work the same as she was accustomed to. Maybe it had something to do with...

Her desk phone rang, saving her from her own broody mood.

As she swung her legs off her desk to lean forward and grab the phone, Rhonda winced at stiff muscles, realizing she wasn't able to be as frisky as she used to—another depressing change.

Crouched down in the teen section of the island bookshop, the girl was going through all the old books, not having any luck finding what she was looking for. She ran her finger along the shelves, pulling out anything that looked like it might be interesting.

But nothing was.

She was bummed.

It seemed like it would be forever before she could grow up and be an adult and get to do anything she wanted. Or be noticed like a real person. She could hardly wait to start the rest of her life, which she had decided would be very exciting. And she would be able to go over to the mainland, alone, whenever she wanted! Grown-ups had all the fun.

Teenagers just waited to be grown-ups. It took *forever*.

Tucked back in the corner of the narrow nook, walled in by corridors of high bookcases, she could hear the proprietor talking to some other customer she hadn't noticed when she had slipped into the maze of the store.

"So you rent one of those shacks with outbuildings out in the valley there?"

The other man had a funny laugh. It made you want to know what the joke was. Curious, she tiptoed down to the end of the bookshelves and peeked around the corner.

"No, I rent one of those shacks with shacks on the hillside out that way," he was still chuckling. "When they first sent me out from the rental office with the key ring, I called back and complained there wasn't even a bathroom in the place!" That fun laugh started rumbling up from his chest again, and she couldn't help but smile though she didn't know why.

"The rental agent told me, polite as you please, 'That's the chicken coop, sir, the house is two shacks over'."

As he laughed with the owner, and she snickered quietly behind her hand, she got a good look at the tourist's back. He was a tall, fit man in bicycling clothes. The back of his neck and his shoulders were wide, but arrowed down to long strong-calved legs from there.

"Well, I'll try to make your welcome a little more friendly ..."

"Jake. Just call me Jake."

"Okay, Jake, come on back. I should have all the island guide books and the ones on our hiking and bicycling trails you asked for right over here."

When the man turned to follow, she saw he had dark eyebrows

to match the dark hair peeking out from beneath his ball cap. He had a handsome profile, square jaw, nice nose, and a friendly white smile on his sun-bronzed face.

She had seen him before.

She had *not* wanted to laugh with him then.

Ducking back behind the shelves, the young teen slipped quietly out of the store while they were in the back. She had passed that Jake man down on the docks one early morning. And he had *not* looked at all friendly then.

He had just looked big and mean, and kind of scary.

chapter nine

Rhonda never did get the chance to find out if she would have recalled her date with the potter, or not, or whether he passed or failed that level of interest test.

Though she had pointedly *not* told her secretary, so it wouldn't pop up on her appointments calendar, Rhonda had not taken into account the machinations of her own dear best friend. The dear friend that was newly married now and lived in an eternal state of bliss, and wanted everyone else to have their very own Mr. Perfect —whether they wanted one or not.

Only by keeping her teeth gritted, had Rhonda been able to stop herself from snapping back after ten days of sweet subtle comments from dear Sam.

"Have you decided what you will wear on your date next week?" And…

"I just saw the weather report and it looks like you are going to luck out. Next Thursday night is supposed to be clear, no showers, and just slightly crisp out. Thought you would be happy to hear."

And…

"Ronnie, there's a shoe sale on at Nordstrom's. Should we go see if they have something stylish but comfortable for your Gallery Walk? We could do lunch."

Sam was blissfully unaware that Rhonda was about ready to have her dear friend fried for lunch. With hot sauce.

Even her best-friend-in-law, Jordan, Samantha's husband, got into the act when she made the mistake of dropping by to visit them on the weekend.

"I heard those Thursday night Gallery Walks are quite the do. More than just galleries, local businesses that display local artworks get in on the show also, serving wine and appetizers. Sam and I have never gone, but we would like to try it ..."

Sam set a hand on her husband's arm, gently interrupting, leaning forward to reassure Ronnie, "But not *this* time, of course. We don't want to intrude."

Rhonda rolled her eyes, took a big gulp of her drink and caught an ice cube in her mouth. She snapped it between her teeth with a loud and decisive crunch.

Sam caught the warning. Her husband didn't.

"You know Ronnie, if your guy is going to be around next weekend, let's all get together for dinner or a barbeque, depending on..." His wife's hand was on his arm again, *not* so gently this time.

"Let's leave that open, honey." Samantha added hastily. "Ronnie can tell us what she wants later." She flashed a nervous smile at her friend—or possibly her former friend, judging by Ronnie's expression.

So it was hardly surprising later—except to Mr. Peter Potter when he arrived for 'The Date' all smiles, charm, warmth, and flowers—when Ms. Rhonda Sayles snatched the flowers out of his hand, tossed them in the sink, grabbed up her purse and shawl and shoved him out her front door, growling her welcome and appreciation.

"Come on. Let's get this over with!"

Oh, he was a clever man, the potter, realizing he had to start romancing and enticing the woman all over again if he wanted to find his way back to her arms and favors.

He never asked where he had gone wrong, it hardly mattered. This was not the kind of woman a man demanded explain herself. In her current mood, she would snarl in his face.

So fiery, tempestuous. He liked that. He liked it more when her fire was directed at him and her temper aimed ... elsewhere, but he trusted his skill with women.

So he charmed and complimented, but didn't flatter. He opened doors, fetched wine and appetizers, but casually, as if it was only his natural pleasure to serve a lovely woman—never as groveling. Finally she quit flinching at his every touch. Then she ceased easing away. When he had the chance to nuzzle a nape, or nibble her fingertips, or held her hand as they strolled, she acquiesced—even granting a smile or sigh.

By the end of the evening he was viewing every painting from over her shoulder, his body pressed close behind her, letting his heat, her senses, speak the language of seduction. They stood close studying every sculpture, his arm lightly draped over her shoulder, around her waist, lightly possessing and pleasing, tenderly touching, and working his way back to his original plan for an evening in her bed.

He hoped he would not have to work this hard all summer, to recapture the lovely brunette's interest again, each time he returned to port. He would hope in vain.

At least the potter had more luck sharing intimacies with Ronnie after that, than her best friend Samantha did having an intimate conversation with her—to get the *low down*.

"Sooo," nearly bouncing with excitement, "how was it?" Sam demanded.

"No comment."

"That good hmm?"

"No comment."

"Oh, come on Ronnie, give. I want all the lurid details."

"No, as in N-O, comment."

"Fine," with a frustrated huff, Sam tried negative psychology. It had always worked on her kids. "I'm not really interested anyway. I was just was being considerate letting you share..."

"You are absolutely consumed by curiosity, dying from it, and you know it, Samantha."

"Well?"

"No comment." But Rhonda had to laugh this time. "Okay fine," she seemed to waiver, "since you *are* an old friend, an aging friend, I will *share* with you. Let's see. The wines served were all local and excellent. The hors 'de oeuvre were either works of art themselves, or delicious, or so-so and cold, depending on the venue. The paintings and sculptures were interesting, diverse, and again all by local area artists." She took a moment to enjoy the steam she saw coming out of her friends ears. "And the stroll around town in the evening was really very pleasant, and not the crush that the fair was.

"So I highly recommend that you and Jordan try the Gallery Walk, it could be quite a romantic date for the two of you."

Sam quit grinding her own teeth and burst out, hands fisted, "But was it for you?"

"Well, I'm afraid I have no comment on that," Rhonda said mildly, her smile serene.

Samantha looked like she was about to have a stroke, or was that a seizure, her face was an alarming color of red.

She shouldn't scowl so, Rhonda thought, it might cause permanent wrinkles, though now might not be the best time to 'share' that information. Sometimes getting even was much more fun than just getting angry.

Especially with dear old aging friends one just wanted to teach a lesson to mind their own damn business on occasion. It was that newly-wed matchmaking disease that was really to blame after all. Maybe there was an inoculation?

"But, what about the potter?" Sam asked before her curiosity exploded like a balloon filled with too much air.

"Peter?" Rhonda placed a finger on her chin, gazed up at the skies with her darker cobalt eyes, and acted as if she was deeply considering her response while she let her friend stew a little longer.

"I would say that he was handsome, courteous, and attentive, without being annoying," as if describing a bottle of mediocre wine.

Sam waited. And waited.

"And? Ronnie?"

"No. Commento. Dear."

It was amazing how realistic Sam's wolf howl sounded, as Ronnie walked away laughing.

Back at her office, Rhonda chuckled over the whole conversation with her friend—or lack of it—again.

After her pre-date experiences with Sam, she was not about to give her the chance to know just how romantic her date had been. Or how handsome Potter had looked in his crisp pressed khakis, belted low on lean hips, molding that sculpted butt so delightfully. His pale blue dress shirt had made the lean bronze muscles exposed where it was rolled on his forearms, and open at his throat, seem to invite her touch or tongue. The added sun bronze on his face made those slow, wicked smiles framed in deep dimples, more sensual. His thick hair was tamed, and more sun kissed from sailing, making her want to bury her fingers deep and make it wild as it was when they were making love—as she had, later.

She noticed that his gold-rimmed green eyes seem to gleam more golden when he was trying to charm and enchant her and tease her out of a mood—and into his bed.

And it worked.

They had had two glorious nights of intense, playful, crazy, wild, and carnal pleasure, until she began to think she had found a winner. And then ...

And then, the damned man had been late again, keeping her waiting for hours for their promised Saturday afternoon and evening sail!

She had let herself be soothed with attention and devotion to her every need after Peter had apologized that his client had been delayed when he tried to deliver his custom order. Rhonda hardly felt she should hold a grudge when his work had necessarily interfered—and/or the sex had been great. As long as it didn't happen again.

But while the potter might be back in her good graces at the moment, dear Samantha would not be so lucky. Rhonda was not about to let her in on her summer dating schedule or details until Sam learned not to meddle in her love affairs—something she had never done. *Before* Sam was stricken by marriage.

Though ...

Just to taunt, torture, tease . . .

Rhonda *might* be persuaded to share a few juicy, naughty details. Her prim friend *might* need help with material for the sexier parts of her book. Ronnie's grin was pure wickedness. Yes, maybe she would assist—and 'share' someday. Not too soon. Sam needed to simmer a little first.

The arts festival may have ended, but summer was just kicking off in the town of Edmonds.

Bett Bone

It was a place that exploded with fun, festivals, events, and vibrancy in the summer like the blooms exploding all over town for the garden competition, while the waters of the sound danced and sparkled as if to join the excitement, and the waves slapped happily against the line of beaches like playful dancers.

Every Saturday in summer there was a Farmer's Market that had grown on the downtown streets to be almost as large as the annual craft festival, with all the local fresh farm fruits, vegetables, and cut flowers, added to local lavender growers soap, honey, and cheese makers. The nearby waters provided fresh and smoked fish which only added to the mix of sights, sounds and aromas.

Handcrafted clothes and accessories vied with the enterprising gal that sold homemade pies, doing a brisk business in fresh cherry, apple, and berry flavors with those thick finger-notched pie crust pastry rims like grandma used to bake. Candle makers displayed pieces almost too pretty to burn in scents of cinnamon, almond, vanilla, lavender, cocoanut, chocolate, really almost any scent you could name. Bakers competed in the sensual and sumptuous temptations with bars almond and maple coated, cinnamon rolls robust, mouthwatering muffins and cupcakes, and donuts or massive pretzels fried as you watched.

Sundays were for lazy jazz music outdoors on the plaza by the guest docks, and a little further up the port a naturalist ranger took kids for walks to see the water wildlife in tidal pools and displays of all the life hiding just beneath the waves in the near shore environment. For some hands on fun they went into the tiny station on the dock and could pet a *Real Live!* Sea Urchin (how come mom & dad call us little urchins?), or see a scary octopus mere inches from their curious noses.

They didn't want to pet that! It had more arms than they did and might grab them and drag them into the tank! Such thrills and chills to tell their friends back home.

Near this little brick ranger building, a concrete pier wrapped its arm out around the northern corner of the port boat moorages, providing a front row viewing platform of all the boats heading into and out of port and of the ferries arriving and departing just to the north. Though its purpose was as a saltwater fishing and crabbing pier, it was a favorite of walkers, everyday sightseers, and tourists, with its wide railed walkway, windscreen displays of fish species and habitat, benches to just sit and view the waters and the mountains across the sound.

But one had to walk with caution and duck to avoid the avid line caster, and beware of buckets with claws climbing out of them. The fishy metal sinks where fish were gutted was a dose of too much reality for some, but the seagulls above screamed for more, hoping for a treat.

If you leaned against the shore side rail and looked back at the rock walled breakwater enclosing the boats you could see, just at the waterline amazingly large starfish clasping the rocks. In the waters between, an underwater salmon hatchling pen floated, to give the young fish a chance to acclimate to the sea and the smells of their home habitat, where they would return to their hometown waters after a few years of adventuring in the deep sea.

And sometimes, if you were lucky, you would see a sneaky frustrated seal cruising those waters, trying to figure out how to get in and rob that enclosed pen of tender young salmon.

Just north of the fishing pier was yet another beach, and more seals, though these fellows were cast in bronze and patiently sat at the edge of the sands with little kids crawling all over their backs, before rushing to build sandcastles, find miraculous shells, and just run and jump and splash in the surf's edge for the fun and love and magic of sea meeting sand.

There were a number of waterfront beaches sandwiched around the port, along with parks, including a marsh wildlife sanctuary behind the port and an underwater scuba park to the far north above the ferry landing.

But all this was just part of the normal fun and hum of summer life in and about the town.

Things really revved up with all the weekend festivals and events, with waterfront festivals, a Scandinavian festival, blooming garden tours, jazz combos, and fun foods, not to mention the fourth of July and fireworks, there were classic car shows and concerts in the parks, and historic, mural, and gallery walks, all in a blaze of sparkling water, crisp sea breezes, and an occasional summer rain to refresh the green, giving everyone a soft summer rest.

Summer exploded in the town and beaches of Edmonds and even the dogs had a glorious time—and their own special dog beach at the southernmost tip of the waterfront.

The San Juan Islands, further up the sound, were another summer tourist mecca.

Ferries disgorged such a constant flow of tourists that one wondered how the main islands remained afloat. More arrived in boats with sails snapping, or bright banners flapping from yachts and cruisers.

Above the boat harbor, on the opposite end of town from the massive lanes of the state and inter-island ferry docks, on San Juan Island, was a small inn looking across a green sloping lawn to the marina docks—a perfect place for a teenaged girl to spend a lazy summer afternoon.

It was a favorite spot for the young teen to lounge and read in the summer, watch boats come in, and even find babysitting jobs from visiting tourists. The inn was owned by friends of her family and they liked her sitting on their lawn, relaxing, and reading. It was an inviting picture, and only a bonus that she could be trusted to talk with a lonely teen tourist or tend and play with restless young ones so a vacation did not stress out parents and make them cranky patrons—all parties benefiting.

She had been alone all afternoon reading, stretched on a picnic blanket. As her eyes moved to the top of another page, movement caught her eye. The teen had been so immersed in her book, she hadn't noticed a boat come in, but a man was strolling up the dock.

She sighed. It wasn't *him*.

Carefully marking her place in *The Secret of Shadow Ranch* with her finger—she did not want to lose the spot where the phantom horse appeared—but she wanted to check the man out to be sure. Training her eyes on his sailboat slip, she saw it remained as empty as it had been for days. Disappointed, but ever curious, she swung binoculars back on the man down on the dock that had just come from that float.

He had a stocking cap pulled over his hair and ears, and sunglasses covered much of his face, but she could see a straight nose, and square jaw covered in a stubble of dark beard, and little more of his face. He had a strong neck, and broad chest in a faded navy t-shirt, with an open plaid shirt over it. His arms beneath the rolled sleeves were tanned and muscled. His shirts hung loose over a pair of grungy looking cargo pants over running shoes. A heavy looking dull green duffel bag hung over his left shoulder and a canvas coat was clutched in his right hand.

Then he turned and stood looking back over the marina as if he was looking for something, or waiting for someone.

Even without his bicycle clothes, she recognized him. There was something in his stance that gave her a little chill up her back. It was the dark haired man from the bookstore, the Call-me-Jake man. She was sure she had heard him tell the bookstore owner that he wasn't interested in boating, or any books on it. An oddity for someone seeking guide books in an island bookstore.

From the look of him right now, he seemed pretty comfortable on and around boats and docks.

Putting away her binoculars before he turned her direction, she found and placed her bookmark, carefully tucked the beloved, battered, and frayed covers of her book in a padded e-reader case to protect her treasure, and packed it, her water, reading glasses and blanket away in her back pack.

Stepping up on the weathered dock, after securing his boat in the marina at Friday Harbor, Jake took a slow look around, green eyes intent, studying each boat and the level of activity in the harbor.

Squinting, he caught himself before rubbing his burning eyes. The contacts were still bothering him, but he would have to wait for the relief of his glasses until his job here was done.

Climbing up the gangway, he strode up into town. He would make a stop at the bank and draw some funds, get a good night's sleep, then he had a long day ahead of him tomorrow. He'd toss some crab pots in his boat and go visit all the coves and niches that surrounded as many islands as he could navigate until he found a good secluded location to secure his crab buoys.

Then he would radio in their GPS coordinates and wait.

He didn't notice the teen trailing along behind him until he caught her reflection, along with others, in the glass doors of the bank. He ignored her—it was an adult tail he was scanning for.

chapter ten

It had been hot and muggy in town, warning the week's sunny weather was about to change; big billowy white puffs like burst popcorn were beginning to rise in columns high in the rich blue sky overhead.

Down at the beach park south of the Edmonds marina the display was even more dramatic. The temperature variance between land and water drug in offshore breezes trying to hoist the huge water gorged sponges of cloudy charcoal to rise up as cooler air pushed in from behind off the Pacific coast.

The battle played out over the sound, the lower levels showing the intense boiling black, gray, with charcoal blued clouds at war below on the front lines over the waters, stirring the breeze and the blood with the exciting fight for the still serene and picture perfect heavens above. The waves bounced in a restless chop, tossing foam and the children playing on the beach laughed louder, ran faster, played harder, as the sun still beat down on the shore.

Deep orange arched sails glowed against the darkening clouds as kite boarders jumped and crisscrossed the broken water in a graceful, if frantic dance, while a ferry crossing the far sound behind them seemed to gleam ethereally white for a moment, as it passed a patch of sun. In the nearby dog park, a pair of golden retrievers leaped ecstatically for a cobalt blue Frisbee before it sailed out with them in competitive and delighted pursuit, plunging into the churning surf to chase it down.

The sunny beach was like a grandstand for the show. From the beach the stacked battle lines could be seen with the bright blue sky on top shooting sun through gaps into the melee below like flaming arrows piercing and highlighting the battle fronts in an eerie glow. On the beach the spectators could feel the heat, the charging atmosphere, yet bathe in the comfort of the stirring breezes, feeling somehow more alive than before. An elemental vibrancy seemed to gust with the breeze and fill all sight, sound, color, and life with excitement.

"Watch me, Mommy! Watch me!"

Rhonda smiled at the excited toddler's voice, unable to resist pausing and turning to see for herself. Kneeling on fat dimpled knees, sand covering his clothes, hair, and cheeks, except where a bright smile with a few pearly teeth glowed, the little boy patted the last clump of sand onto a ragged sand tower then picked up a little yellow bucket of seawater, and with great drama and sound effects, dashed it on his creation.

"I'm a wave, Mommy," he chortled, "See, I'm a big wave!"

Such glee, she thought, such joy at young simple pleasure. Her smile faded as she moved a ways further down the beach above the tidal sands and dusted off an old bleached driftwood log to sit for a while. It was so easy to forget simple pleasures, she would sit awhile and watch and maybe remember—or at least calm her darker thoughts.

Happiness? Laughter? More. Joy.

The word seemed to leap in Rhonda's head and drift and settle in as she looked around her at the playing children, the laughing dogs, the man freeing a colorful kite into the freshening wind. Good old-fashioned joy. Simple. Happy. Special. It was everywhere around her—but not in her. To her it seemed more like a fascinating stranger.

She'd come down to the harbor to meet up with Peter. He told her he'd probably be working on his boat, but if he finished early he might join up with some guys that had invited him to play beach volleyball with them.

The troubled skies looked like the weather might become too rowdy for their plan to go sailing, but they could always find something to do . . . inside. Though, Rhonda admitted, she might have had a little too much indoor sport last night. Her muscles were still hung over.

When she didn't find Potter at the boat, which was locked up tight as usual, she was neither surprised nor pleased. She wasn't about to wait around for him like she had done the last time when she had accidentally fallen asleep for hours, stretched out on deck in the sun, waiting. She decided a little stroll, down the boardwalk over the high arched steel bridge into the marina park, might ease her stiffness.

It was as good a reason as any to go see if he was down there playing beach volleyball. She was almost hoping she didn't find him there.

And she had not. Surprise, surprise, her date had vanished again.

This was *not* how she was accustomed to being handled—not to mention—he had left no note taped to the boat for her and hadn't called—yet.

When she didn't find him down on the beach, she decided to do a little vanishing of her own. Reaching into her bag she pulled out her cell, turned it off without checking for messages, and stuffed it in the very bottom of her tote. She would take the afternoon for herself, wandering along the sand and among the sea grass and strewn logs of the shore. She had found the perfect spot to observe and yes, to brood.

But here Rhonda had found something else.

Joy.

It was everywhere around her; she could feel its gentle hands reaching inside her to pat, stroke away the hard places inside her, tease away her natural cynicism, easing, knowing. Oh, she had plenty of fun, wicked fun. But simple joy? Joy was a stranger, only an occasional visitor to the front door of her soul. For once, instead of slamming up a 'no trespassing' sign, she eased the door open. A little. Just a tad. With the chain still on, she smiled at herself. She watched the boiling gray black heavens and recognized what probably mirrored the current view inside that room she was guarding so closely.

But the bright orange sails that flew and flitted through the gray, what would those be? Hope?

She stretched her legs out into the warm, dry pebbled sand, leaning back on her silvery log, her eyes half-closed to savor and absorb, and let the swooshing sound of the waves cajole her and *hope* her thoughts could find some matching steady rhythm.

Kevin and Shelley, with Timmy leaning forward from the

backseat, were surprised to catch a vacated parking spot when they pulled into the Marina Beach. It was one of the boy's favorite spots to go on their Big Brother/Sister day, though Tim referred to it as his day with his 'main men'.

They were glad to find the close-in spot as they began to unload all the towels and folding chairs, the cooler, frisbees and balls, from Kevin's SUV. Timmy took the toys and food basket, of course, and charged off leaving Shelley and Kev to wrestle the rest out and lug it over the grassy berm to a picnic table down by the sand.

"Isn't that Sam's friend Rhonda over there?" Shelley paused, resting her load a moment, and shaded her eyes to see more clearly. "Yes, it must be. I can see her high wedged sandals. Who else would dress so nice to walk in the sand?" Shelley laughed, delighted.

"Yeah, I think it is ...," Kevin glanced over then stopped.

The melting ice water sloshed loudly against the cans in the cooler he was carrying, as he stared across the beach, frown lines showing on his forehead over his sunglasses.

"Who is that guy she's talking to," he muttered, as if to himself.

Shelley turned back and noticed the man crouched close beside Ronnie, then turned back to Kevin with dancing eyes and a mocking grin.

"With *Rhonda*? Why just another nameless, handsome stud in her harem, I'm sure." She chuckled again and picked up her chairs and kept heading for the section of beach Timmy seemed to have claimed. "Come on, Timmy's waving at us. He must have found the perfect spot."

Kevin rested another minute, watching the couple down the beach, before hefting the cooler and following. After getting their gear set up, he still seemed distracted.

"I thought Rhonda was seeing that artist guy."

"You mean Peter Potter?" With a huff of laughter she chanted, "Peter Potter the potter with the pickled pecker, err, potted pepper," slapping a hand over her mouth, she gave up.

"Yeah," Kevin drawled dryly, green eyes twinkling at Shelley, "both from what I hear. But," turning back to stare down the beach thoughtfully, "that guy is not Potter."

An Arts and Crafts AfFair

San Juan Island

There had been a mid-summer storm last night that had lashed the islands with a dazzling light show, grumbling thunder, and swept down small limbs, flooding thirsty fields and meadows, puddling on all the roadways.

Today everything was bright and fresh and green again and she had gotten on her bicycle and gone exploring the island, pedaling to a point that held her current interest. And if she hadn't seen the branch that had fallen and cracked the tiny window on the old shack, she told herself she never would have trespassed—any further.

"OMG!" The teen whispered to herself, hearing a noise outside the shack.

She froze, ears straining.

Just as she was blowing out a relieved breath, sure she was imagining things, the teen heard a dog bark nearby. She jumped a foot, but it wasn't until she heard a man tell the dog to hush that she almost wet her new pink panties.

This was a really stupid idea! Why did she *do* things like this?

She knew better. Really, like how *many* times had she been grounded?

The dog made another woofing noise, closer to the front.

Tiptoeing carefully, she didn't dare turn her cell flashlight on, she edged into the shadows against the far back corner and almost shrieked when the rough wood wall opened behind her. Swallowing her gasp, she peered into the darkness of a small hidden back room. It wasn't much wider than a closet, with a workbench lining one side.

Hearing a man's voice again outside, she stepped over the threshold and slid against a wall, slowly closing the door all the way.

It was *very* dark.

It was a good thing she wasn't afraid of the dark. She had courageously given up her nightlight at least five years ago. She shivered and wondered if that was a cobweb across her face.

She could hear her heart thumping. It sounded a lot louder in this really dark place—that felt like it was getting ever smaller.

What you don't know can't hurt you. Yeah, sure mom, like duh, why do they have intelligence agencies? Walls could close in and crush you whether you could see them doing it or not. It wasn't like one of those if-a-tree-falls-in-the-forest kind of things if you happened to be under the tree when it fell—noisy or not. She felt a little tougher having banished another parental gem of wisdom.

Noise. She hadn't heard any for a while she realized. Or maybe she just couldn't hear from back in this little room—over the sound of her heart pounding like a parade drum.

She would wait to make sure. But when she thought she might have felt a spider on that cobweb that might be across her face, she decided she had waited long enough.

Aiming her cell down toward the floor she turned on the flashlight, and swiped across her face. Nothing. Phew. And she found she could hear better with some light. She could hear that dog, but it was far away now. Over her non-fear of the dark, the teen's curiosity jumped back in first place. She spread her light over the opposite wall.

A row of glazed pots lined the workbench, but they were unlike any she had seen before. These must be secret new designs, she thought. They looked like wide mouthed vases painted and glazed in bold colors and abstract designs. But when she happened to peek inside one, she saw they had an inner wall that circled around half way up the inside from the base of the pot. The inner wall was divided into individual pockets around the whole interior.

What could be the purpose of that?

It must have some special reason; it must be tons of extra time and effort to create such a fancy double walled pot. She tried to picture how it could be used. Maybe the pockets were to hold different bundles of more delicate flowers around the rim, while the center section could hold big, long stemmed roses or lilies, or ... whatever. The pockets were all deep and looked glazed so they must each be waterproof. Or maybe, she pondered as she moved down looking in each pot...

Wait, this one is different she noticed looking in the last pot on the bench. Its inside was smooth and completely finished like a normal vase, only narrower inside. Doing a comparison she saw it had the same inner dimensions as the ones with double walls. An empty container with clay remnants along with a putty knife and an opened box of sandwich bags sat beside the last pot. She was just picking up a can of paint glaze when she thought she heard more noise from outside.

Tucking herself beneath the work bench, she shut off her

flashlight.

Oh joy. Super dark again.

Crouching in the dark, trying not to breathe too loudly, she concentrated on the mystery of the strange pots above her, hoping to get her heart to quit beating so fast and loud.

If I get out of this without getting caught, she silently vowed, I'll.... She considered and rejected all the things she should never do again and couldn't come up with one she wanted to sacrifice.

When the shadow fell over her, she tried to ignore it.

Rhonda was immersed in her own thoughts sitting on the beach, on her self-revelation that after all the years of a life of self-critique, planning, and goal setting, it had all been about her business, her career. Never had it been about her personal life, and never had she made a personal needs list—and if she had, it would not have been topped with 'find simple joy in life'.

Career versus marriage. That had been her early personal choice, and maybe her last major one.

In the baby boomer generation, Samantha and Rhonda came of age in a time of all out social and cultural, even physical, battle.

The civil rights struggle had led to the Equal Opportunity Act, which was also a huge boon for women. Woman finally had an equal right to a *good* job opportunity, college education, and even eventually to their own credit cards. It gave them new financial and legal contractual force—they no longer had to marry a man to provide a financial front man or to contract for something as basic as a car or house.

Their high school graduation class met a rapidly reshaping revolution. Their male classmates were buzz cut by the draft for the Vietnam War, or dropped out as long-haired hippies. For the females, still required to wear dresses to school—no slacks, jeans were for workmen—there was the traditional route of marriage, and new competition: college and career, even free love as flower children.

Samantha had taken the traditional route of marriage and kids, almost before she realized there were now other options. Rhonda went for college and career, and ...

"I'll take the Free Love, of course, and lots of it, thank you very much."

But even that had to take a back seat to her career ambitions. She was dedicated to a plan and a set of goals that she worked toward steadily. She was a self-confessed workaholic, one had to be to succeed in what was still a man's world, needing to be twice as good, twice as sharp, work twice as hard.

And Rhonda had done it. Meeting every business goal she set, following her plan to great success.

And now she had it all.

But . . . what was *it*?

And why had she gotten this far in her life and not realized *it* was somehow seeming like not enough?

When had joy and happiness become so damn important? And why, now?

"That is an awfully big scowl for someone enjoying the beach. Are you worrying about being rained out?"

Suddenly the deep male voice reminded her she had been sitting brooding in a shadow—someone's shadow—and the voice was much deeper and huskier than Peter's. The shadow shifted and moved around to take a seat beside her on the weathered driftwood log.

"Excuse me, do we know each other?" Rhonda didn't mind that her voice sounded waspish.

"No," he drawled in that deep voice, white teeth exposed in a smile beneath mirrored shades and a ball cap, "but we would *like* to know each other."

His confidence annoyed her.

His voice and smile—not so much.

And the protest she had been about to automatically snap back at him died on her tongue when she spotted the legs beneath his shorts. Thick, darkly tanned, hard, thigh and calf muscles. The man was a hunk.

Hmmm.

Rhonda scanned higher, sensing she had admired this form somewhere previously.

chapter eleven

"I didn't mean to eavesdrop," he shifted a little nearer, a mischievous quirk to his smile, "but, did I hear you requesting some free love? Lots of it? Because I'm all in for that. Way in."

The mischief in his smile widened to wicked as he watched his innuendo register on her face.

She saw it also, staring into his mirrored sunglasses at a dazed woman, mouth open.

"I wasn't sure if you were asking me, or...," he continued in that same amused, quiet, husky voice, "Well, regardless. Just saying. I'm available, experienced, and eager. Just say where. Now is good for when, for me. How about you?"

"I... you... Are you applying for a job?" She was too stunned to get her lips to work.

"Did I mention that you'll find I'm a very *hard* worker?"

"You're terrible!" She bit back her laugh.

She should have blistered him with her tongue, but she had to admit she enjoyed his brash humor. It reminded her of someone—herself, actually. Then the thought of giving this man a tongue lashing sent her thoughts careening off in the direction he was leading.

The sound of children's squeals and laughter down the beach, snapped her to her senses. She gave herself a mental slap. There are kids nearby, Ronnie girl, watch your dirty thoughts—especially if she was letting some of them slip out out loud.

Giving him her back, she stared out at the churning clouds and water, hoping he would think he offended her, and if ignored, would leave. She hoped that happened before she burst out laughing at the charming rogue.

"Okay, well just let me know when you are ready," he murmured, unrepentant.

Instead of leaving, he just scooted down from the log, stretched his long, strong legs out in the sand, with the log as a head rest, he folded his arms across his chest, and most likely closed his eyes beneath his shades.

The gall of the man! Was he waiting?

Waiting until she was *ready*?

She couldn't hold it back anymore, and when she started laughing, she found it hard to stop. She couldn't remember when she had laughed so long and hard.

How was a woman supposed to go back to her brooding when she had such a man waiting to give her lots of free love.

"Oh, just go away," she finally managed to get out, half exasperated. "I'm not going to be ready today." To her horror, she almost giggled, but managed to cough instead.

"Are you waiting for him?" It was a casual question.

"I don't wait for any man," she snapped automatically, before glancing around, then pinning her frown on the man lazing in the sun, beside her. "What do you mean him? Who?"

"That guy you waited to join you for dinner at the marina restaurant, a month or so ago."

"I was *not* waiting. I was winding down after the fair, enjoying some private time." Her voice was too defensive to sound sincere, she realized, but couldn't seem to stop herself. The man did something to her nerves. The man ... wait!

"You! Was that you at the next table?" She remembered a dark haired man catching her eye and attracting her interest.

And giving her a lazy, heated once over, right in front of Potter. She had returned the favor—in front of her late-for-dinner date.

"Sure. I just linger around near your beauty, hoping someday you will notice me." His grin was hard *not* to notice.

"You are the most ridiculous man!" She huffed, secretly charmed.

"And you are the most ridiculous woman. We are made for each other. Fate." He shrugged.

"I'm ridiculous?" Her cobalt eyes flashed and heated.

"Of course. Look at your shoes."

He didn't need to run his hand down her leg to point out where they were located! She shivered, then slapped his hand away.

"See? Now who wears shoes like that in the sand?" he asked so irritatingly calm and reasonable.

"These are my boat shoes," she turned an elegant ankle and admired her high wedge sandals that had sturdy red canvas strapping crisscrossed Grecian style to just above her ankle.

"Sexy." His voice was flat. "Not very practical."

"They are cork!" Indignant, she tapped the thick wedge as if to prove a point.

"Ah," unimpressed. "So they won't mar the boat deck?"

"They float! They're cork." Dense man. He sounded like he coughed. Or was that a laugh? "What?"

"I was just trying to picture you floating head down in the sound with your red shoes bobbing on the surface. I guess they would mark your position like a buoy." Another suspicious sounding cough. "But wouldn't a life jacket be more effective? Though, I guess, clearly not as stylish."

"Wretch. If they float I won't lose my shoes."

"Ah. Well, as long as you float also, I guess that would be crucially important."

"Are you laughing at me?" Rhonda frowned.

"Sure."

He smiled, then added, "Are you ready yet?"

"What?" Temper was replaced by blank surprise on her face, then storm clouds boiled in her narrowed cobalt eyes like the ones in the skies above them.

"NO!" Like a snap of thunder.

He laughed, shrugged. "Okay. We'll wait."

"Go wait somewhere else," she growled. Arguing with the man took way too much effort.

"Actually..." He popped up off the sand in a display of athletic strength and grace and stood looking south toward the dog beach. "I probably have someone waiting for me." His voice trailed off as if he was uncertain. Probably a first for him. 'Sure' seemed to be not only his favorite word, but a definition of his personality.

"Well, don't let me keep you." She was *not* disappointed.

"Oh, no rush. My date is a bitch," he said casually, tucking his hands in the pockets of his shorts.

"I'm sure you deserve each other," she said with unwarranted sarcasm. She wanted him to leave didn't she? No, need to sound bitter.

"Hey, have fun," she tried for a friendlier tone. "By the way, do you have a name?" She regretted it the minute she asked. Who cared?

"Sure."

She looked up at him expectantly, but when he just stood there smiling, she huffed out an angry breath. Two could play his game.

"So do I." She snapped, waved and ground out between her teeth, "Good. Bye." And turned her back on him.

His delighted chuckle rankled, but she heard the sounds of his feet jogging off in the sand, and breathed a sigh a frustration.

From a distance, she heard him shout back to her.

"My date is a dog, Rhonda. See you around."

It was *not* funny.

Clearly he was not only a lingerer, but a first class eavesdropper. And for a moment, the tiniest moment, she just might have been jealous of a dog.

She didn't know why she laughed.

Further up the beach, Shelley and Kevin had been drawn into a beach volleyball game by young Timmy.

"Bummer," he'd slogged back across the sand, shoulders slumped, after being rejected as a player in the adults only game forming on the beach.

"They wouldn't let me play. How's a kid to have any fun?"

With exaggerated melodramatics, Timmy flopped down on the sand like the world might as well end for all he cared. Casting a sly eye sideways, he suggested, "You guys should play."

"We're good," Kevin replied, not wanting the kid to feel more left out.

"No, really man, you and Shel should play. Then I would have someone to cheer for, something to do watching. If I can't play, hey, the least you can do is play and make fools of yourself so I have something to laugh at."

"Wow, Tim, what an enticement." Standing up and brushing sand off her bathing suit bottom, Shelley surprised them both.

"I'm game. Want to help me entertain the kid, Kevin?"

Frowning, he slowly unwrapped himself from his comfortable

sprawl, rolled his shoulders, and sighed, "I guess. Show this kid how it's done."

Kevin was the one boasting, but Shelley had a secret smile of confidence of her own. In high school she had captained a women's volleyball team that had been state champions.

But no one needed to know that. Better to demonstrate for these unsuspecting males.

Rhonda happened to catch the action, when she glanced down the beach.

She had tried to recapture her broody mood, but that man had ruined it for her. She watched the activity on the beach awhile longer before heading home.

Spotting a volleyball game in progress, she scanned it to see if Potter was playing. He wasn't.

"But I am just curious, I am not waiting for him," she said firmly, in case any shadows were lingering nearby, then felt like a fool when a seagull turned and stared at her.

"Eat sand," she told it.

Turning back to watch the game, she recognized a few of Sam and Jordan's friends playing.

Shelley had just rotated to the front left corner defending the net. She looked so tiny amongst all the big males, but Rhonda noticed that while she was small, she had full feminine curves and well-toned arm and leg muscles, pale skinned against the cobalt blue of her one piece swimsuit.

If nothing else, Shelley was built to distract the men's concentration.

Just as Rhonda had the thought, Shelley crouched slightly side on to the net, arms loose to her sides, ready, tensed, looking like a woman that was serious and knew what she was doing. Rhonda couldn't pull her eyes away.

An opposing player, a big beefy guy, leaped tall and blocked a return, slapping the ball down hard at the net. Shelley was already shooting up high, straight arm punching her stiff fist up from her right...

"Oh!" Rhonda laughed out loud. "Good shot! Way to go, girl!"

Even from a distance she could hear the young boy's gleeful

shout.

"Way to go, Shel! You pasted him!"

He was not referring to the volleyball—Shelley had missed that shot.

She had missed it because a man had charged forward from the back line to 'help' her and, trying to reach over her head, had intercepted the force of her fist with his chin.

The red-haired male lost—Kevin was out cold in the sand.

"I don't know whether to yell at you for invading my space, or whether to apologize." Or whether to laugh, Shelley thought, because really it was kind of funny seeing him flat out in the sand staring up at her dazed and stunned wondering who hit him. But she kept her laughter silent, though she did give him a clue who had flattened him.

"But since I have already decked you," she managed with a straight face—she was an attorney, after all—"consider yourself chastised for crowding me." His green eyes widened.

She knelt down beside him, unaware of how the sunlight made her blonde hair glow like a halo around her angelic looking face. Or that along with the concern in her blue eyes, that flash of humor also showed.

"I really am so sorry, Kevin." She brushed red mahogany strands of hair off his forehead, and sand off his check above the bag of ice she had fashioned from their cooler. She was a little clumsy, her own right hand was wrapped in another ice bag. That square chin of his was like striking stone, but nothing seemed to be broken on either of them—except maybe someone's ego.

"I guess I should have told you I was a volleyball champ, huh?" She murmured to him gently as she dusted sand off him.

"Then maybe you would have stayed back." She didn't say, *"Where you belonged"* this time, as she was trying to comfort him.

She supposed it was a lost cause.

The man would probably never speak to her after this, much less look her in the eye.

"I...," he grimaced, shifted his jaw slightly, "sorry too. Your play, shoulda trusted. Hell of punch." Tried to smile, couldn't manage it.

"Tim happy?" he mumbled.

She couldn't lie to an injured man.

"Ecstatic."

The storms that had been threatening all day broke over the town that evening.

And over at least one head—the delinquent potter's.

"There was no excuse for abandoning you like that, sweetheart."

Rhonda's growl was more that of a lioness—one that hadn't been fed—than anything soft or sweet of heart. But she bit her words back. Arms crossed, leaning on her doorjamb blocking him outside, she waited to hear what his story would be—this time.

The downpour she kept him standing in would have felt warm and cozy compared to the ice chips her eyes were hurling at him.

He could have pulled his poncho hood up to protect his head and face. She suspected the reason he didn't was to try to play on her sympathy so she would let him in. Fat chance. She was rather enjoying seeing him standing there looking like a drowned rat. Rather appropriate, she thought.

"I received an urgent call from a client and had to rush out and deal with a problem. I should have called you right then. Again, no excuse, but I thought it would be better to go see how long it was going to take to sort things out. So I could let you know."

That earned him raised eyebrows, tighter lips, and another arctic blast from those eyes bluer than any glacier.

"It took a while longer than I expected. But you'll be glad to know I got everything all taken care of now to my client's satisfaction."

She didn't budge in position or expression. She was neither glad, nor gave a damn.

"And I did call you, then. Repeatedly. Both here and on your cell."

If he expected brownie points, he better wipe that hopeful look off his face—or she would. She didn't offer the information she had shut her cell off and deleted her messages unheard.

"I guess you didn't get my messages." Faced with silence, he took a step forward, suggesting, "Let's check your phone. I bet we'll find them."

Her expression sent him back two steps.

"Listen, Rhonda, I am really sorry. I hate it when my work interferes with our time together . . .," Potter saw that excuse had been used too many times, even with this businesswoman. "I'm begging you for a second chance."

Her long elegant fingers tapped against her elbow where her arms were still crossed. According to her count, it was more like his fifth or sixth chance. He better beg harder.

"I promise, no matter what comes up, I'm done working for the weekend now. The rest of it belongs exclusively to you. I'm all yours now," he tried one of those wicked smiles, edging closer. Lowering his voice, a hand reaching out to her, "Just think, you can have your way with me. A willing sex slave. Sound good, baby?"

He stepped forward as she finally stepped back.

Only his knuckles would show bruising from the door slamming into them. She had been aiming for his face.

The most painful bruise from Kevin's injury turned out to be the fact that Timmy told every kid in the shelter, in living color detail, over and over and over, just how his 'main man, Shel' had created the purple, black, and green decoration on Kevin's chin.

Most of the guys had seen Shelley, knew how small she was. They were all massively impressed—with her.

Him? Every time they admired his coloration, they tried to hide their snickers—not very hard, in his opinion.

He could hardly blame them. Kevin was pretty impressed himself—with her.

He would send her a bouquet of flowers next week with a card saying he was sorry for hurting her hand. He might even be tempted to add that he would kiss it better once his jaw recovered, but he wasn't sure yet if she would appreciate the joke.

Or if it was one.

He blamed the pain meds for making him a little goofy. Or was that ... punchy?

He laughed, winced, then decided he better take a few days off to rest then toss the pills.

He needed a sharp, un-drugged head soon to deal with some things.

chapter twelve

S helley had not slept well.

With all the fresh air and exercise the day before, and the steady beat of the rain on the roof all night—a perfect combination for restful sleep—she should have. Normally. But instead of restful, she was restless and regretful, wishing she had not punched the lights out of the man that was starting to mean way too much in her life.

She had admired Kevin from her first contact with him coordinating the sentences of troubled teens between her office, social services and his Youth Shelter. She had enjoyed his company again later, when she had spent time with him as part of the package of taking on the painfully young Timmy as a Big Sister.

After that first, second, then third, fourth, and etcetera contacts she had been charmed by his personality, entertained by his humor, impressed by his dedication, softened by his gift and attention, and —not to be scoffed at—had the serious hots for his body. No denying that!

Her senses started to sizzle whenever she was near him, her nerves jumping with each touch or accidental brush of contact. When he fastened those green eyes on her the world seemed to whirl, her insides swirled into a spiral of heat, muscles melting, heart speeding, breathing something that needed to be concentrated on—was forgotten.

All the signs were there; she was fast falling under his spell. And not wishing to slow or stop herself.

Then she had punched him!

Good lord, she could hardly believe it.

Would he ever forgive her?

Had she lost all chances with him?

Would he ever even speak to her again?

Poor man could barely speak at all right now.

Shelley had tossed and twisted her body and thoughts around all night long, wishing it didn't matter so much, hoping it wouldn't, but unconvinced. Finally surrendering to the realization she was never going to resolve her worries and get any sleep, she climbed out of bed to a gray and damp dawn. With Sunday chores to do and restless energy to burn, she might as well be doing something useful.

Control what you can, she reminded herself, an essential lesson she'd had to learn for emotional survival as a criminal attorney.

She had vacuumed, emptied trash cans, washed windows, scrubbed toilets and tubs and floors with a vengeance. Towels and clothes were sorted, washed, dried, folded, neatly put away. Working with uncommon speed and determination, Shelley was thankful she could follow routine like an automaton. Her concentration was zero; her mind constantly nagged with the thoughts that had kept her sleepless all night.

Stacking the clean dishes back in her cupboards, she finally closed the last door, tossed aside her towel, and leaned with arms braced on the counter, blowing a stray strand of hair out of her face.

She was *such* a liar.

Shelley kept telling herself she was falling for Kevin.

It was bull. She had *already* fallen—hard—too late to escape any pain.

And he had fallen hard, also, she recalled with a strangled laugh that turned to a groan.

Oh yes, he had fallen. Not *for* her, but *by* her—by her fist. No changing that.

Only thing to do now was keep going, wait for the consequences that were out of her control. Stripping off her sweaty cleaning clothes, she dumped them in the washing machine on the way to take a shower and get herself cleaned up.

By the time she had showered, dressed, caught her damp hair in a neat ponytail and was crossing the parking lot, grocery and errands list in hand, she suddenly stopped and realized the weather had changed dramatically. Air now scented with that wonderful post-storm fresh aroma, the sun was back bright and cheerful and not too warm. It put the spring and pleasure back in her step.

The overnight thunderstorm slept in late Sunday morning under a thick soft gray blanket, finally rising and, after a light shower, departing in late morning.

Birds hopped out from beneath dripping shrubbery chattering with excitement announcing the sun was coming back. Fluttering their wings, ruffling up feathers and dancing about twittering about damp nests, but finding the lingering puddles of cool water most refreshing.

The sun not only came out, as church bells rang in the town, but burst through with an exuberance that was stunningly sweet and fresh. All the flowers wore crisply colored petals, every green brightened and more lush, all of nature dusted and washed clean.

It was a renewal.

A Sunday so fresh and bright it was as if God had come out to bless and forgive all sinners—whether on the beach or pew—and grant them a new beginning. A fresh start on a day as gorgeous as heaven could ever be—with all yesterdays forgotten.

At least that was what Potter must have hoped when the skies lifted and he saw an irresistible sailing day forming. Leaving nothing to chance or delay, he called a marina cafe and ordered a picnic lunch and bottle of wine. After straightening the boat and stowing anything he wanted out of the way, he dressed in his white cotton polo, shorts, and canvas deck shoes. He headed up to the cafe with his picnic hamper lined with cloth napkins and wine glasses.

Potter had a cab deliver him and his basket to Rhonda's front door, then sent it away. Though it would've been easier to leave the hamper on the boat, it clearly spelled intent to take it and demonstrate there'd be no more delays or waiting—and allowed some flexibility. Confident she would find the day and his plan irresistible, he'd at least have nourishment while he camped on her steps praying for that door to open.

Bett Bone

When the morning turned to sparkling brilliance, Rhonda moved out to her tiny condo balcony to savor her coffee, croissants, and Sunday paper. It didn't take her long to realize that it was a day meant for sailing—and she was *not* sitting on the deck of a sailboat with the wind blowing through her hair.

There was a simple solution to her yearnings.

Riffling through the paper, she found it in the classifieds.

Bringing her phone out, she made a call.

"Well, hell, it's barely noon! He didn't have to be so snippy about my asking for a test sail *today*. *That* salesperson sure lost a big fat commission. No way am I going back to that dealer to buy my boat!"

She reached for her paper to call a few more ads.

"Hmm. No answer. They're probably all out sailing," she huffed out a frustrated breath, having tried the last of the numbers for private owners with boats for sale. Reaching for her coffee cup, she found it was empty, dabbing up the last flake from her pastry plate, she sat back and crossed her arms beneath her chest, staring out at the lovely, heartbreaking day.

"I admit it *was* a financially reckless idea, I guess," Rhonda comforted herself, musing out loud. "If I buy a boat in the middle of boating season I'll pay a premium with little time left to enjoy it, and a whole winter of storage fees". She was just wondering about renting a boat for the season when her doorbell rang. She would also need a sailor. So immersed in her own plans, Rhonda didn't even think to check before opening her door.

There was a rat on her porch!

But he *did* have a sailboat handy.

Being in the right place at the right time, turned out lucky for the man only because he had the right equipment. But it did *not* turn out to be a day of forgiveness for the potter, after all.

Her agreement was subject to conditions—and penance.

"Three hours, starting now, and *all* sailing. Then you go back home to your island. And don't count on there being any bouncing berths involved, so just keep your damn twitchy hands to yourself, or lose them! And any future chance with me."

He could be traded for her own boat later.

Whether it was an impulse driven by the fresh start feeling of the day, or the fateful coincidence of having something she meant to do being tossed directly in her path, Shelley pulled to the curb on her way to the store in front of a lawn sporting an open house realty sign.

She'd always thought real estate was a good investment—despite the markets. If you needed somewhere to live, it seemed a waste to toss the rent money to someone else rather than letting it slowly build something for yourself. That was her reasoning when she purchased her condo a decade ago, thinking she would only stay there five years at the most. It was small, but met all the needs of a woman that spent the bulk of her time working—first for the public defender, and later for her former opponent, Jordan's prosecutor's office.

Always intending to have a house someday, Shelley found that time had flown with her busy career; that *someday* had never quite gotten onto her schedule. But something young Timmy had said awhile back must have lodged in her subconscious, because she found herself noticing real estate signs and ads more of late. Still with the feel of being something that would be nice at some future day. Closer, but not yet. Just getting a sense of the market and going rates, however—

Here she was.

Shelley had no one waiting on her, no job demands today, no reason not to take a peek, get some information. She desperately needed to keep her mind distracted, anyway. It would feel good to do something purposeful for her future—something she had control over—something more fun and far reaching than just chores.

"Why not?" This looked like a good place and time to start her search.

The simple ranch house had a nice big yard, which was one of her requirements. It was several decades old but appeared to be trim and well-maintained. Shelley wouldn't want a fixer-upper, or a house someone else had recently remodeled to their own taste. She would be happy with something that had all the basic conveniences in working order. Being outdated or showing a little wear was fine with her, as long as it had the potential for her to work with someday when she was ready to do her own remodeling, as the urge or need arose.

For the near term she just wanted an easy no-hassle transfer from her condo to something with a backyard of grass, instead of a parking lot. Somewhere she could plant a few flowers or putter in the yard whenever she wanted. Somewhere with room to have more friends gather casually.

With her expectations in mind, she jumped out of the car and strolled up the walk to see if she could match any of them—and her budget—and fine tune what she was seeking.

Waving over her shoulder when Potter dropped her off before heading back to the islands, Rhonda breathed a sigh of relief before skipping up the gangway. As she walked to her car she was glad to have avoided any pressure to define the future status of their relationship. They'd gotten along fine in a friendly enjoyment of the sail today, but if he had pushed, she would have told him to take a hike. He seemed to sense that when he mentioned he would be back in town in a week or two and she made no response.

"Should I just give you a call later next week?" He asked quietly.

"Fine." Her tone not indicating if she would answer the call, or not—for good reason.

But the sail itself had been fabulous! What a day!

Now she had that charge of energy and sassy mischief that always seemed to come with being pleased at having gotten her own way. The afternoon was *so* much *too* lovely to waste catching up on any more brooding.

Turning her car toward Samantha's house, she'd go visit her friend, torment her a little with her high spirits. Sam was always trying to gauge how Ronnie's relationship with Potter was going. She wasn't about to share her current indecision, but she *could* give her a few details of prior dates. *Juicy* details to assist her dear friend in writing some wild sex scenes for her book. Surely her overly prim friend could use some good material. Her grin was more wicked than vengeful when she thought of all she could 'share'.

Rolling down all the windows and opening the sunroof, Rhonda turned her car radio to her favorite rock n' roll station—and cranked it. Trying to keep her foot from landing too heavily on the gas pedal, she sang along loud and lustily.

So what if she was out of tune? It was a day meant to cut loose and let the wind blow wildly through your hair.

Samantha heard the deep thumping bass tones before her friend had even pulled into the driveway. Coming out her front door, she stared, laughed, waved, then after listening a moment, grinned.

"Is that really Steppenwolf?" She shouted over the music, happy to hear the sounds of their youth.

Rhonda just laughed and continued singing "Born to be Wild" at the top of her lungs, before turning the car engine off. The sudden silence was startling.

"So," laughing, Sam asked, "been out cruising the strip, lady? Come on in. I'm afraid Jordan's not home. He will be bummed when I tell him the wild woman came to visit and he missed it." Leading Ronnie through the house to the back deck, pleased to see her best friend, Sam couldn't wait to catch up. "So, Ronnie, tell me what you've been up to."

"Oh my dear child, have I got a story to burn your tiny little ears. Better get the drinks. You'll need one. And grab your pen and notepad. We can work on some naughty ideas for your book."

Stretched out later in a chaise, with a frosty drink in her hand, Rhonda didn't look like a troublemaker—unless you saw the devilish sparkle in her dark cobalt eyes.

"Yoga," she said lazily in response to Sam's awkward, pink-cheeked query, not the least fooled that it was just writing research.

"Yes, all that slow careful bending, and stretching, and . . . flexing. Mmm. It is quite sensual and stimulating exercise you know, Sam." Her smile was slow and wicked.

"Okay. Yoga." Sam made a note on her pad, soft blond hair falling forward to hide her flaming cheeks. "Good exercise for increased flexibility and mobility," she noted briskly. "Got it. Thanks, Ronnie. This should help with my . . . ah, the segment I'm currently working on."

Rhonda watched beneath her lashes, amused. Even after two kids and married now to a very virile man, her prim little pal had trouble talking about things she clearly had no trouble enjoying in private.

"Speaking of bending and flexing and such," the brunette tormentor sipped her drink adding, "I have an excellent example to share. Maybe you can use it in your book."

Rhonda dramatically framed her story. "The sun was setting, bleeding all over the sky when we moored at a wooded, isolated inlet where the boat could drift at anchor with the bow facing the glorious clouds and colors in the west.

"Potter said he had a big surprise for me—and he certainly did! He was in the stern pulling up a net. I was leaning over the bow railing, and the sunset was so intensely crimson that it turned everything pink, the white hull and sails. Even my skin was pink."

Probably the first blush Ronnie ever had, Sam mused, but kept that thought to herself, asking instead, "But it isn't even sunset yet, Ronnie…"

"Not the sail today, the first sail with Potter. You begged to hear the details. So, as I was saying, I was leaning over the bow rail, wearing that bikini I have with the little ties on the hips…"

"You still wear that?" Sam gasped, shocked. She had not had the nerve to wear a bikini since her thirties. Even then she had always hidden in her yard to sun bath, dragging a towel over herself every time a passenger jet flew over at thirty thousand feet on its way in to SeaTac.

"The new one, of course," Rhonda huffed indignant Sam might think she'd wear an old suit, yet impatient to get on setting her dramatic scene. Each year her new bikinis had quick release ties on the hips, of course. Sam knew that.

"You destroyed the mood."

"Sorry, Ronnie. Go ahead," Sam poised her pen over her pad.

"So the picture is: bent over the bow rail in my bikini, brilliant sunset backdrop, and a bit of a breeze flutters across the waves and sent a chilling shiver down my heated skin." Maybe she should be a writer, Rhonda thought, impressed with herself.

"Then," dropping to her husky, sensual voice, "Big, warm hands clasped my hips from behind and eased me back against a hot, hard, male body. My ties had unraveled in his hungry fingers. The scrap of fabric fell away, leaving me bared! Pressed tight against a Hot. Rampant. Naked. Man!"

Samantha dropped her pen and clapped her hands over her ears—but only for a moment—she didn't want to miss anything.

"As his hands slid forward to cup and caress my breasts, and free them to the last light of the sun gods, he leaned over me, flexing me further over the railing. Then those hard male hands gripped me by the hips and his first hard thrust tore away my breath and nearly sent me headfirst into the crimsoned waves—"

Sam choked, turned ten shades of sunset, and kept her head down, pretending she was madly scribbling this all down on her legal pad. *Oh my goodness!*

"Are you getting all this down?"

Sam nodded, unable to look up at her friend's eyes.

"Got it," she mumbled. "Bent over, breeze, male puts his peter... No. Peter Potter put his heater in you and warms your bare pink body, right before he knocks you over the bow into the fluttering waves." The last words were a little garbled in Sam's gasping giggle.

"I tell you, Sam," Ronnie ignored the mockery of her storytelling skills, "Flexed like that definitely added to the pleasure. I swear Potter sent me halfway to heaven. You really must try yoga."

"Okay. I get the picture." Sam winced at her own words because she really *did* get the picture—a little too vividly. "But what was in the net?"

"Chilled champagne and caviar, of course, which we did eventually get around to enjoying. Have you ever had caviar licked out of your navel, Sam?"

"Ronnie! Enough!" Sam shouted, eyes scrunched, both hands thrown up to cover her ears—almost—she only listened a little.

chapter thirteen

It was so horribly sad.

Such a waste of precious human life!

All week Shelley had been working on cataloging all the police, lab, and coroner's reports that had been landing on her desk as steadily as the deadly beat of a funeral march. And as she assigned each case number, she knew a funeral was taking place somewhere nearby for each one.

Drug overdoses. Doses that would not normally have been fatal except for the extremely pure product hitting the streets recently, all from the same source. The lab reports confirmed it. The prosecutor's office was compiling these case files for when they caught up with the source that was bringing the uncut product into the local dealers. When they caught him they planned to place criminal charges for each death as a separate charge against him —make him pay for his death toll.

This was not someone passing a few joints, or a dime of coke, this was someone dealing wholesale murder—and he knew it!

One of the detectives had even questioned whether this might be some fanatic that hated drug users by shipping product so pure that, even after being cut through the local distribution chain, it remained fatal—trying to kill off all the drug users.

Though many of the task force thought it was more likely that a new brutal drug cartel was trying to shove its way into the territory by providing the highest potency product.

Whoever was involved, Shelley would like to give them a few doses of their own medicine—their own *fatal* medicine. But those were personal emotions, not her opinions as an assistant prosecutor. She tried to keep them separate, but it gave her sleepless nights and stomach aches as the death toll kept mounting and they still had no actionable leads.

At least she wasn't a public defender anymore, so she would never have to dread defending the bastards doing this.

Finishing with her pile of paperwork, she pinched the bridge of her nose between her fingers to ease the pain in her forehead when an office worker breezed in and plunked a big bouquet of flowers in the just cleared space on her desk. Barely glancing up, she pressed harder, rubbing at her eyes, and said, wearily, "Wrong office. It's not my birthday."

"Your name is on the card, sister, birthday or not you are stuck with them." And left.

Card?

Shel looked up and saw a huge bouquet of roses instead of the normal budget floral bouquet that Jordan Campbell ordered for every staff member's birthday. Reaching up she plucked the card free and pulled a handful of petals closer to capture their scent. *Mmmm.* It even eased her headache.

She read the card, blinked, looked up at the beautiful lush bouquet and felt her throat thicken, a sting in her nose and moisture blur her eyes. It was a reaction she'd never had to bouquets received from colleagues for birthdays or to celebrate a winning case.

Roses.

From Kevin.

How special. How sweet!

She grabbed at a tissue and dabbed her eyes, trying to swallow the lump in her throat.

Or..., Wait!

What if this was some classy kind of kiss off, a goodbye-it's-been-real kind of message? Grabbing another tissue, she blew her nose. How was she to know?

"Just enjoy the damn flowers, idiot. Smell the roses," she told herself. She needed them right now—beauty to counter the morbid cases that littered her desk. Sniffing their sweet aroma, she sniffled even more from emotions too battered and close to the surface. She had emptied her box of tissues before she was ready to face the world again.

Across town, another woman was receiving a floral bouquet in her office. Three decades older—approximately, she would never tell—Rhonda was also years more experienced in receiving male floral apologies. Her reaction was not to get all choked up, though the sound was similar.

When her grinning receptionist placed the flowers on her desk with a flourish—she snorted.

"Just toss me Potter's card; take them out front until you can get them sent to a senior home," she waved them off impatiently. She glanced at the card.

"Wait! Let me take a look at them first." Carnations. Nice smell, if simple. "Okay, go," she ordered her harried assistant. "Take them with you."

Leaning back in her leather chair, Rhonda crossed her heels on her desk, and read the card again.

Ready yet? Was all it said; all it needed to say.

She was irritated Peter would try using flowers; but amused and intrigued the beach guy did.

And she was reminded she had some issues to deal with.

Tapping the card against her chin, she thought back to last Sunday and her visit with her best friend.

"Really, it is not funny, Rhonda. You can't go around having sex out in public. Right out in the middle of the sound for everyone to see!" Sam had been outraged.

"It wasn't the middle of the sound but a little cove too far for anyone to see anything."

"People with waterfront homes have binoculars and telescopes, you know, to watch passing ships, and..."

"Well, so they got to watch something less boring..."

"Ronnie!"

"Okay, fine. But don't tell me you and hubby haven't ever had outdoor sex."

Sam gasped. Narrowed her eyes.

"We have very respectful married lovemaking, not wild outdoor fornic...," Sam waved her arm for the word she couldn't bring herself to say.

"You mean married people never have wild sex? Just respectful, boring..."

"We can be wild and still have respect! And my husband's

lovemaking," Sam stressed the term, "is never, ever boring!"

"Well, I can believe that," Rhonda took the wind out of her sails, "I just find it hard to believe you have never done it outdoors. Respectfully."

"Seriously, Ronnie, don't you ever have more romantic times with anyone? You have been seeing this guy all summer. How is it really going? How is he doing?"

"How is he doing? I would say he is still in training." She gave her friend a smile, not adding that he was barely getting a passing grade on his training so far. She didn't really know how she felt about Potter—or her life in general at the moment.

And didn't want to discuss it.

"But is it serious?" Sam persisted.

Rhonda responded in a way she knew would turn her friend off the topic.

"Well," she had drawled, "he does have some very nice equipment. Should I describe it for you?" Her smile was wicked.

"NO! Never mind!" As intended, Sam thought she was referring to his body, not his boat.

But even though she had managed to get Sam off the topic last Sunday, it was a topic she couldn't continue to avoid. She needed to make some decisions about what she wanted on numerous levels, and not just how to react the next time Potter called for a date.

Was she wasting time on Peter? Since she didn't want a long term commitment, though, what was there to waste?

Maybe she was just too demanding? Though why she should not be escaped Rhonda at the moment, but maybe she could ease off a bit, cut the guy some slack. She had found herself getting tired of the constant chase, she was a jaded female rake, apparently.

Or just a lazy one. It was easy to see the same man for the summer, especially since he wasn't around all the time bugging her. Maybe she should drift along with a just okay relationship for now.

Especially since she could do that drifting on a sailboat.

So Potter would get a stay of execution, for now.

But she still needed to figure out what she needed to get her life in general going in the direction she wanted—as soon as she figured out *what* she wanted. But she would have to save those crucial questions for another day.

Shelley Airton felt like she had been granted a reprieve—having misplaced her normal confidence—and she was uncomfortably nervous.

She tried for casual as she shrugged off her wrap, baring herself to the unforgiving sunlight, draping her cover close at hand over the end of the poolside chaise.

"Nice body," drawled a lazy male voice.

"Oh, thanks," she glanced down at her brightly colored suit. "I got it on sale at..."

Flushing, registering his words, startled blue eyes flashed up into laughing green ones, and a very wicked, if still bruised, smile.

"Nice bikini too," Kevin added, giving it another uncomfortably thorough appraisal before nodding. "Very nice."

"Thanks. Um . . . Is this, I mean, I thought..." Shelley waved her hand as if trying to wave off her embarrassment.

"Yes?" he teased.

"I thought this was a business meeting." Her blue gaze made a question of her statement.

Kevin looked at the pool, then down at his own bronzed half naked body, and just gave her an amused smile.

"Um, you know, just a collegial type get together sort of business meeting," Shelley's mouth, thankfully, stumbled to a halt. "It's not?"

That is what she had assumed when Kevin called her office to set up this Friday night dinner, when he suggested they grill steaks at his place and take advantage of the pool to cool off after a week of work.

She *told* herself it was only business, but had been unable to suppress a little thrill, regardless. Especially after he warned, firmly, "Do *not* bring Timmy." But he probably just needed a private conference with her about the young scamp.

Still, she ran out at lunch to buy a new swimsuit.

Now he slowly shook his head, copper and gold highlights glinting in the sun off his dark auburn hair. Then his smile faded, his eyes and voice softened, serious, when he looked straight into her eyes.

"Does it need to be, Shel?"

Mesmerized, for a moment she forgot her question. "What are

you saying?"

"I'm saying I respect you professionally, Shel, and don't want to put you in an uncomfortable position if that is how you prefer it. But I thought—hoped—that we had, or could have, something more."

"Friends?" Her voice sounded thin.

His grin flashed a set of white teeth and a pair of sexy dimples in his tanned face.

"I already count you as a trusted friend, you should know that. My boyish charm must be slipping if you haven't noticed I'm angling for something more personal than that."

She couldn't help but laugh. "And just what are you charming me into, mister?" She asked, blue eyes saucy and sure once again.

"Well, now, lass," he let a soft burr roll seductively in his voice, "I wanted to spend time alone with you without distractions. Distractions like a young lad that shoves in between us every time I try to get close to you. I want to be private with you." He moved in closer and slid his arms loosely around her waist, bare sun warmed skin sliding around her barely clad body.

'I'm hoping we will have a meeting of the minds," his breath brushed across her lips as his head lowered, lips smiling as they touched her nose, the corner of her mouth, his green eyes owned hers as he whispered, "A meeting of the minds . . . and maybe bodies."

She barely felt the jolt of his lips nipping at hers before he clasped her waist, lifted her and tossed her in the water, diving into the pool after her. He was still laughing when she came up sputtering. When she threw him a glare, he shrugged and grinned shamelessly.

"I had to cool off fast. I forgot we were in public, lass."

"So you threw *me* in?"

"Well, now, I couldn't leave you up there alone attracting other men with your beautiful body, now could I?"

Oh! He was a green-eyed charmer, all right!

"Let me help you cool off then." She slapped a wave of water into Kevin's unrepentant face, laughing until he grabbed her ankle and pulled her under. It was a wild, playful battle before they drug themselves exhausted from the pool to go char steaks on the semi-privacy of his balcony.

Letting their suits dry on them in the waning sun, the playfulness of the pool moved to a soft flirtation—flirtation without words.

Sifting around each other as they prepared their meal on the small balcony, the bared skin of an arm touched, brushed a shoulder raising shivers—not of chill, but subtle sensation. Their conversation was quiet, casual, relaxed; but nerves danced a tight rope of mutual awareness. Laughter was soft, low, slow; eyes cast the silent glances of deepening attraction.

As she husked the corn cobs, she was aware of the motion of her breasts barely contained in the small bright triangles of fabric——as was he. As he bent to pull drinks from the cooler, he was aware of his half-naked body being measured and admired, feeling the stroke of her eyes caressing the muscles along his spine and bared thighs.

Both were thinking of later when they would go back inside his apartment to dress—or undress—but neither dared speak of it yet——out loud. Only in the gentle touch of her hand as she brushed an imaginary insect from his hard bronzed shoulder, only when his fingers lingered on her check as he curled a stray strand of blonde hair back behind a delicate ear.

Only with eyes catching, shying, and dancing back to latch on each other full of awakening heat.

The meal itself was another teasing feast for the senses.

Beef medallions were grilled wrapped in crisp salty bacon, lightly seasoned then topped in the last few minutes with a fat slice of tomato to heat and hold in the moist blend of melded flavors. Foil wrapped and roasted corn on the cob dripped juice and butter down their chins as they bit into the crisp kernels releasing the flavors and memories of childhood joys and picnics.

Rather than salad, Kevin had artfully skewered fresh chunks of green pepper, fat mushrooms, and plump prawns for grilled kabobs. Leaving the unopened bottle of wine on the counter, they chose a pitcher of fresh iced tea floating with mint leaves and sliced lemons, crisp replenishing nectar to their thirsty young bodies, after the play and exercise in the pool.

With a soft sigh in her throat, Shelley finished her last bite.

"That was absolutely, incredibly delicious!"

Watching her lick her fingertips, ignoring the napkin in her lap, not wanting to miss a single drop of flavor, Kevin watched her tongue flicker gathering the last bits of pleasure and thought she perfectly described what he was seeing.

Delicious. Absolutely, incredibly delicious.

"Yes," he murmured, barely registering her thanks as he gazed at her—her pleasure his. Then rousing himself, added, "You are most welcome. Anytime."

"So what's for dessert?"

Shelley was teasing, patting her tummy, too full for another bite. When he didn't respond right away, she glanced up to check if he thought her serious, but his intent eyes stalled her breath, his answer clear in their gleaming green depths.

You.

You are dessert.

She felt locked in that gaze, aware of him stretched out on the deck chair like a lazy lion with a thick red mane, subdued but dangerous with those hunter's eyes that hypnotized. Shelley felt her body respond instinctively, eyes widening, a tiny shiver rippling down her spine, her nipples pebbling as if she had a chill.

"It's probably a little cold for you out here," his eyes quietly flickered over every part of her, noting bumps raise on her forearms, and elsewhere, "with dusk falling, the mosquitoes will be out to snack on us at any minute." A small smile curved his lips, "and you look much too tasty in all that pretty skin. Shall we go inside and see what we can find as dessert?"

She swallowed—or would have if her mouth wasn't suddenly dry—rising to follow his half-bare body into the kitchen, she was more than ready to volunteer.

And she would need to, she realized, recalling his earlier words that he would not press her for more than she wished in their relationship. Setting their plates down on the counter, she turned to see him check the fridge then idly begin opening the upper cabinets to see what was in them, she watched his back and shoulder muscles shifting with his actions.

"Maybe I should have gotten a watermelon?" he was mumbling when her arms slipped around his waist from behind, and the hard tips of her breasts teased his bare back, her breath a warm whisper against his shoulder as she licked lightly, then murmured, "You seem tasty. I think I will have you, sir, for my dessert. That is if you don't min..."

He had turned in her arms with a groan of male pleasure and triumph, caught her closer, his lips brushing, claiming, and demanding, before she ever finished the sentence.

They managed to make it to his bedroom, but left abandoned

dishes, and a trail of still damp apparel discarded along their path, behind.

Shelley had expected wild, carnal, dangerous sex after he swept her up and stripped them both as he carried her to his bed.

And it *had* been dangerous!

But not in the way that she expected.

She'd had scorching sex before. But it had never burned clear through her organs to reach her heart, turning it to cinders.

He used his strength to lift, cuddle, cradle, claim, and cherish. His mouth and hands trailed nibbles and a showers of kisses over her body, as if she was an exquisite work of art meant to be breathed and tasted for ultimate pleasure, their joining and melding of flesh a sacred right.

He took her past heat, past excitement, past expanding, rippling passion into a land of cherished oneness that left all her barriers shattered and vulnerable, before tenderly, lingeringly, claiming possession of all that was left of her body, heart, and soul.

She almost feared she might never be able to gather all the pieces of herself to take home with her when morning came, finding they had become completely fused and bonded into his being and possession. And she would regret having to come back to earth after being turned into and treated like a goddess. She was not sure if she slept or just fell into a dazed and wondrous coma.

When she woke sometime later before dawn broke, curled in his arms, buried against his chest, his hand gently stroking her hair, trailing her spine, and softly shaping the curve of her hip, she panicked. If he made love to her again she was afraid that she would completely disappear, dissolving into smoke, or liquid, or steaming into mist, never able to find her person again.

When she panicked, she talked—babbled really—snatching any safe topic, expecting any minute he would silence her with his lips, roll her beneath him again for more sweet torture. But he listened, with care and interest, content to share stories and talk quietly in the peace of the night, cuddled together.

Somehow she found herself telling him verbatim all that had happened, all that was said and she felt when Timmy had come to do chores one day to 'pay off his credit' for his bouquet for Candy.

Kevin had smiled at the eleven year old's man-of-the world attitude.

But Timmy was just a child, wearing disguise, as Shelley's story of the day showed.

"I like vacuuming. It's kinda of like mowing a lawn," Timmy confided. "Only you don't get the smell."

Smell? Shelley wondered. "Gasoline?"

"Nah. Cut grass. That's a great smell. Like kids laughing and playing all day, that's what it smells like you know." He shrugged as if embarrassed and turned to wrap the cord carefully making sure there were no twists.

Shelley stifled a smile. Well, that explained his unique style of vacuuming. She wondered why he went down one side of the hall, turning at the corners, and coming back the other direction. Instead of just pushing the vacuum back and forth, Timmy vacuumed most of her rooms in those odd diminishing rectangles, humming some strange tune as he went. Wondering what strange tune it was, she realized now that it was mowing sound effects. *How funny*. But her beige "lawn" looked nice and fresh—though it clearly didn't *smell* like fun.

"Did you used to mow your lawn a lot?" When he didn't respond she set down the stack of mail she was sorting through and glanced over at him.

Timmy was focused on making sure the cord plug was precisely aligned and snapped in as if the world depended on it being just right. She assumed he hadn't heard her when he rose and pushed the vacuum down the hall to place it back in the closet, until she heard him say quietly over his shoulder, "I never had a lawn."

And suddenly her neatly "mowed" carpet no longer seemed funny, but left a tight knot of sadness in her heart.

Turning to Kevin, now, her lips brushed his chin, before nestling her cheek back against his warm chest.

"This may seem strange, but ever since then I've found myself noticing real estate for-sale signs at houses with big yards, that I don't recall ever noticing before. I confess, I've even gone to an open house that was on my way one day. I think I'd like a house." Her voice trailed off as she thought about big yards filled with laughing boys Timmy's age.

They lay silently a while, touching, then his body fell still and his chest rose slow and steady in sleep. Shelley was relieved. And terribly disappointed.

But not as disappointed and confused as she was late Saturday morning when she finally awakened again to find him gone. There was a note in the sparkling clean kitchen beside a hot pot of coffee and her carefully dried bikini.

Had to leave you sleeping beauty.
Feel free to use the pool today.
Please lock up when you leave.
Kevin

chapter fourteen

L ove 'em and leave them.
⠀⠀⠀⠀⠀That was Rhonda's motto.
Though 'love' was clearly a euphemism in her book.
But what about Peter? Why did she linger? Just lazy?
Probably, she decided.

She had fully intended to quit procrastinating about leaving him and decide on some clear direction for her life. Before he called her again.

But she blew it.

Oh, she had gotten a start on wondering why she seemed to be acting out of character. Why she felt unsettled, unfinished, somehow drifting through life at the moment, like a boat that had lost its oars.

Was this a mid-life crisis? Or was she using that term too loosely when she was so close to retirement.

She wondered if the fact her closest friend had suddenly gotten married was weirding her out somehow? Though why that would be, she had no idea.

Sam was married now.

And so what?

Ronnie was truly thrilled for her friend. And it wasn't as if she didn't still get to see her as often; or as if Sam had ever been her companion in Ronnie's brash and bold social life. Not prim little Sam, the dear woman.

So why?

Why did it make any difference now that her friend had someone to love her?

Why did Ronnie feel some strange empty place, some need, not for the weakness and trap of love, but...

Affection maybe? She had friends for that.

For a dependable shoulder once in a while? Not to cry on, heaven forbid! But to lean against, to rest with? Sounded like a wayside bench on a long hiking trail.

No. the fact that Sam had married shouldn't have anything to do with Rhonda's sense of satisfaction.

Unless it was because Sam seemed to have a new plan for the rest of her life.

A direction.

And Rhonda recently realized she had already done and accomplished everything, met and surpassed every goal she had set when she was younger and...now what?

What do you do when you have finished all your to-do lists? Reached all your goals?

Apparently she needed another plan, another list, new direction for the rest of her life. She had never thought when she was younger, determined, striving, that she would actually get everything on her life's to do list checked off satisfactorily. Who did?

Figuring out what to do now, besides spending her life laying around sipping drinks in a sailboat all the time, seemed daunting. Her brain seemed to be without focus, bouncing thoughts all over the place—and she did not like losing control. So she put it all off.

It gave her one item for her new list: *Do life.*

She'd buried herself all day Monday, working on a business proposal. One that she'd hired plenty of underlings to do as competently, but then she wouldn't have a good excuse to keep procrastinating. She'd sent her assistant out for some take-out for a working lunch. Her efficient assistant had switched Rhonda's line over to her own office before leaving. The constant ring was so annoying, Rhonda finally snatched the phone up to answer it herself.

Potter.

She hadn't yet decided if she wanted to see or talk to him or not.

Too late. She was talking to him.

She was even agreeing to see him that weekend, suggesting they go see his work in the Seattle gallery with Samantha and maybe Shelley. Before he could respond, she said she was busy on a proposal and would chat on the weekend, hanging up.

She shook her head, slightly disgusted with herself for her indecision, but at least she had set up a group date so she could keep a little distance.

And Sam would quit bugging her about a gallery jaunt.

She shouldn't have done it.

It was an invasion of privacy.

She knew it.

Her curiosity had been too great, and led her astray.

Or had it?

No. Something was not right.

She hated feeling this way. She hated knowing it about …

Him!

Why did it have to be him?

Now she was miserable; now she would have to—

"Green eyes? That's it?" Frustration laced Jordan's voice.

"And suspicious activity," the detective tried to avoid the prosecutor's eyes when he finished his report.

"Suspicious? Suspicious how?"

"Maybe smuggling?"

"Smuggling what? Where? Do we have dates, locations? Where did the tip come from?" Jordan ceased his rapid fire questions at the complete lack of response from Detective Mallory.

"The note just said, and I quote, 'maybe smuggling, question mark' end quote."

"Brilliant. So we have a tip that tells us that a green-eyed man is…"

"…Acting suspiciously, and maybe smuggling," the detective finished the prosecutor's sentence with a shrug.

A long beat of silence filled the meeting room while the prosecutor's team and the two detectives twiddled their pens, and chewed on their thoughts.

Detective Mallory finally heaved a sigh, and broke the uncomfortable silence.

"Listen, I know it's vague, but I thought it was worth getting together. We know that we have a big and increasing problem with drugs being smuggled in along the coast here. But it hasn't been in the papers or on the news, so the public doesn't. That means that there aren't the usual crazies flooding us with vague, useless tips like this. And let's be honest, we don't have the first idea who, or where exactly, or how, ourselves.

"So, given all that, I thought it was a serious valid tip that someone knows something and is trying to alert us, however insufficient the tip is. Maybe it's someone they know personally and don't want to get on the wrong side of, or someone they feel bad about reporting yet feel they should do *something?* They are probably thinking that now that we know there is a problem that we will look sharp and catch them without having to get further involved. Waiting to hear if there is an arrest. If not, maybe we will get more help." The detective threw his hands wide and shrugged.

'Yes, you're right. And right to bring this in," Jordan nodded, scraping a hand through his dark hair, then leaning forward to brace lean forearms on the table.

"No one knows we are already on alert and still clueless. At least this is a clue, if nothing more. Okay. Green eyed men. How many of those could there be?"

Shelley looked down, doodled on her legal pad. Kevin had green eyes … The same green eyed man she hadn't heard from all week since his rather unromantic note.

"Hell," Jordan said, "they could be wearing green contacts! Let's save that one for the moment, until we get some suspects and move on to the other." Rising he stood by the whiteboard on the wall, and wrote down a heading.

"Okay, smuggling what? Drugs? Art? Explosives?" He wrote the list as he spoke. "What else folks? Give me some ideas, then we will break them down and check for recent activity on any of them."

Shaking her thoughts loose, Shelley volunteered, "People. Either illegal immigrants, or terrorists, or human trafficking for sex slaves, but still we don't know if the smuggling is smuggling in or out when it comes to people."

"Okay, Shel you call the INS, see if there is any activity recently on any of those fronts. I'll call the ATF about explosives, and a scan of the Internet for chatter. Detectives, get some short term help okayed by your chief then check the pawn shops for art and your contacts for rumors, and run some regional database checks for police activity on all except the drugs. Let's see if we can pin down quickly if there is anything besides our drug investigation we need to worry about and assign someone to, so we can get our focus back where we already know we need it. I'll call your chief, as usual, and update him on this meeting. And if you get any more clues, don't hesitate to call us together, Mallory. Thanks, guys."

"I do have a Colonel Mustard in the Billiard room with a candlestick, if anyone is interested?" Mallory was great at easing tension with laughter.

But Shelley couldn't seem to find a smile, much less a laugh.

All week she had rifled through the phone messages Elsa handed her, checked her machine at home, hoping for the right one. But it was never there, and now? Now she didn't know what she would say or feel when, or if, Kevin called.

He had studied the Edmonds waterfront, and beyond, thoroughly.

It was essential to seek the weaknesses, know the tides, trains, and ferry schedules. He needed to know where and when the public gathered, and why they were there, what they were doing. He needed to know when the crabber went out early in his skiff to pull his crab pots, and when the port security car made the rounds, and how carefully they *looked* around.

Most of all he needed to know what looked normal, what was ignored as insignificant, and what created curiosity and questions, much less set off anyone's alarm bells in the area. It was well known that potential witnesses, questioned whether they had seen anything, responded with any *unusual* person or event, rarely providing what they had actually seen going on that they considered usual, normal, under their radar, and hence, without suspicion.

From the morning and afternoon scuba divers at the underwater park to the north, or the nearby midden shell beaches appearing only at the lower tides, he watched and gauged it all. He traversed the rocky bulkhead of the railroad tracks from north to south as they passed in and out of town past the ferry station, the train station, the marsh and marina, the people and dog parks, all the way down to the isolated rock walled beach.

Barely large enough for a single skiff, he had discovered the beach outside the chain link fence dividing the dog park from tracks and a forested bluff south of town. That private spot had evidence of usage by an innocuous pile of silvered driftwood that, on closer inspection, turned out to be a low makeshift shelter, and a single votive candle nestled deep in the rocks that he had found on another occasion. That area was an important hidden niche to be aware of.

He watched the security police and their trained dogs working the ferry holding lines, he visited the length of each dock and pier in the marina. As a seemingly dedicated birdwatcher he circled the marsh around, noting how the thick tree-height cattails screened both the water and many sightlines.

He knew the core of town itself, and its many alleys, spending the bulk of his private investigations above the town, as a friendly sweaty jogger running the wooded trails of Yost Park for his health.

He found that there were linkages across the main roads into town were one could jog across from parks in the north to the south on one wooded trail after another, arching over most of the town, yet virtually invisible, jogging or walking the greenbelts that divided what had seemed to be non-stop residential areas. He had heard that black bears had suddenly appeared in back yards to snack on pet food and bird feeders, and now he saw how they could travel unnoticed on the edge of downtown.

He needed to understand the terrain and its population in dawn, day, dusk, and dark. But he needed to slip through the areas almost unnoticed, as a sailor, tourist, jogger, dog walker, or birder; so there was no way he could run around wearing bear bells in the dark. So far the worst things he had startled were fenced barking neighborhood dogs, a few frogs, birds, herons, raccoons, and a deer. He *thought* it was a deer—something large had crashed away unseen through downed limbs one night in the forest.

He wasn't getting much sleep, but he was as fit as he had ever been, as the whole town undulated up from the waterfront. Even the main business core was four to five blocks uphill from the waterfront.

But when his muscles wept, he remembered the reward, the payoff, and pushed harder, always alert, always observing every detail and nuance. Even when it appeared he was just out enjoying a casual day in the sun and outdoors, or on the water.

"Hi. Come on in. I just need to grab my purse, and... Hey, what's wrong, Ronnie?"

"Nothing."

Well that was a lie, Sam thought.

Even that forced smile couldn't conceal the flattened look in Ronnie's normally vibrant cobalt eyes.

Sam heaved a sigh, "Okay, if you say so. Is Shelley going to meet us at the gallery?"

"No. Change of plan. She had some emergency meeting, so we will have to do it some other time," Rhonda stated with a finality that told Sam the question of them going today anyway was definitely closed. Maybe a boyfriend problem then? Though Sam didn't dare ask that, either. Not with Ronnie having once made it very clear to her that *Rhonda* was *not* troubled by men, *men* were troubled by *her*. So in the mood her friend was in...

"We will go downtown to Seattle," Ronnie stated, "and I will buy you lunch at some arty bistro, and we will take in the..."

"Sights?" Sam jumped in.

"Stores," was the firm response. A defiant glint finally lit her best friend's eyes.

"Right," Sam forced a smile of her own, thinking she should put on more comfortable shoes.

At least shopping would put Ronnie back in high spirits, regardless of what was weighing on her mind.

Rhonda had not been completely honest with her friends about the gallery trip cancellation.

"Samantha and Shelley are really looking forward to going to the gallery in Seattle with us to see your works on Saturday."

Rhonda took a sip of her wine then lifted her knife and fork to cut into her tenderloin before looking up to ask, "But they asked me the name of the gallery and I was a little embarrassed to admit I didn't know. Which one is it?" She put a piece of steak in her mouth and closed her eyes for a moment to savor the tenderness and exquisite seasoning. She loved this restaurant; the potter must really be trying to make points with her.

"The one on Fourth Avenue," he answered vaguely. "Hey, do you have to work tomorrow? I'll be busy with deliveries part of the day but I'd planned to take you sailing in the afternoon. We can go over to that cove we found and do a little skinny dipping, play around a little..."

"Sorry. I have a full day tomorrow. I didn't expect you to be here until tomorrow night. Friday is going to be too busy for me to go sailing, much as I would love to. Would you see if you can get the waiter's attention, please? I better lay off the wine and drink coffee instead as I can't afford to be fuzzy headed tomorrow."

"Sure, sweetheart." Ordering her coffee, he turned back, scratched the back of his neck, and concentrated on preparing his baked potato from the condiment dish, saying, "Listen...uh, I may not be able to make it this Saturday. Something urgent has come up that I need to deal with I'm afraid." He never looked up, so he continued oblivious to the frosty glare aimed at him from the iced over cobalt eyes of his dinner companion. "That's why I popped over early, so I could devote plenty of time to you tonight, tomorrow, and Sunday."

"I. Beg. Your. Pardon?" Each word snapped like an icicle.

"Huh?" He glanced up and still didn't seem to realize that death was imminent.

"You made a date to go to the gallery with me and my friends on Saturday."

Glancing around nervously at the other diners, he leaned forward and lowered his voice. Though his words were quieter, there was a distinct tone of irritability that he couldn't disguise.

"No, actually, *I* made a date to spend time alone with you, Rhonda. *You* are the one that invited your friends and decided to mess up our sailing date on Saturday." Trying to lighten the mood, he gave her a small smile and shrugged his shoulders.

"Hey, babe, galleries are work for me." He reached to cover her hand with his and gave her his special smile, "I just wanted to come play with you, babe. I even brought clay." He winked at her.

Rhonda wanted to take some very solid, heavy, glazed clay and break it over his smug damn face.

"Fine," she smiled sweetly back at him, though it seemed her teeth were bared rather threateningly. "We will just go without you. I'm afraid you will just have to 'play' with yourself on Saturday.

Babe." She did not wink at him.

"Ouch!" She did not return his smile either.

"Give me the name of the gallery."

"I told you it's the one on..."

"The name." She was firm.

"I don't remember the damn name, okay? It's on my paperwork at home. I just drive..."

"Excuse me." Rhonda rose and set her napkin on the table. "I need the ladies room."

And she did stop in at the ladies room—right before she walked out the restaurant door leaving the potter to suck air waiting for her return.

She had waited until she was in the privacy of her car to start calling the man every vile name that came to mind. Finally, she calmed down a bit. Yes, the gallery trip was her idea, but he had agreed to it right up until he found a way to weasel out.

"Evasive lying bastard! He did it again. Every time I ask him a question he evades it and tries to distract me with sailing sex." Adding in a mutter, "Or clay sex." It was a pattern she realized she had been noticing subconsciously for some time now. She would ask a personal question and he would distract and divert her, never giving her a direct answer.

"And I ask him about the gallery he has been telling me he sold so much to? A big client and he can't remember the name? That is pure bullshit!"

"And!" She took a finger off the wheel, as if pointing it at him, "And he is the only artist I have ever known that does not seem eager to promote his work, get the support and interest of everyone he knows, and everyone they know, to support his art. There is something very fishy about this guy."

Rhonda had always operated on the 'trust but verify' principle in her business. She didn't usually bother with her men because she never kept them around long enough for it to matter—they just weren't that important.

"But this guy," she told her car, "is pissing me off trying to play me. Well, he is in for a little surprise."

She hadn't really had a very big work day planned for Friday, but Potter's assumption he could just show up and rearrange her schedule after all the times he hadn't been where he was supposed to be had seriously annoyed her.

First thing Friday morning she sat down at her computer and looked up art galleries in Seattle. She printed off the list. Only one appeared to be the one he might be referring to near Fourth Avenue. She had some business she could take care of in Seattle so she gathered the files and took off well before lunch.

After completing her business, she headed over to the gallery. The gallery was actually located just around the corner from Fourth. Strange he hadn't mentioned that.

A sales associate greeted her.

"I came in to see some pottery done by Peter Potter. I believe you show his work?"

"Oh, yes. He is so talented. Come right this way, ma'am."

God, she hated being called ma'am—it sounded so . . . *old*. Though, to the twenty something girl, she must seem ancient. Her annoyance changed targets when the girl brought her to the pottery.

The single, solitary, *one* piece of pottery.

"Here we are. Peter is a truly innovative artist. The additional design elements that he builds into his art make it unique and gives it a lasting stability and strength suitable for use in either residential or commercial design. As you can see, this is no teetering pot. It is built to last and become an heirloom and a lasting artistic investment." The sales associate gushed on and on as Rhonda cocked her head from side to side and stared at the *single* pot.

She turned her head to glance around at the rest of the display area. Yep, just one pot on display. She very distinctly remembered him talking about his big shipments to the Seattle gallery. She distinctly recalled all the trips he had made over to the mainland to deliver pots he had finished for the Seattle gallery.

"Excuse me, do you have more of his works in back that aren't on display?"

"Oh no, this is the only piece we are fortunate enough to have, but the artist will make it up for our clients in customized colors to match their design needs on a special order. What colors would work better for you?"

"Black and blue," she muttered under her breath.

"Pardon, ma'am?"

"Nothing. Are there other galleries in town that display more of his pieces?"

"Oh, no," she said with pride. "We are the exclusive dealer for his works in the Seattle-Tacoma area. He may have another gallery in Bellevue on the eastside that I am not aware of, but only here, in Edmonds, and on the San Juan Islands can you see his works."

"Interesting." The man was lying to someone. Either the gallery owner or herself.

"Yes, isn't it? You can see here that the piece is designed to rest on its side for a more dramatic contemporary piece, or upright as a standard vase design. He accomplishes that by using a very labor intensive double wall construction on the lower portion of the pot to add weight and ballast. Not only does it give it flexible design but is part of what makes it more stable for commercial installation. It won't be easily tipped or knocked off a display base. I like the look of it in this tilted position best . . ."

"So," Ronnie managed to insert, "I can see this must be a bestselling work with all those special elements. How many of his works have you sold already?"

"Me?"

"This gallery."

"Oh, well we have had a lot of interest, there were some people here from one of our prestigious hotels looking at several of these to use in their lobby ..."

"They bought several. How many?"

"Oh, well, not yet, but..."

"How. Many. Pieces. Has. This. Gallery. Sold. Total."

"Well, none. Yet. But..."

"Thank you. Why don't you give me your card so I can call if I am interested?"

When she got back to her office she handed the list of all the galleries in Seattle to her assistant.

"Please call each of these galleries except for the one I circled. I want the following questions asked:

Do they now /or have they ever had any pottery art by Peter Potter. If so, how many pieces do they have now, and how many have they sold? Please type up the answers on a separate sheet unless all the answers are no and zero. Thanks. Please don't put through any calls from Mr. Potter until I advise you differently. Just say, 'She is very busy, babe'. Be sure you don't forget the 'babe'.

"Yes, ma'am."

"And don't call me ma'am anymore. Call me babe."

"Yes, babe."

"Try not to giggle when you say that. It is most undignified."

But by the time Rhonda barricaded herself in her office, her sense of humor had vanished.

She pulled out a legal pad and began making notes on deceptions/suspicions about Mr. Peter Potter the potter.

? Too Convenient Name? The first Item on her list.

???=sex vs. direct answer?

How many times had she asked him a question and received some rousing raw sex instead of an answer? Granted, she had hardly complained at the time, and she certainly hadn't kept count. But she knew she had been curious enough to ask some things— simple things, ordinary things—several times, on several occasions.

Some were of the nature of how long he had lived on the islands and such, vaguely personal. Most were questions about his art, his work, and she heard a lot about shipments and deliveries—at least some false, as she had discovered—but little about inspiration or specific designs he was working on. What man, what artist, was not eager to brag about their work and fame, or at least try to promote their works to every possible patron? Rhonda had plenty of money and influence, and Potter was aware of it, but not only did he not use it for his career, he seemed, now she looked back, to block her interest and efforts to support his work. It just didn't add up!

She recalled asking him if he used his boat to make deliveries to the Seattle gallery—the now mysterious gallery—curious if he was able to write off a portion of his sailboat expenses as business expense.

Had he answered? No.

She'd assumed he was too busy thinking about checking that out with his accountant, to answer. Rhonda had suggested they combine business and pleasure and offered to sail with him on his next delivery to Seattle. He had winked at her and admitted that the gallery owner was a little sweet on him and he didn't want to crush her future hopes by bringing a beauty like Rhonda with him. Then . . . well, more raw sex as he told her why no woman could ever compete with her. She had enjoyed the play, ignored the flattery. And...Forgotten the rest.

Picking up her phone, she buzzed her assistant.

"Call that gallery I circled also, but just ask for the name of the gallery owner."

"Okay, babe."

Nice to have obedient employees—maybe.

Now she thought about more of Potter's deceptions. She had to ask herself, just how long did it take to set up one damn vase? All day? Maybe he had finally gotten bright enough to use sex to promote his art, but she seriously doubted it. It didn't fit his pattern with her, but it did fit his pattern of deception and misinformation.

Responding to the buzz of her intercom, "Yes. A corporation? Thanks. Google the corporation later when you have a chance."

Well, that was interesting. And just one more mystery. A corporation he called 'SHE'? Not!

So what was he really doing when he lied about his reasons for breaking all their dates?

She wasn't really concerned about another woman—or if there was another woman the guy must have the sex drive of a battery operated bunny. She certainly didn't lack that kind of attention from her lusty lover.

It really wasn't funny, the man was a skilled liar, but she couldn't stop laughing.

After all, all Rhonda had to do to get laid was to ask him a question.

Almost any question!

Sobering, she realized the man was a very smooth operator and there was something very strange about the way the man managed his artistic career, almost as if it was a hobby.

Or a cover for something else?

Rhonda decided she would start being more observant and objective.

Maybe she needed to see what he was up to when she wasn't with him?

Meanwhile... She would have to ask him another personal question. Like, *Do you have a pet?*

That should get some action.

"What is so hilarious?" Her assistant set the gallery list on her desk. "Sorry, all no and zero. Babe."

Rhonda just shook her head, then snorted as she thought up more innocuous questions.

chapter fifteen

Timmy sent a text message to Shelley the following Saturday morning, just a *Hey, how R U?*

He had to wait an hour before she texted back that she was working, and couldn't get away. But he was cool with that. Just glad for the contact. He tried not to remember how he had felt a week ago.

In his mind he thought of it as Black Friday. He didn't want to *ever* feel that way again!

"There's a serial rapist guy out there!" He told the man. "I heard it on the news." Timmy's lips were tight, his jaw firm, but his voice had quivered just a bit, so he tried to clear his throat.

"Really. Gosh, I hadn't heard that. Must have been on a different channel or the internet," his driver responded, concerned. He had wondered why the kid was so set on a ride.

"Yeah, well," Timmy turned to stare out his car window. His fingers were drumming a tattoo on one leg, his other knee was bouncing. "It was down south a ways." Oregon, or southern Oregon, almost California, Timmy recalled.

"But you know those guys travel a lot. Maybe even making a break for the border. Canada." Tim added, nodding wisely. "Like, you know, and they see a pretty lady like Shelley, well..," Timmy had to pause to swallow, tried to sit up straighter, stop his knee from bouncing. "Well, we men just need to check and make sure everything's cool with her, you know?"

Even the serious subject couldn't stop the driver, a full grown male, from a small smile at the eleven year old kid that was a full grown protector beside him.

"Yep, we gotta look out for our friends," he agreed.

"Yeah, like Shel's my main man you know." Timmy used his forearm to swipe sweat off his forehead, fiddled with his seat belt. He didn't remember there being so many stoplights between the shelter and Shelley's apartment. Or maybe they were just all red tonight. He had ridden with Ms. Rhonda once, she knew how to get places fast! He wished she was driving, but she hadn't answered her phone either.

When he finally pointed his driver into the apartment complex, he was craning his head to spot Shelley's parking space.

Empty.

He blew air into his cheeks and tried to let it out slow. He was glad her car wasn't there. If it had been and she still hadn't been answering her phone that would be bad news. But she should be answering the cell if she was out somewhere. She had hands-free.

"Her car here?"

"Nah. Maybe we should drive around the lot, just check for sure."

"No problem, kid."

They searched the whole lot. No car. It was getting dark.

Timmy wasn't feeling so good now, realizing that just because her car wasn't here didn't mean Shel wasn't hurt and here in her condo, unable to answer the phones. What if that serial dude attacked her and stole her car? Her cell phone? He stole her purse!

"We could have the building guy let us in her place," trying to keep the panic out of his voice. "Might as well since we are here already. Right?" The manager had seen Timmy hanging with Shelley a lot, he would probably be cool with that.

"Sorry, kid. Can't do it." The building manager told him. "I can't let you in her place."

"But, see, she isn't answering her phone. I've been trying for hours. And if she was just out she would answer her cell, or text me, and I've called it a zillion times. Nothing. Voice mail. She doesn't call back. And I tried to get our friend Kevin and he doesn't answer his phones either, so he can't help her. She doesn't do this. You have to help me. I called other friends and can't get any answers, and..."

"Okay, okay. Easy kid."

The manager softened when he saw the tough little guy was either going to start crying, or vomit. And he was the kind of kid that would vomit if he broke down and cried in front of anyone. He gave the kid his office phone to try the tenant's two phones again while he waited. But there was just no response

"Here's what I can do, kid. You can't go in, that's trespassing. But if you two will wait here in the office, I will go do a welfare check."

"Place is clean, undisturbed, no one home, kid," he reported back what seemed like hours later. "If I see her, I'll have her call you."

"Don't bother, she has my text messages. But thanks, man." The breath of relief Timmy blew out sent a pile of papers skidding off the manager's counter.

But when he got back to the shelter, he still didn't know where Shelley was. Just one place she wasn't—home. He tried Kevin's cell again. Nada. Ditto on Shelley's that night.

When he called Shel's cell the next day, she answered sounding normal—and safe.

Timmy was too embarrassed to admit he had been a little worried about her.

He hoped her building manager didn't rat him out.

Tim wished she would mention where she'd been, but she didn't say anything about that, or why she hadn't returned his calls that night.

Though Shel had returned all his messages this last week. That was sure a relief. They still hadn't caught that serial guy on the news.

Shelley had promised to take him to the beach soon. Timmy hoped he'd get to see her maybe paste Kevin again. Cool.

But she didn't say anything about him going with them. In fact she didn't say *anything* about Kev.

Weird.

"Well! Some sleuth I am!"

Rhonda was still chastising herself.

She tended to share her thoughts out loud with her car when she drove—who else was there to tell? And she liked the way her empty car kept her secrets. She especially liked the fact it never *ever* argued or talked back. She'd had the tongue removed from that talking slut on her GPS.

She had gone down to the marina earlier that day, and gotten a call on her cell from Potter.

"Did we have a date today?"

"No."

"Oh, I thought you were down here at the docks for me."

Damn. He must have spotted her right off.

"You are too full of yourself, Potter," her voice indignant. "I live here, remember? I've been coming down to the marina and beach to walk long before I knew you. Goodbye."

She had failed horribly at her first attempt to sneak around.

"If I'm going to spy on Potter, I need a disguise, like the time Sam and I pulled off our little caper." Slowing her car to turn and change direction, Rhonda thought about how well their clever disguises had worked that time—too well!

At least this time she didn't have to worry about being mistaken for a bank robber. Though . . . she chewed her lip as she turned into the warehouse parking lot, "Maybe I should let Sam's husband, Mr. Handsome Prosecutor, know that I am going undercover this time?"

Then she started laughing, picturing his face.

She could easily imagine what he would have to say.

"Ms. Sayles," he would state officiously, trying to hide a smirk, "going undercover is *not* a disguise for you, I regret to remind you. Where else *would* one expect to find you *except* under someone's covers?"

She had liked the guy from the start.

Even when he had rejected her seduction that time that she tried to protect Sam from him. Thank God, that hadn't worked!

No, she'd keep her concerns about Potter to herself for now, in case he was being sneaky just to hide another affair from her.

As she locked her car, she started preparing a list of what kind of disguise she needed. She had never been inside this store before, usually she just dropped her prior year's wardrobe off at the loading dock—or had her secretary do it. But Goodwill was probably just the place to find something no one would ever expect to see her in—she needed old, baggy, clothes, and, she shuddered, some clunky cast off ratty shoes. A padded vest to wear under her clothes for added bulk might be good, and she had to be sure to find one of those derelict hats that looked like a bucket for her head. She should get a wig too, but for something that close to her skin, she wanted something fresh and new. She thought a swingy pageboy in a silver streaked gray would do the trick.

Rhonda couldn't help grinning as she entered the warehouse store. She was looking forward to the potter's next time in port. She loved to sleuth. But this time she'd leave her trench coat at home—and stay far away from any banks!

The girl on the dock stood partially hidden behind a cluster of huge tarred and roped logs sunk vertically off San Juan Island. They secured the individual floating docks and anchorages of the marina that were subject to the rise and fall of the tides, below the high fixed dock anchored ashore at Friday Harbor.

She had the budding breasts of a young teen, but the round waist, straight hips over long tanned coltish legs and knobby knees of childhood still. Her thoughts and emotions were just as frustrating and confusing a mix of childish dreams and maturing awareness. She had suffered the angst of endlessly waiting for her body to grow into a woman's, and the exhilaration of her first massive crush—though in her young and starry brown eyes she called it true love. Unrequited, but she still believed in fairy tales.

Or had.

Perched above her atop the tarred posts was an old and plump gray and white yellow-beaked gull. They both had their eyes focused on the last sailboat at the end of the dock—or rather the handsome bare-chested man loading it.

The gull angled its head to watch his hands, alert for any sign of food or bait.

The girl with the windblown wispy hair was memorizing every other inch of him, to take home and dream about as she waited to grown into the woman the man would notice and fall desperately in love with.

Or she *had* dreamed that.

Many times the girl and gull had watched and waited, still and quiet while the waves splashed against the docks, the winds rocked the boats, and the tied lines and riggings clanged lazily and discordantly against a dozen masts. No matter how many times they did, neither ever saw what they hoped for. Yet.

But while the gull was ever patient and optimistic, the girl's eyes had taken on a different kind of watchfulness. She was beginning to wonder if the handsome prince in her fairy tale wasn't something else in disguise.

Someone else. Someone not handsome or princely at all.

She had hoped she was wrong, she had felt the pangs of doubt, but her maturing mind was overruling her childish hopes—and she was feeling the grief of that loss.

And ... finally, she had taken tentative action. But it was not enough.

She watched, wishing life and knowledge were as easy as her school tests, where answers were clear. Right or wrong, true or false. But becoming an adult had a downside she could not deny.

Responsibility was a two-edged sword. She looked forward with excitement to the day she was old enough, responsible enough, for her parents to let her have the keys for the first time to drive their car.

But there were always rules to follow to keep everyone safe, and they had to be followed. When they weren't, someone had to take responsibility for acting, to protect others. Everyone had a share and a stake.

So she watched. She needed proof, or a strong lead, then she had to act again, and pass on what she knew to someone old and wise, and responsible enough to known how to handle it. Because as hard as this was, she had to do something, though she was still just a kid.

Just not as silly or as stupid a one—anymore.

The man seemed to shift his sharp green-eyed glance toward shore momentarily, as if her thoughts had stabbed him in the back. Then the gull jeered at him and he turned back to work, his handsome mouth tightened, a scowl wrinkling his weather tanned face as he hoisted another box carefully from the dock and stowed it deep in the small cabin of the sleek sailboat.

"... and that volunteer tutoring program with the software company that you got us linked into has been a big hit. Almost a third of the boys in the shelter have signed on already and I expect more will soon. They like the young instructors and seem to look up to them."

"Good," Kevin nodded, then tipped back on his chair legs, feeling a little strange sitting on this side of his desk. He had refused his swivel desk chair, telling his assistant shelter director to stay put. He had only come in for an update; he had to leave again soon. "Did the Y include the guys on that big picnic, like they promised?"

"Oh, yeah. Even bussed them to it. They had a great day! Spirits are pretty high around here for now, which has kept problems low and easy for me."

"You're doing a great job, Brad. I knew you would. Sorry, to leave you in the lurch like this, but..."

"Hey, boss, no problem and no explanations needed. You need to be gone, I know it must be important. I'm glad to help out, and have to admit, this is great experience for me."

"You are handling it well, Brad. Thanks."

"Well, it has been easier with money in the bank, I can see that. We've been able to add computers and E-readers with all the anonymous donations coming in this summer. And more kids happy, job's easier." Brad smiled and shrugged.

"Yeah, but don't discount your abilities, buddy. *You* are keeping the guys happy, taking over for me lately. Anything else I should know before I desert you again?"

"Well . . ."

Kevin rocked forward and planted the chair legs back on the floor, leaning over the desk. "What? Tell me. I can see you're troubled."

"Well, it's about Timmy."

When Kevin jumped from his chair, Brad waved him back down. "No, hey, sorry. He hasn't gotten in any trouble. Nothing like that to worry about. He's just ... down. Not his normal happy, cocky little self, is all. Maybe I'm borrowing trouble."

Kevin shook his head, got up and wandered over to the window and stared out, arms crossed over his chest.

"I guess I've spoiled him a bit," he admitted with a quiet sigh, "but he is our youngest, and such a great little guy. Now, I guess, he is missing the attention with me gone so much lately."

"He is that, but this seems to be something more than that. Weekend before last he got a little . . . frantic, I guess is the word.

He's okay now, but still a little down like I said. Just thought I should mention it."

"Weekend before last?" Kevin murmured, his back still to the room. It wasn't the view outside he saw now, remembering. He knew why that weekend was burned into his mind—and body. But he couldn't figure why it would have anything to do with Timmy. He tuned back into what Brad was saying.

"He had been trying to call that A.D.A. he's so fond of, probably trying to wheedle his 'main man, Shel' again into taking him somewhere for the weekend, though she wasn't scheduled," he said with a little grin for the precocious kid. "But he couldn't reach her. She didn't call back."

Kevin's head dropped to his chest. He had talked her into shutting their phones off so they could have a little time free of work calls, private time without the constant outside interference.

"And he tried calling you, see if you knew where she was, but couldn't reach you. He kept trying and trying and couldn't reach her, didn't get any response to his messages. Guess he tried a few other folks, couldn't get through there either. Long, short, the kid got frantic, for some reason he had convinced himself that something bad had happened to Shelley, because she always at least texted him back, even if she was too busy to talk.

"So we finally let one of the volunteers drive him over to her place late that night, to reassure him. Told the kid adults have their own private lives, but he was asking if he could have a missing persons report issued on her, crazy kid! She wasn't home, car wasn't there, manager even checked her apartment to say all okay there, but the kid was a total mess until he finally got ahold of her the next day. So, it's all okay now. She even took him out to the beach last week. But he still seems down for some reason."

Had she told Tim about them? He wondered if she had told the kid they had been together. He had only called Shelley twice since then, but she hadn't returned either call.

Was he in trouble with his two favorite people? If he was, he deserved it.

"Just thought you should know. Kid's young, maybe getting too attached to her. Don't know if we should do something about that, maybe get the kid a different mentor before it gets worse?"

Guilt flooded Kevin's system. Hard to know sometimes what was right—or *most* right.

"No, Brad. Leave it with me. I'll work on it when I get back. For now, where is Timmy? I'll stop and say 'hey' to him before I leave again."

chapter sixteen

Rhonda thought the cane was a nice touch. It was an aluminum cane with a rubber grip and had a four legged tip for the elderly instable. It had seemed like an excellent idea until she realized she couldn't get up and sprint away dragging it behind without blowing her cover.

She had been watching.

Rhonda saw him come from his boat carrying a box up the gangway, then slipping out of her sight between two other boats on that slip. She was surprised to see him climb onto the deck of some stranger's boat and remove the dingy tied on top, lower it into the water, and place his box and himself in it.

Was he stealing a boat?

Should she call someone?

She decided to wait and watch him first. He clearly couldn't get too far rowing that tiny thing; she doubted he planned on trying to leave the harbor in it.

And what was in the box, a pot? Maybe he was just delivering some of his artwork to another yacht in the basin—something purchased during the art show? She tried to parallel him on the boardwalk as fast as her four legged third leg would hobble without drawing attention, keeping track of his progress along the ends of the boat docks.

Then she lost him.

Someone was putting their pleasure boat in the water, and pedestrians were not allowed to cross while the boat hoist lifted the strapped boat overhead from its trailer, to swing it down into the boat basin.

Pacing slowly down the boardwalk once traffic cleared, she

failed to find Potter in the hundreds of boats. Giving up she went back to her bench near his sailboat and waited for him to return, until it started getting dark, and she had to leave. She did have to go home and get all dressed up. She had a late night date with Potter for drinks at the marina bar. She could hardly wait to ask him how his day had been.

Later that evening, just as she expected, the dog flat out lied to her again!

So she did a little lying of her own.

She hadn't really suddenly developed a debilitating migraine. And she wasn't really sorry they would have to cancel the fun he had planned on his boat until next time. But she didn't mention that 'next time' might be delayed—so she hadn't lied about that.

Yet.

Jordan was on the phone when Shelley responded to his summons. Spotting something new in the corner by the window, she went over to check it out. It was an amazing sculpture. A driftwood like pier post formed the pedestal for an amazing likeness of a seagull hunched on top, wings tucked in. Carved of wood, the detail was incredible. Shelley reached out to stroke her fingers across the detailed carving that defined each feather, almost expecting to feel warmth.

"This is exquisite," she told him after he hung up the phone. "It looks alive."

"Think so?" Jordan rose, grinned, and reached for a remote. "Watch this."

Shel squeaked and jumped back a foot when the more than lifelike gull turned and cocked its head and pinned her with a beady eye. "What the..."

"And this...," showing off, Jordan turned the remote to his wall mounted TV and Shelley was looking at a stunned blond staring back at her.

"Why, that's me! And that is here, this office. Amazing! You don't have to feed it fish do you? "

Laughing, Jordan turned off the remote and stepped over to join her by the bird. "It does look real, doesn't it?" He reached out to stroke an intricately detailed wing.

"There was an artist that had a booth at the Art's Festival and he hand carved these incredible bird decoys, then hand painted them so beautifully that, before he knew it, he was selling his Mallard Duck decoys faster than he could make them. It had been a hobby, crafting them in his spare time and selling them to duck hunters, then suddenly decorators were coming in and buying them for dens and offices, and he had to quit his day job and started carving full time. He branched out from ducks to geese, then pheasants, eagles, then gulls when he started showing at the arts fair here. Now he does custom requests.

"I fell in love with his work and bought a Mallard for my home office on the spot, and heard him talking to another client who wanted to modify them for security cameras. So I thought about it and was back the next day and custom ordered this guy. He just arrived, but Elsa has already named him Gordo. And don't ask me why because I haven't a clue. Which reminds me..., have a seat."

Settling himself back behind his desk, Jordan leaned back in his chair. "We have received another clue. Just as brief as the last tip, and in the same handwriting. It seems our green-eyed man owns a boat."

Sitting down more abruptly than planned, Shelley had realized that her green-eyed man did also. The same man she had barely heard from in weeks. The one that seemed to have vanished from sight. The one whose phone call she hadn't returned because she didn't know what to say now to a green-eyed man who seemed to vanish mysteriously.

And now he was a green-eyed man with a boat.

Shelley hadn't been able to get their lovemaking out of her mind —or heart. But she also hadn't been able to forget those quiet words they had shared in the dark when they had spoken of dreams and hopes. When he talked about the shelter and what it meant to him and what it meant for his boys.

And how he'd vowed to do *whatever* it took to keep it funded.

Every time she remembered that vow her mind had flinched, as it did now. Shying away from the possibility that her green-eyed man could ...

"Do we know what kind of boat he has?"

"No, Shelley. Not yet, unfortunately. These vague tips are torturing me." He was not alone in that!

Jordan had just walked her out of his office to collect any

messages from Elsa when his secretary looked up at Shelley with a mischievous little smile.

"So what's with you and that Kevin MacClarty, Shel? Lots of rumors about you two," Elsa teased, warm eyes, sparkling with affection.

The blush that spread up Shelley's face was that of a young girl. Feeling the heat, she covered her cheeks with her hands, flashing a startled glance at Jordan, but he had already turned back to his office.

The suspicious direction her thoughts had been drifting made her instantly wonder if Kevin's apartment was being watched. Did someone report that they had spent the night together? Was that why Jordan had made a point of telling her not to share tip information with Kevin? Was he under serious suspicion? Were the tips really so vague, or did Jordan feel he had to keep info from her if she was involved with a . . .?

"Come now, girl, don't look so startled." Elsa coaxed. "Did you really expect to get flowers from a man delivered here and not have rumors start swirling around the office about you two?"

"Oh," Shelley just stared for a moment, took a deep breath, then stuttered. "I, ah. We really are just, ah. Well, you know that boy I mentor? He mentors with me. Friends, that is what we are. Because we spend time together. With Timmy! Time together with Timmy."

Elsa laughed until she nearly had to wipe tears from her eyes.

"Oh, girl, you have it bad. I can see it in your face. But, if you aren't ready to confide in me I'll quit teasing you. Here are your messages, hon." And as Shelley grabbed her messages and escaped down the hall to her office, Elsa called after her. "Oh, there is one from lover boy." Then she giggled, when Shelley pretended like she didn't hear her.

Elsa loved to meddle in the lives of the office personnel, just like they were all her own kids. She mothered and meddled, all because she cared about them. These lawyer types tended to work too many hours and take everything too seriously. She wanted them to have some fun and love in their lives. They needed the balance.

Just look how love and marriage had turned her boss around? And just in time. Jordan had become extremely obnoxious, but she had loved him like a mother anyway.

Though he could still annoy her at times.

Jordan liked to stay informed on the lives of his staff, also—for

Sam's sake of course, he claimed. He just wished Elsa wouldn't refer to it as the 'latest office gossip 'all the time.

But *he* was just as interested in being 'informed' as Elsa was. She'd seen him turn back to his office so Shelley wouldn't catch him grinning. And she had noticed, even if poor embarrassed Shelley hadn't, that the man had *not* closed his office door all the way. She knew he was back there listening. With a chuckle, she corrected that to *informing* himself. Just getting *the low down*, of course.

The call had come while Rhonda was in the shower.

She had been expecting it—and expecting not to answer it no matter where she was.

He had told her he would call today to arrange for them to get together. She knew he wanted to pick up on the fun he had missed the prior evening. She had told him not to call too late or she might have other plans. She had pointedly not informed him what time 'too late' would be.

And he had laughed, anyway, as if she was teasing.

Being Rhonda, she was of course *not* teasing about that, and anytime he called today would have been 'too' late, but he managed to *really* goad her temper this time.

Not only did he push the timing of his call to what he probably considered the last possible minute, but when she did not answer he had the gall to leave a voicemail *informing* her of what restaurant to meet him at, and what time *she* was to be there!

Ohhh! That made her *very* angry. Angry enough to torture a man that richly deserved it. She called back on a line she knew he wouldn't answer, but would eventually check for messages.

"Oh Potter, I'm so sorry I missed your call, darling. I was naked when you called. Naked... and ... damp. Damp and ... dripping, actually. Expecting you... here...not a phone call. Oh well, c'est la vie. Again, so sorry to have missed you when I was so prepared for you to come."

She paused to let her full meaning sink in, then continued in a less throaty, breezier, tone with a carefree little laugh thrown in, "So... why don't you give me a buzz in a week or so and maybe we can go have lunch at that charming outdoor cafe that's opened down by the yacht club. Gotta run, bye."

The cheery tone completely disguised the hard splinters in her cobalt eyes.

Keying in her code, she transferred all her phone calls to voicemail, then she grabbed her purse and headed out. Heading for the bar of the restaurant that he had mentioned. She would be gone before he arrived; but she expected him to hear about it.

She would make certain of that, she thought, her smile more than a little evil.

"So many men, Ronnie girl, and so little time!" She chanted her mantra to herself, but somehow it sounded a little tired to her ear this time.

When she reached the archway leading into the lounge, an intimate candle-lit and darkly mirrored niche of the seaside restaurant, Rhonda paused a moment checking out the patrons. She spotted her target, one of several she knew would be available. With a slight smile and a slowly seductive sway of her hips, she sauntered into the room past him.

"Ronnie, darling!"

Glancing back over her shoulder, with a questioning raised brow, she stopped and turned a smile on the gentleman beckoning to her.

"Arthur! I didn't see you there! How *have* you been?"

Sharing a drink and a few laughs with him, she asked a tiny favor. He was more than happy to help. After Rhonda left for her dinner plans with her friends, he kept his eye out. He saw the man she was currently tormenting come into the bar, asking the bartender if she had arrived yet.

"Excuse me, are you looking for Ronnie?" Arthur saw the man stiffen at his purposely familiar use of her name. "She's been in tonight, having a few drinks, and we had a bit of fun, if you know what I mean." Arthur winked, before adding, "But she's gone now. I think she left around the same time as the man paying her so much attention."

Coming out on her deck an hour later with a platter of burger patties in her hand, Samantha caught her husband in a tight embrace with her best friend.

Seeing his wife, Jordan pushed Rhonda back a bit and teased,

"Ronnie, I know you are Sam's best friend, but that doesn't mean she'd approve of you playing with her favorite toy." He grinned shamelessly at his wife.

"I'm jealous," his wife said.

"You are not," both Rhonda and Jordan stated flatly and almost in unison.

Rhonda had been confiding her serious concerns to Jordan while Sam was working in the kitchen.

Knowing Ronnie was not the hysterical type and very savvy about men, he took her seriously and promised to have the potter's background looked into. Aware that issues might arise that might possibly be linked to one of his office investigations, they had both decided it was best not to mention her suspicions to Sam, yet. Jordan suggested that it would be best for now, if Ronnie was willing, for her to continue on as if interested in the potter. Keeping a view inside, while he checked out the guy. She agreed, eager to help.

"Thanks Jordan," she'd stepped up and gave him a big hug. "I knew I could count on you, like Sam does. You are my best-friend-in-law. Thanks again."

Touched, he squeezed her back. "You can always count on both of us." He said as his wife arrived.

Stepping away from Jordan, going to take the plate of raw burgers from Sam, Rhonda said, "No, I am the one that is jealous."

"Jealous?" Sam laughed. "You want my husband? Sorry, you can't have him," she grinned at her friend.

"Oh, I know that!" Rhonda laughed. "Believe me, I already tried my best, while you were locked in jail," she added quickly. "He wasn't buying. He turned me down flat, wouldn't even humor me. Just told me upfront that I wasn't and would never be his type!"

"I'm sure he didn't mean to be rude," Sam offered, more concerned with her friend's feelings, than defending her husband. Rude-to-Women had been Jordan's middle name, after all, back then.

"Oh no, he wasn't being rude. That time," Ronnie qualified. "He was just being honest. That was the time he took me to lunch to find out everything I knew about you. Now that I know why, it was kind of cute, actually. Reminded me of when kids ask their pal about someone they have a crush on. I'm surprised he didn't ask, 'Do you think she'd like me?'."

Jordan, obviously having eavesdropped while he had his back to them at the B-B-Q grill, snorted a laugh before inserting with a sheepish grin, "I wanted to," heading into the house for the buns, "but I was trying to play it cool."

Both Rhonda and Sam smiled fondly as he disappeared into the house.

"Well," Rhonda sighed, "You sure don't ever have to worry about what that one is up to when you aren't around. That is a one-woman man, if I've ever seen one!"

Sam couldn't believe her luck either. She hadn't even wanted a man, and then she had ended up with the best.

"That's what I'm jealous of," Rhonda interrupted her thoughts. "That dreamy, happy look, that sound devotion that you both have for each other. I've never seen you so relaxed and happy, Sam. I thought I had when you were with your kids, but now when you are with your kids and Jordan, you just glow like a damn fluorescent light bulb. Maybe even like Halogen!"

Ronnie always teased when she was embarrassed at showing her feelings too freely, her affection too seriously.

"I know. I am. Thank you," Sam said softly. "And add you, my friend, and life is perfect."

"Ditto. And I've always been content, lucky really, sharing your kids, but...I guess I'm just a little jealous of what you and Jordan have. I honestly didn't think that there were any men like that left around. Loose, anyway. So I didn't miss not having one of my own. In fact, the concept that a man might be worth having around, under your feet, for something besides sex is still new to me. I've been giving it some serious thought."

From anyone but Rhonda, that would have been joking, but Sam could tell she was serious, and from Ronnie, that last comment was earth-shaking.

"Your potter friend?" Sam gasped. "You mean you're serious about him for, well, you know, other reasons?"

Rhonda threw back her head and laughed until she started to choke and had to constrain herself. "Oh, Sam, the look on your face! You have to be the only mature woman that is getting regular sex that can blush at just the thought of the word!"

Returning from the house, Jordan glanced at his wife's pink face, and decided to turn it his favorite color of rose red. "You should see her when she's having it." He confided. Yup! Sam's face matched the roses behind her. So cute, but she'd get him later, for sure.

"Hey!" Sam stuttered, embarrassed, but a good sport, "You two quit picking on my sense of propriety." Pointing her threatening finger at Jordan.

"As you wish, Miss Prim," Rhonda nodded, using a familiar nickname.

"So don't try to sidetrack me. I know your tricks. We were talking about getting serious with a man. Are you getting serious about Peter then, Ronnie?" Sam was clearly excited about the idea.

"Oh, I think you could truthfully say I am having some very serious thoughts about the potter." The irony in Rhonda's voice went right over Sam's head, but Jordan heard and caught it. "But regardless, what I meant before was not that I am serious about him, only that I am seriously thinking of evaluating my potter for potential... ah, future action. But, not there yet."

"Oh." That sounded like a more sensible, less drastic interim step for her friend's personality. No need to go into shock, yet.

Seeing Sam relax and regain her lovely ivory complexion, the imp in Rhonda was unable to resist adding wickedly, "Though I do hate to get serious and distract any man when he is focusing ... hard."

Sam just dropped her head and shook it wearily while Rhonda and Jordan laughed out loud. They knew her weak spot and they loved to tease her. Secretly, Sam loved the way that they did.

"BURGERS ARE READY." Jordan called out, rescuing her. "And Rhonda," he mock scolded, "No 'buns' jokes from you today!"

Sam strolled over and wrapped her arm around her husband's waist, then with a wink, a blush, and a grin at Rhonda, slipped her hand down and gave his buns a playful squeeze.

Detective Mallory was a man with an optimistic outlook on life——a rarity in his line of work. He maintained his through the satisfaction of a diligent and dedicated work ethic balanced with a happy and supportive wife and family, a job in a small town atmosphere, and—above all—an easy sense of humor. He was able to laugh with others at life's sense of the ridiculous, and especially enjoyed a good laugh at his own expense—though he was not one to pull practical jokes. But others did, and if it eased the tension of their jobs, even if it made him look a little silly at times, well, he was good with that.

But not today, for god's sake.

There was serious work to do today, and it was time to put playful jokes aside and concentrate. So he couldn't restrain an edge of irritation in his voice when he was interrupted to take an urgent phone call and found himself talking to a child that identified herself as 'The 21st Century Nancy Drew'.

Teeth gritted, he held the phone to his ear as his eyes scanned the squad room seeking guilty grins or quickly lowered heads, but everyone seemed to be hard at work leaving him with only one target for his anger. And with no hint of a disguised or distorted voice, that target was a child. Trying to control his tone, and keep his voice calm and even, he thanked 'Nancy' for calling.

"Nancy, being a detective yourself, I'm sure you know how busy it can get when you are in the middle of a case. Why don't you give me your phone number so I can get back in touch to work with you just as soon as I am able, honey."

He probably shouldn't have used that term—it was most likely against some sexual harassment rule—but right now he was feeling more than a little harassed himself. The child's voice sounded the same age as his daughter's and he called her 'honey' all the time. Unless she had been unwise enough to put one of her friends up to this …

"But I have an important clue," the young girl was protesting.

"I'm sure you do. After all, that is what we detectives do— gather clues. But, Nancy, right now I'm afraid I have a Priority Clue I'm working on…"

"But I don't have time to mail this one."

"I'm sorry, maybe you could … What did you just say?"

"I said I don't have time to mail this clue like I did the others," 'Nancy' replied patiently.

Detective Mallory had to stop himself from jumping out of his chair and yanking the phone off the desk. He calmed himself. "Ms. Drew, are you possibly calling about a man with a certain eye color?"

"Yes, the green-eyed man. With the boat. That's me! Good, you got my notes," she sounded both excited and relieved. "I have figured out his pattern, you know his mode of operation, and he is doing it now! "

"Hold on just a moment. Miss Wonderful 21st Century Nancy Drew, do you mind if I record this?" He felt a grin split his face from ear to ear when she agreed. He turned the recorder on before adding, "Would you be offended if I called you 'honey' instead of Detective Drew? It's shorter, and what I call my dear daughter."

If 'Nancy' had a solid clue for him, he might love her almost as much.

chapter seventeen

A silent and expressionless Detective Mallory passed a sheet of paper to each member on the task force before taking his seat at the conference table. When he had contacted the prosecutor to request he immediately convene a meeting, the detective had not revealed a hint of what he had to discuss beyond the need for urgency. And he did not speak now, sitting, he waited for them to read their brief report, wanting each to react individually.

Report from Detective Mallory:

RE: suspected smuggler tips - green eyed man with boat

From confidential source: 21st Century Nancy Drew a/k/a Honey (for short-ok'd)

Source is a young female, approx.: pre-teen to teen age that previously contacted us in two separate hand written tips.

RE: Pattern of person-of-interest's criminal behavior as analyzed by source/ in her wording:

Day 1 - He goes into town to the bank, and other places - but bank always starts the pattern.

Day 2 - Next day he goes out all day fishing, actually when asked he said he is crabbing but he only has two cheap collapsible crab pots on his boat, not stacks of them like the serious crabbers. On these outings he does always dress like a fisherman though, chest waiters, flannel, stocking cap, and does usually bring back at least one good sized crab, after being out all day.

Day 3-4/5 - Next two days, sometimes three, but usually two from dawn to dusk he spends working in his private studio No one is allowed there, it is secluded at the back of his fenced property.

Day 5/6 - Then he packs sealed boxes into his boat, usually late at night or early before dawn, or sometimes in the late afternoon if it is very foggy - but always when the docks are empty- and the other boats are berthed or out working.

Day 6/7 - Then the very next day he leaves, either at dawn or as soon as fog lifts a bit on the morning outgoing tide. He isn't dressed as a fisherman on these trips, but in nice casual clothes, and he is usually gone at least overnight, if not longer. I think that is when he goes to the Mainland. And whenever he gets back he is more relaxed and nicer to people and doesn't do anything much, or in any pattern I can see for days, or weeks, until he goes to the bank again, then everything happens in the same pattern.

Urgent! The pattern has started again "doing it now"!

Report compiled from phone transcript of "urgent" tip.

As each person finished reading, the most common reaction Mallory saw was for their eyes to immediately snap back up to the top of the page to reread the source description. Eyebrows bounced up almost in synchronicity as he watched them all silently mouth the words '21st Century Nancy Drew?' in disbelief.

The room remained uncomfortably silent.

Leaning forward, keeping his face absolutely blank, his eyes down where his big neat hands were folded on the table, his voice neutral, Detective Mallory relayed additional information.

"The source advised me that her great grandmother had given her a set of her childhood books, the 1930s era Nancy Drew Series. For anyone unaware, Nancy Drew was a young woman that solved mysteries. The 'inspiration', the source informed, and I quote 'for her sleuthing and selection of a code name'." Mallory had to pause and tighten his lips for a moment then, without looking up, continued.

"I was able to verify that this source is definitely the same source that mailed in the previous handwritten tips unsigned. The call was triggered by the urgency of another impending departure on another smuggling trip to the mainland, as the pattern has started again, according to this source." Then head still down, maintaining his posture, Detective Mallory ceased speaking and waited.

And waited.

Finally, Prosecutor Jordan Campbell cleared his throat and spoke, skipping over any discussion for the moment of the source's credentials. Or age. Or 'inspiration'.

"Mainland. Yes, that does rather stick out. Clearly the boat and the, ah, source are located on an island off the coast."

"Well!" An eager Detective Roberts jumped in. "That should make it a lot easier to narrow things down," he sounded relieved. "I mean how many islands can there be?"

His excitement seemed to fizzle under a table full of unenthusiastic, if not annoyed, gazes.

"What?" Young and enthusiastic, Roberts was the other detective assigned to the task force. While well versed and familiarized with his local jurisdiction now, he had only transferred in fairly recently, having spent the whole of his youth and early police career in the Midwest.

Jordan cut in firmly before anyone could respond.

"First, for the purposes of narrowing our focus, let us assume for now that as the tips were sent here, we need only consider the adjacent area, which would be the islands in the sound and straits off Western Washington."

One of his staffers snorted, then, at a stern glance from his boss, said, "Well that should help. How many hundreds of islands *is* that exactly, sir?"

Ignoring him, Jordan spoke quietly into his intercom requesting a map from Elsa, then addressed the room, his voice as steely as his hard gray eyes. "It seems clear from the tip that we only need to address the islands of the range I have outlined that have a harbor that can support a town with a bank. We will narrow our initial list of initial possibilities to islands that have banks. In the San Juans, for example, while there are hundreds of islands, I can only think of three that are likely to meet that criteria. Someone on my team," those steel eyes pinned the sarcastic staffer, "will verify that and contact all banks and compile a list of the island branches. Immediately. Leave now and work until it is complete."

After the chastened man removed himself, red-faced and now wisely silent, Jordan sat back, his tone more collegial.

"Detectives. I think you might best work with the Port Authority. We need a list from them that covers: a) boat slips rented to island residents, b) island homeport boats that have used the guest dock in the last six months, and how often and ... Hell! We don't even know what *kind* of boat we are looking for. Do we yet, Mallory? No? Terrific. If…," he waved his hand, "…she calls again, please pin that down. Anyway, where was I? I seem to have forgotten what 'C' was." Leaning back he raked a palm over his dark hair, concentrated a moment, and then shrugged. "Maybe the port will have suggestions of what else to consider. If you have any problems with them regarding confidentially of their clients, please tell them how urgently we need a list of just the slip numbers, and the names of the home base islands. And we need it yesterday, of course. Maybe we can sweeten the pot a bit by offering additional patrol 24/7 to the port security when we expect an incoming boat? Starting…,"

Detective Mallory spoke up, "The informant intends to text message the cell phone number I gave her the minute the boat unties from the dock for the Mainland trip."

"Okay. From then. Which reminds me, you said this tip was a phone in, any chance you got a location or name off the caller ID, Mallory?"

"Negative. The number was from a prepaid throw away phone purchased with cash at one of the largest WalMarts on the mainland. Kids are smart these days. The call was placed from the parking lot of the same store. So, nothing there."

"Well, bring that boat list in as soon as you get it and I'll supply the manpower to cross check the islands and get us a working list to start checking out. Thanks."

The rest of the team laughed as they rose to leave, knowing just who the staffer was that was getting *that* assignment.

Before heading for his own office, Jordan heaved a sigh, and rested his palm over his face, covering his grimace. He assigned himself the job of contacting the Coast Guard to give them a heads up that his team expected to need assistance. Tracking an unknown boat, from an unknown island, to an arrival at a guessed-at port. Hell! And he would *not* divulge any hint of the source of this tip. He had already passed Rhonda's friend's name and her comments on to Detective Mallory at the end of the meeting.

"Not *another* suspicious female?" The harried detective commented.

"Look on the bright side," Jordan teased, but his smile was tight, "if God were merciful, this could be our guy with a boat? But I wouldn't bet on it. At any rate, you will be doing Ms. Sayles a favor, if you check him out."

"Ooh-la-la! Anything for her, of course!"

Jordan had his assistant prosecutor, Shelley, in his office.

"As I mentioned to you, Rhonda Sayles, who has been... 'dating'... that potter she met at the Arts Festival earlier this year?"

"I met him. Peter Potter. His sailboat is at the Edmonds Marina."

"Exactly. Well, Ronnie privately shared with me that she has lost trust in him, and more to the point, thought he might be up to something that was, at minimum suspicious activity at the port, and possibly even that his art and pottery might be a surface cover for something else.

"She says she went to view a supposed shipment of his art to a gallery in Seattle and found one piece and in trying to confirm other information from Potter, nothing he said matched up. She says she knows it probably sounds silly, but as she has made it clear to the potter that she will help support and promote his artworks. So she says the fact he seems to be secretive and even negative about giving her information to help him, added to his lies about it, tells her that his art may not be his real function here.

"As she is very intelligent, and she has checked and found he is not where he says he is, she has become highly suspicious." He paused a moment and grinned, "She says every time she tries to ask him the most simple questions, he diverts her with wild sex rather than answering. Confessing that at first she had no complaints, but is wise to him now and doesn't trust him."

"If *any* woman is capable of thinking objectively during wild sex, it would be Rhonda," Shelley grinned back at him. "She is probably an expert, or something. But seriously, boss," she shifted forward in her chair, her demeanor shifting to match her words, "Ms. Sayles is savvy about men. She has a developed skill at reading men, especially handsome men, she has probably heard every line there is, and she is very smart, very sharp. I cannot imagine her bringing her concerns to you unless she is highly suspicious.

"And this is a woman," Shelley continued, "that is a CEO of a highly successful business that she created and developed herself. This is not the kind of woman that would cause trouble for a man because of something petty, or the woman scorned type of situation. In fact, I'm surprised that with her lack of trust, she hasn't dumped him flat yet. That's more her style."

"We discussed that. She says the only reason she hasn't is because she wants to find out what he is up to. And you don't need to remind me how brilliant she is, remember, she helped Sam outsmart me once already!"

Shelley laughed with him, remembering Ronnie had outmaneuvered this prosecutor getting an innocent woman into his jail and keeping her there.

"Anyway, I talked to Detective Mallory, another of Rhonda's fans, and he took it seriously also. They sent a detective to the port to ask a few questions. Let me share his report on Potter's sailboat berth with you and get your impressions on this.

"The company that holds the lease on the berth is a small boat sales company located in Vancouver, British Columbia, a little more difficult for us to check into, but we do know from the port that it says that it leases the space so that it can bring clients down on trial cruises when they are purchasing one of their boats. They want to avoid bringing a client down and being unable to find an available spot on the guest docks at such an award winning port. Thus avoiding a disenchanted client which is not a good sales prospect. So it's worth it to them to have reserved space. And they apparently pay their bill annually in a lump sum, in advance, rather than monthly like most. They say this allows them to buy their US dollars at a negotiated exchange rate and not have to worry about variable currency rates changing their cost budget."

"That makes good business sense."

"It does," Jordan nodded his agreement. "However . . . they rarely use the space."

"What?" Doesn't a space like that cost a fortune?"

"To not be used? Yes, I would think so for a small company. And this company says that particular kind of space, an end of dock cross space is necessary for their needs, even though more expensive, since the boats they bring down may be either yachts, or sailboats, of variable sizes, so the outer dock works better for them than uncovered sailboats slots inside against the boardwalk.."

Shelley nodded, stating dryly, "Also way more private way out there where the boats and roofs block being able to see them, as opposed to all the people that walk the boardwalk looking down into them all the time."

Jordan smiled, "Precisely! We're on the same track, I see. That's why I wanted you here; to be sure I wasn't just seeing ghosts for Sam's friend. We are keeping my wife out of the loop for the time being, in case nothing comes of it. She doesn't have much of a poker face," he admitted, smiled fondly thinking of his ever blushing bride.

"Anyway, back to how often the berth is used. They have never used the space more than four times a year for a day of docking for their trial cruises out of Canada. Recently, once a year has been the norm. When they bring their boats in, Canadian registered, they are of course subjected to a very thorough customs inspection.

"Now, an interesting change, maybe related to slow sales, but, see what you think. For the last two years the company has contacted the port to put their berth into the LOAN-A-SLIP program. This program allows the port to act as a rental agent so to speak, subletting the unused space to meet needs of other boaters, for an agreed time. This works to the benefit of both the holders of the berth, with the rents being deducted from their lease fee, and gives the port added short term guest docking without losing a long-term tenant due to low usage.

"So for the last two years the small boat company has contacted the port putting their berth up for sublease from the weekend before father's day, which, as you know, is when the Art's Festival runs, through the weekend after the Canadian Thanksgiving holiday. Which means in effect from mid-June through mid-October..."

"But," Shelley interjected, "I don't know much about boats, but isn't that the prime boating and boat sales season? When they would need it for themselves? Do they just get the best rates then? And with sales slow, just need the money?"

"All valid questions. Here's the other bit of interesting," Jordan paused, "coincidence? For those same last two years an American citizen and resident has written the port the week *before* the boat company offers the space and has requested that same type of location, outer end dock full width, for exactly the same time period. *Exactly* the same, weekend before Art's Festival through middle of October. Bingo!

"Port has a perfect match at the top of their list, one transaction, perfect time and space match, no hassle with re-renting space every few days or weeks and all the extra accounting that entails. The winner is Mr. Peter Potter, both times, and it is even less trouble because it is an American registered boat."

"My, what a *most* convenient ... coincidence. Two years in a row, even."

Jordan watched Shelley's face furrow in thought and waited.

"And ... since it is an American citizen and boat," Jordan was nodding encouragement as Shelley spoke, "then I bet that changes the customs scrutiny ... which, if he leased the spot directly from the Canadian company, would be treated like another boat potentially coming in from another country!"

"That was my read, also," Jordan agreed. "We'll need to double check all our facts, but it's just another possible question about Mr. Potter's activities. And when you link that to another bit of information I received a while back, makes me think we need him looked into more thoroughly. Apparently there was a drug dog that alerted on the parking area that corresponds with where that dock gate opens to the public, though the adjacent parking area is reserved for the boat tenants. There were no cars in the area when the dog alerted on a routine patrol. When they took the dog down that particular dock row, it seemed to be running back and forth the length of the dock without a specific target. They wondered if it was a false alert, or if recent rain had blurred the scent. But interestingly, Potter's sailboat was out of port a few days, and wasn't there at the time.

"Anyway, based on your concurring reactions, I'm going to have the detectives look closer at this. And just so you know, I have already informed Ms. Sayles that we have a one-way highway here. Anything she learns she tells me. Anything we learn . . . we won't be sharing with her."

"Got it. But I never tell anyone anything I hear in this office anyway, unless you order it."

"Even a friend of yours that we have worked with in the past?" He asked hesitantly.

Shelley wasn't offended, he was just checking if she included other law enforcement or consultant types. "No one, Jordan. Not Kevin, not detectives, unless you approve it. No one. And...," she held up a hand to stop his apology, "I appreciate your interest in my input, and I already know you trust me completely. It never hurts to have absolute clarity, does it?"

Shelley gave him one of those sweet smiles that belied what a tough, seasoned professional she was. He would never quit regretting the way he used to treat her as an opponent, and never quit being thankful he had the sense to hire her.

"Kevin, huh?" he said softly, leaning back in his chair to stretch with a grin. He had heard that rumor. Apparently there was something to it. Sam thought they made a cute young couple. But then his wife didn't know everything the prosecutor did.

Rhonda breezed in, trailing a man.

"I hope you don't mind that I brought a date, Sam," she called out as she came down the hall. Jordan popped out of his office and directed Rhonda and her guest to the dining room, "Sam is in here, Ronnie, just putting the finishing touches on the table. It's Potter, isn't it?" Jordan reached for the man's hand and pulled him into the dining room with them.

"Sorry, I didn't call, I hope you have enough. Oh! Oops! Looks like you already have another guest coming," Rhonda looked embarrassed when she noted the extra place setting.

Sam opened her mouth, but Jordan spoke.

"Actually," he said smoothly, "Sam was hoping you would bring your date and set an extra plate just in case."

Sam blinked at her husband, closed her mouth, and smiled quickly at Potter. "Oh, I think that was the timer, excuse me," and rushed off to the kitchen before Rhonda looked up and caught her smile or her eyes. She could never look Ronnie in the eye and fool her.

She fussed around in the kitchen with things that didn't need fussing with, while Jordan seated their guests and got them drinks, then slipped into the kitchen to "see if his wife needs help".

"Jordan?" she turned questioning blue eyes on him. "I thought the man in your office was joining us for dinner?"

He looked at his wife, sighed, raked a hand through his dark hair, paced two steps, turned, put his hands on his hips, and gave his wife a very stern look.

"The man in my office does not exist. Understand?"

He waited until he received a solemn, silent nod from Sam.

"I have to go warn him to stay in the office. Sorry, honey." He turned to slip down the hall, pausing when he heard a soft, "Jordan?"

When he turned warily, fully expecting anger, hurt, or some reaction, his sweet wife just held out a chicken breast on a napkin.

"Give him this to hold him until later," she said quietly.

Jordan shook his head slowly, whispering, "You are a treasure, sweetheart." Heading down the hall, he wondered again how he had gotten so damn lucky.

They had moved out to the patio for drinks after dinner, enjoying the sights and scents of the back garden on this perfect summer evening.

"If you folks will excuse me a moment," Jordan rose, hoisting his empty beer, I need to do a little recycling trip to the boy's room, then I'll grab us some more beers."

It had been uncomfortably tense, Ronnie and her date had been sniping at each other over an argument they'd had on the way over. After Jordan left, Samantha tried to ease the taut silence.

"Didn't Jordan do a great job with this yard? Come, let's walk back and I'll show you the back garden plantings. Please let me give you the tour, Peter. Ronnie has seen it, but there is always something new in bloom."

Seeming to be willing to mend fences, or at least be courteous to his hostess, Potter stood and gathered Rhonda's hand, "Sure, let's go take the garden tour, love."

Jordan stepped into the kitchen, pulled a cold beer out of the fridge then headed down the hall. Opening his office door, he entered the darkened room without turning on the lights. The man standing just back from the window looking onto the back deck and yard, was silhouetted by the bright outdoor light that slatted through the wooden blinds, tilted to give a clear view out, while keeping the interior cool and private.

"Well?" Jordan asked, handing over the beer.

The tall, broad shouldered man murmured without turning around. "Yes, I have him on my radar."

"Good."

"What is Sam's friend's problem?"

"Ronnie is annoyed with Potter. Apparently he plans on going to Vegas this weekend on a business trip and won't take her with him. She said, and I will quote so you don't miss the flavor, 'But it reminded me of how long it has been since I was there. I guess I'll just take some handsome hunk down there to *play* with this weekend, since Potter won't be available for fun.' Potter thinks she's joking, but Sam says she definitely is *not*."

"Tell the lovely Ms. Sayles I'm available. Not joking either."

"I'll set it up," Jordan responded just as seriously.

As Sam walked her guests back through the plantings, they came to a small secluded grassy spot in a far corner, surrounded by shrubbery and shaded by a roof of lacy, leafy branches.

"How lovely! I don't think I've ever seen this before. I had no idea you had this lovely spot back here behind the shrubs." Rhonda admired the private screened niche surrounded by fragrant white azaleas, roses, and honeysuckle climbing a screen beside a wood shingled potting shed.

"Yes," Sam said absently, staring down at the lush pad of grass, instead of the flowers. "This is a lovely spot back here, isn't it?"

"So pretty and fragrant and private", Ronnie agreed.

Sam, still fascinated by the patch of lawn, agreed, "Private, yes, it's very private. Especially when the neighbors are on vacation."

Rhonda looked at shrubbery hiding a fence that completely screened the niche from the neighbors, thinking it was an odd thing for Sam to say. Glancing over at her, she noted her friend looked very flushed, but she had a little smile on her face, her gaze still fixated on the grass.

Jordan found them, handed around chilled long-neck beers then swooped his arm around Sam's waist and gave her a hearty kiss on the check. Grinning, he added his appraisal of the lawn and said, "Has Sam told you this is our favorite..."

"Picnic spot!" Sam interrupted, quickly, her face aflame.

Jordan threw back his head laughing, and squeezed his shy wife closer to him, agreeing, "Right. Best picnics we have ever had." Looking over at Ronnie, he winked and said quietly, "Especially when the neighbors are gone."

"I see," Rhonda grinned rather smugly, but Sam wouldn't look at her. "Yes, your wife and I were just discussing some of our favorite *outdoor* activities the other day, but Sam failed to mention this lovely place. So you come out here and picnic with your husband, Sam? How sweet."

Something in her tone turned Sam even redder, raising her chin to state rather defensively, "Yes, when the neighbors are on vacation and there is no noise from their yard," her husband's eyebrows rose and his lips twitched, "then we find it most pleasant, to picnic together here. As a married couple." Sam nodded, as if to convince herself all was right and proper.

Rhonda threw back her head and laughed.

"Well, then next time I come by and ring the bell and don't get an answer, I'll just pop back here to see if you are …ah, picnicking . . . outdoors. I'll bring my camera."

chapter eighteen

Rhonda relaxed back into her first class window seat for the flight to Las Vegas with a contended sigh. She thumbed through the in-flight magazine while she waited for the plane to finish boarding. The empty aisle seat beside her gave her hope for a peaceful trip—false hope she realized as a large man took the seat. Not looking up from the magazine, Rhonda couldn't help but be aware that the man smelled divine. But she was a wee bit jaded with men at the moment, initially divine or otherwise, so she kept her face averted.

He must look as good as he smelled if the way the stewardess was fluttering around him making an idiot of herself was any indication. But he did have a voice that vibrated in a woman: a deep, rich, sexy drawl, maybe with a hint of the south in it somewhere.

But she refused to be drawn, keeping her face in her magazine pretending to read until the stewardess left, then longer still. Until she felt his gaze on her, and her bouncing pheromones refused to settle down and leave her alone. She glanced over casually, and choked on a gasp.

He looked as good as he smelled and sounded. There was just one damn problem.

"You? Not you!"

He just grinned at her anger. "Miss me, did you? I see you couldn't forget me."

Arrogant, insufferable. "My god, what are the chances I'd take one tiny little flight and get stuck with *you* beside me!" She hailed the stewardess, close by, of course. "I'd like to change seats, please." It was pure Rhonda: a demand, not a question.

The stewardess blinked at her, looked at him, and then stared back at Rhonda as if she had lost her bloody mind. "But ... I'm sorry, ma'am." That word! "The plane is full. There are no empty seats."

"Just my luck," Rhonda grumbled.

"Yes," the stewardess gave the man another long, admiring look. "I wish I could change seats with you myself, but it's not allowed."

Her seatmate coughed into his hand while Rhonda scowled. "Then you better start bringing me drinks the minute the plane is airborne and leveled off," Rhonda huffed. She tried to twist away from him and face the window, but her seat belt humiliated her, and paid for it. Fortunately it didn't have ears.

He coughed again, and cleared his throat, when she growled.

"Are you laughing?" she accused.

"No, ma'am." He liked the way she winced at the word.

They were both silent for a while, though his silence came with his lips turned up at the corners. Hers were a mirror image—reversed.

As the plane rose out of SeaTac, islands were suddenly swimming below in the Sound. Crisp mountain ranges on either side fenced them in, as if trying to prevent their escape to the ocean. The scene was lost when the plane climbed above the blanket of cloud and headed south.

He finally spoke quietly.

"I guess I'm not quite what you ordered."

Her head snapped around to see who he was speaking to so sweetly. He was looking straight into her eyes.

"I ordered?" She asked, heavy on the sarcasm. "I beg your pardon, you ..."

"Yes. A handsome stud to play with in Vegas?"

When she just stared at him he added, "Jordan sent me?"

Oh, lord! That is when Rhonda realized she was stuck with the man she thought of as a beach dog—for the *whole weekend!*

"So what happened in Vegas?" Jordan asked as soon as they were alone.

Eyebrows raised, surprised.

"You didn't get the report? Damn those..."

"Oh, yeah, sorry. I got that, and I'm impressed. Thank god we have at least one strong suspect and connection to focus on now. Maybe we can pick up the rest of the network with surveillance on those guys. No. What I meant was," Jordan lowered his voice, smiling slightly, "How did it go with Ms. Sayles?"

"Who?"

"Rhonda," Jordan reminded with a touch of impatience.

The other man stopped walking, turned to face Jordan and shook his head slowly back and forth. Then he shook his finger back and forth like a metronome in Jordan's face. "Shame on you, Mr. Prosecutor. You know what happens in Vegas, stays ..."

Jordan interrupted him with a groan. "Oh, come on, she's my wife's best friend."

"Then ask your wife."

"She told me to buttonhole you. Ronnie is not speaking."

The other man grinned. "I'm not surprised. But..."

"But what?" Jordan was nearly dancing to get the scoop. To stay informed, of course.

"Well, I just hope Rhonda isn't surprised when she learns that not *everything* that happened there stayed put."

"Huh? What are you referring to?"

"Gosh, I'd love to tell you Jordan, but I'm afraid the Vegas truth-in-advertising police might put a warrant out on me. And that wouldn't be wise for someone in my position. So, see you around."

Jordan just sighed, knowing he was beaten. How could that man be so charming and annoying at the same time? Well, Ronnie was bound to spill it eventually. She didn't usually care who knew what she had been up to. In fact, she was usually eager to tell all in graphic detail – just to see Sam blush and squirm.

Jordan turned and headed for his office. Ronnie had actually done a great job helping them get a lead in Vegas. He hadn't even called her yet to thank her for all her help. Maybe he'd take care of that right now.

As he passed his secretary, Elsa, on the way to his office, she narrowed her eyes.

"I know that look. You, mister, are up to no good."

"Professional duty," he responded sternly, closing his door behind him.

And maybe he might make his wife happy as well. There was *always* a reward for that.

Unfortunately, Ronnie had only a few words for him.

"Thanks a lot for the escort." Not said with gratitude.

"Man, this kid I knew did that and found a gargoyle! Is that cool, or what?"

The boys were excited. Too excited. The noise level was raucous as they dressed, shoes flew through the air, along with paper airplanes and a jock strap or two. It felt like a typical boys dormitory, and that was good news. Kevin had decided a few days earlier that they deserved a treat—some real fun.

The Shelter was located north of Seattle in a corridor of urban sprawl sandwiched between the Interstate and the old north-south highway that grew more paved parking lots for the surrounding strip malls than grass. Its scenic beauty rated in fractions on a scale of one to ten. So most of the youths' sports activities took place indoors where the air was dusty, stale and sour.

"How many of you have spent a day outdoors, competing and having fun and picnics on the beach and breathing fresh salty air? Show me your hands."

No hands shot up, though one did hesitantly wave with a question and eyes full of hope. "Did you say beach? I only went to a hot dog stand by a community pool."

"Okay, how many of you want to go do what I said this Saturday? Show me…"

All the hands were already raised and waving eagerly, except one kid that always waited to see what everyone else did. The boy next to him grabbed his arm and raised it for him telling him not to screw it up for everyone.

"Great. This Saturday we are going to go a few miles north to the coast town of Edmonds to enter the Annual Street Scramble Event. It's a race up and down the hills of the town, and along the waterfront, where you will use a map to find things, like in a treasure hunt, but what you have to find are answers to clues. The most found, over the greatest distances traveled, win event ribbons. But just to make it more rewarding I have a signed football, basketball, and baseball mitt, for our top three and some other prizes for finishing. Everyone gets a picnic and maybe a game of volleyball on the beach, depending on how crowded it is."

The sound level rivaled that in the Seahawks stadium during a game.

The real reward for the boys, they would realize later, was being a normal part of a community event and their sense of belonging.

Beyond the day of outdoor exercise in fresh air, it was a chance to sharpen mapping skills while experiencing healthy competition and teamwork, which they would treasure long afterwards—just because it was *not* a normal part of the lives of *these* youths.

He would give them a sense of independence from their pack, creating individual initiative, by splitting the boys into pairs, each with a college age volunteer counselor to go along with them to guard against any mischief, but letting them map their own routes and strategy. He didn't expect any problems as the boys would leap at the chance to test and challenge themselves with plenty of 'normal-boy fun' available. Old fashioned fun and bragging rights. This rare opportunity to be normal kids.

"Thanks to a generous donor funding us," Kevin murmured to himself, as 'fun' wasn't included in the budget allotment. He was desperate to give them more opportunities like this. And even more desperate to keep the shelter open.

Shelley had turned surprisingly silent, recently. It seemed she was giving him the cold shoulder treatment since the night Kevin had made love to her.

He *had* called, just not the next day, and sent flowers to her office, *eventually*. He had done everything a woman expected—though he had been a little slow about it. But he had been out, taking care of things. She should understand that as a career woman.

Kevin did not get it. Had he offended her somehow? Had he moved too fast? Maybe she wasn't ready for so much intimacy yet … Maybe?

Hell, he had no idea what was up. Maybe she was just busy, maybe he was just imagining it was personal and chilly.

She had said 'busy' on the one text message she had responded to after all his phone calls that she hadn't taken—or returned. But only the one text, and only the one word. "Busy'. No 'hey'. No 'miss you', no 'sorry' she was busy, not even a 'luv', 'later'. No chat. And she hadn't even signed her name. Just 'busy'. The single word she had given him in the few weeks since he had made passionate love to her all night long ... Surely he wasn't that bad?

And young Timmy still looked at him like he was evil incarnate.

He had finally had a discussion with Timmy and admitted that the night Shelley had been missing, she has been with him—all night.

He hadn't meant to make a confession. He assumed the kid already knew after all the time the two of them spent together—without him. Yes, he did need to separate himself from them for a while. But he felt more like he had been dumped by both of them. Of course, he was not being logical, but dammit he missed them!

Didn't they miss him? Even a little?

No point asking the 'other man in her life' what the trouble was with his Big Sister. Timmy seemed to have decided that Kevin was trying to harm or steal Shelley, and all Kevin's words of wisdom about adults caring for each other, and needing to spend special time together, without it stealing any of their caring for a dear friend, had met a stubborn little stone face.

And a warning.

"You just keep your special time, and your hands off of my main man, or you'll answer to me! If she wanted you, she would be answering your calls, don't you think?"

Well, Kevin had some serious 'busy' to deal with himself, anyway.

He would have to wait 'til later to fix his problems with the two of them—still convinced they *could* be fixed. Though it sounded like young Timmy was going to fix him first. He almost laughed, but the hurt was too raw.

"So, how do I look?" Rhonda struck a pose on Sam's doorstep, arms stretched gracefully to the sides as she did a slow twirl so that the full benefit of her outfit could be modeled.

Sam couldn't find quite the words to describe 'the look'. Though she should have been forewarned, her friend had dragged her along as she shopped for each individual piece. Still...

"Beautiful, as always," Sam chickened out. It was true. Ronnie was expertly groomed, manicured, her makeup perfect, as always. *She* was beautiful, her clothes and accessories *were* beautiful. Sam just wasn't sure it was legal to wear them all at the same time, on one body.

"I think it looks rather arty." Rhonda twirled one more time just to watch her skirt flare above her stiletto heels.

"Arty," Sam repeated, folding an arm across her waist, to prop her elbow, and a finger on her chin, as if she was thoughtfully and seriously considering the possibility. She started her survey at Ronnie's toes so that it would take longer before she had to meet her eyes and, hopefully, give her time to think of something to say. Red stiletto couture heels, under a red-purple-orange-yellow, Sam gave up her attempt to name all the colors swirling and slashing in the full length, flared skirt. It was made of sheer gauze; that much became clear by the time Sam reached the knees. She hoped Ronnie had at least a mini slip beneath, but just in case, she would avoid checking in bright sunlight.

Cut in snug from low on the hips, up the cinched waist, molding Ronnie's breasts tightly—except the uncovered part displaying abundant cleavage—was a purple topper that looked like it had been stolen from a ballet class. It was of such a thin knit that every skin pore seemed to show, not to mention... Rhonda clearly needed a coat; she appeared chilled.

Over all this drama there was a wide heavy belt cinched low and snug on the hips, made of braided leather with one end left to dangle, fringed and beaded, swaying over—well, where Sam hoped that slip was—like the rope girdles the medieval women wore. A multitude of bangles and bracelets, some with bright charms coated each arm beneath the three-quarter sleeves, and Ronnie's neck was buried under necklaces of all variety like the old gypsy women that used to wear their wealth. None of these necklaces, however, covered the exposed skin of the deep cleavage, except to taunt.

Sam gained time by detouring around the face to the earrings swaying like miniature wind chimes from Rhonda's ears, then studied the complicated hair style. Most of the long, dark, shining hair had been swept up, with a few curls left down to tease. A highly patterned and colored silk scarf spread across her friend's forehead then seemed to braid into the hair in some kind of loose coronet, with the ends left to float free and flutter down her back. All together it was...

"Be honest now, "Ronnie smiled confident of the forthcoming awe.

'*Owww*' was closer to Sam's reaction. "Oh look," she stalled, "you have a bright yellow leather purse! I don't remember you buying that."

"Oh, this old thing? But it is one of my favorites. So vibrant. It always catches the eye. Well?" Another twirl with everything floating, fluttering, dangling, jangling, swaying, and vibrating.

"Truly, I think you have . . . outdone yourself, Ronnie. It's so arty and ... unique!" Especially on a woman about to start collecting Social Security benefits in the near future, Sam thought.

This whole 'arty' thing had started when Sam had shown Rhonda the brochure for the annual upcoming Writers' Conference. As the keynote speaker was a favorite author of theirs, and that portion of the weekend conference was open to the public, Samantha asked if her friend might like to attend the luncheon and keynote speech. Rhonda was thrilled and agreed.

Then suddenly, in a seeming rush of affection, and desire to show her full support for her dear friend the 'unfinished author' as she put it, Ronnie had late registered for Sam's full course of classes that day, just last week.

When she drug Sam off shopping the day they canceled the trip to that gallery, displaying her lover's work, Ronnie had gotten the notion she needed something 'arty' to wear 'around all those *creative* people'. Sam had assumed Ronnie had meant to wear only one or two of the pieces she'd purchased that day.

"Don't worry," Rhonda had told Sam when she learned they would be going to class together, "I know how important this is to you, and that you need to concentrate and focus completely. I'll just sit in the back corner by myself, and not distract you. I just want to share the experience so I will understand what you go through better. Honest, you won't even know I am back there. I'll be as quiet as a mouse."

Sam trusted her silence; just her clothes would be screaming from the corner. Holding back a sigh, she stepped out and pulled the door closed, heading for the car.

"Don't you need to dress first?"

Samantha looked down at her comfortable loafers, pressed khaki slacks, and navy cashmere twin set pullover and cardigan. Patting her navy briefcase, she said, "I appear to be. Yes, everything is here."

Including Sam's 'arty' navy, rust, and tan patterned socks just barely peeping out from the crisp hem of her slacks.

"Let's get going, we don't want to be late for registration and orientation for the conference. And parking will be a bear. I understand another event is also going on at the center this morning."

chapter nineteen

The gull drifted on the draft uphill from the center of town, head cocking side to side seeking unguarded chips or sandwiches—but it seemed too early for lunch. All the playfields were full of running, jumping specks of those tiny, careless humans; every curb was lined with shiny metal people movers; masses of people had moved into the building below, and would erupt again later.

It was a target rich environment. The breeze was light but steady now, up away from the harbor, so waiting was easy and should prove rewarding.

Inside the building below, careers and dreams were being built and nourished, while others were being crushed under the brutal weight of reality—depending on course and content. The Writer's Conference attendees bounced between lectures that inspired the spirit, to ones that punched with hard truth, and back again like dribbled basketballs, unsure whether their writing efforts would foul out or ring the hoop and drop a winner. But if nothing else seemed certain that day, it was that persistent effort and patience were essential. A lesson the bird circling above could teach them all.

Outside the building, it seemed as if Nature was paying out rewards points for all the nasty stormy days it had ever spent. Morning fog had burned away from the higher rim of town, replaced with the rare brilliance of sunlight from a summer already in bonus time, refusing to surrender its grasp or leaves to fall. Rattling the only half-yellowed leaves it kept defiantly treed still, summer taunted with a breeze too pleasant for fall. The town folk rejoiced in the bright gift, grateful it came on the weekend for once. People filled the sidewalks with steps that sprung instead of slogging, grabbing onto the seduction outdoors for one last walk, jog, or stroll, or race for distance and time to gather answers to clues, in a city wide scavenger hunt, in the annual Street Scramble Event.

The bright black eye of the gull had caught the flow of bright orange splotched humans flowing out and spreading down into town from the playfields earlier, but had determined the papers in their hands didn't look edible. If it could have read the word 'Scramble' printed on the neon orange vests, it might have wondered if that meant 'eggs' and equaled tasty, but there was no appealing scent, so he just floated and watched, waiting for something to happen.

Something was bound to happen with so much activity.

The circling gull was not alone in its watchful, waiting intent.

Down in the harbor, fog still ruled, but it was weakening and sneaking away in fat drifts of mist.

Further out on the waters, away from the warmth of land, the light wind sweeping through the strait and sound had cleared most of the fog already, and ferries crisply shuttled peninsula traffic and tourists between the fog wrapped shorelines.

At the edge of the fog line, sailboats jostled for position to escape the rock-walled port marina to sail out for another day of play on the bright end-of-summer waters. Other craft waited patiently to enter the port to tie up for a day's visit and entertainment in charming downtown Edmonds.

The bright barrel shaped sails of the kite boarders were being prepared to lift into the sky from Marina Beach further south, where they could experience briefly the bird's eye view of the circling gull. Today, the sails even had tiny wireless cameras attached to record that unique view for the van with darkened windows, parked early and alone, at the deserted beach—deserted, except for a few very alert and fit walkers and joggers.

There was even one hardy old soul sitting at one of the bench tables inset along the boardwalk that traversed the length of the port, seemingly enjoying his newspaper and a cardboard container of steaming hot coffee, despite the fog.

In the salt marsh, that paralleled the back of the port inland, there were an unusual number of bird watchers, and they seemed unusually determined considering the visual conditions. They also sported less silver hair, harder, younger bodies, and seemed to prefer electronic tablets to crumpled spiral notebooks, on the whole, to jot down what they were seeing through their binoculars. They talked to themselves, mumbling into their shoulders a lot, also.

As the sun started to roll the remaining fog back closer to shore, another bench table set in front of the guest docks acquired a coffee drinking, news reader. She seemed fascinated by the hundreds of gulls that settled on the sunny rock top of the breakwater that shielded the entrance to the port.

She guessed they must be there for breakfast, as the Bait Shop was positioned nearby. Or maybe they just liked to check out and gossip about the boats passing though. They were a noisy, cheerful group. A bit of chatter would start at the far end of the rocky ridge, then spread up to the other end until it sounded like all the gulls were laughing. Then it would quiet down until the gull cries and chatter would start up again elsewhere and spread throughout.

The woman watcher couldn't help but smile a little. She suspected one gull told a funny story or naughty joke and it spread down the line until all of the gulls were laughing, cheerful in the morning sun.

Another lone gull graced a pier at the end of Z slip in the marina, eye beads alert and watchful. But unlike the one circling over the town above, this particular bird had no intention of ever leaving his post in search of food.

His prey would come to him.

The watchful gull in the marina was named Gordo – a name, that if it were a real bird, it probably would have detested.

And it was not laughing—just watching and waiting with infinite patience.

He sat at a picnic table, away from the chaos and crowds near the Parks and Recreation Banners—the sponsors of the event —where all the eager scramblers were registering. His orange vest, map, and clue sheet were on the table before him. Head down, he appeared to be studiously studying and analyzing the map, making routing notations on a notepad, most likely writing down whatever he seemed to be muttering to himself. He was too far from the others milling about for anyone to hear what he was saying, or see what he was writing, other than to note his lips moving and his hunched posture, as if guarding his route like prized answers in a crucial test.

His body language and large fit physique discouraged intrusion, along with the concealing wall of his highly reflective sunglasses that made anyone approaching feel like they were staring themselves down. Clean shaven, he had a hard square don't-mess-with-me jaw. A flat black baseball cap covered his head, turned backwards.

Despite appearances, he was intensely aware of everything going on around him.

He knew when the flood of teenage boys arrived with the red-haired man and his college assistants. He knew when the man registered himself for the event, along with all the kids, and collected his orange vest. And he knew that shortly after that, the man with red-hair reached for a pager, moved away from the crowds, and made a cell phone call.

He watched as the man went over and was clearly apologizing, making his exit, *had to leave*, etc., etc. He couldn't hear the words, but they didn't really matter. The man had effectively registered for an event where he didn't need to show up, or check in, for another few hours.

Then the red-haired man left.

An intriguing alibi—except for the kids. He wondered what excuse they had been given for his abrupt departure. He made another notation, head down, muttering to his map—or his chest.

He watched one young tow headed kid watching that man leave with wounded eyes, tight lips, and hands braced on hips, before turning away and shrugging as if he really didn't care anyway—though the hurt could clearly be read in the set of his narrow, almost fragile seeming, shoulders.

The main suspect was on the move.

Along, no doubt, with any number of other unidentified and unsuspected connections.

He had sailed from San Juan Island. A helicopter trailing, spotted him tacking into the Kingston Boat Harbor, across the Sound from Edmonds, and anchoring his sailboat near some crab pot buoys.

Then a report from a different source came in that he *might* have rowed ashore and *might* have been spotted boarding as a passenger on the ferry to Edmonds. It was an unconfirmed report that came in after the ferry had already arrived, docked, and was preparing to unload.

As resources were rushed from the marina to the ferry dock, the officials at the headquarters' media command center paced nervously, itching to be actively involved in the search, yet forced to just listen as another report came in from the field..

"Our camera above the kite board is getting in as close as wind allows to Kingston Harbor. It's showing a dinghy with two teens working near the suspect sailboat pulling in crab pots. Can't tell if there is any connection, yet," reported the operator from the closed van down at marina beach.

"Keep watching as best you can. We didn't think to put any more resources over on that side of the sound, unfortunately."

One of those forced to watch and listen at the command center, as the detectives, DEA, and field agents coordinated in the search, was the Prosecutor. Jordan Campbell had no active role yet, except as part of the task force group involved in the earlier overall drug smuggling investigation and in any future prosecutions. But he was a man that felt it was important to involve himself in every phase and aspect of a case, not just the ending.

His assistant prosecutor, Shelley, was there also—just as edgy and looking extremely pale, for some reason.

What Jordan was pondering right now was what was going on in the suspect's mind. Did he know they were on to him? Were these evasive moves, or just another drop-off or pickup site they were unaware of? The DEA agent had mapped with GPS and confirmed the crab pot buoys the suspect used before up in the San Juans.

But Jordan's gut told him the man was on the run.

So why hadn't he made a run in his boat for Canada?

That Jordan did not know unless the guy was too worried about international border security, or getting trapped on another island—Vancouver Island—in British Columbia. He suspected the man might have figured his chances were better slipping into Edmonds, where he had contacts, and unwitting pals that could help get him away into the inner U.S. mainland where there was still the option of a remote Canadian border run, or switching to the east coast, or high-tailing it over the easier border into Mexico.

Or *unwilling* contacts to assist him.

That was Jordan's greatest worry.

After an in depth background check had been ordered on the suspect after his Vegas trip, they had found that he *had* no depth!

Peter James Potter had the history of a two year old. Rhonda's instincts had been right. As had their tipster on the island. He had tripped the DEA agent's radar earlier, also, as they tried to trace an international distribution chain.

So if Potter was on the run, he was dangerous.

When Ronnie had reported she had a date scheduled that weekend with Potter, the authorities had decided it was time to take him down, hoping to catch him coming in with a big shipment and nab any connections they could.

Jordan had ordered Rhonda to make herself scarce, worried Potter might try to force her to help him, or seek revenge, if he was cornered. She was to stay away from home, close her business, and stay away from any of her usual haunts in Edmonds this weekend. She was not to answer her phones and turn off her cell phone.

A squawk came from one of the monitors in the darkened van. The technician grinned at the sound effect he had rigged to alert him when the motion sensor gull camera at the end of Z dock became active.

"Well, Gordo, let's see what you've got," he said as he spun his chair around to check the screen. "Hopefully it's not just some girly gull come to visit."

The feed showed a sailboat easing up to the end of the dock on its small reserve motor. He waited until the boat registration numbers came into view, then cursed and grabbed up his phone.

""Who the hell is watching that sailboat?" He yelled into the handset, then listened a moment before responding.

"The hell it is! If it's anchored in Kingston, I'll eat my hat! There is a sailboat of the correct description and registration numbers pulling into its berth on Z dock, here in Edmonds, right now! I'm patching the live feed though to headquarters now," his fingers flew over the keyboard as he spoke.

Verifying the boat on the screen at the command center, Detective Mallory did a little yelling of his own.

"Where are your kite boards?"

"They had to come in. Wind died on them." The tech countered, "Where is your helicopter?"

Mallory grimaced.

"They had to pull it in to refuel. Should be back on scene in thirty more minutes. Then we can…"

"Hold up! See that?" The tech interrupted as they all watched a feed from Gordo the Gull. Two teenage boys were tying up the sailboat, and then giving each other high-five hand slaps. Pulling out a roll of cash, they divided it between them laughing, then headed up the slip.

"Those *are* the kids that were crabbing near the boat in Kingston," the tech confirmed, waiting until his mike was turned off to curse.

Mallory cursed also before broadcasting to the field agents.

"Alert to all marina units. DO NOT, repeat, do NOT stop teens exiting from Z dock. Stay in place, maintain cover, just give us their direction. We will have patrol pick them up away from the boats. Repeat, hold positions."

Mallory listened as each watcher muttered an acknowledgment for the microphones hidden on their chests.

Being teenage boys, the two were easily apprehended at their first stop – food. They were quietly put in a patrol car with their drinks and fish burgers from the Beach Café. They both seemed to see the whole thing as a great lark.

"Hey, this crazy dude just showed up and gave us tons of cash to steal his sailboat! Pretty wild, huh? We just had to sail it over here. Is that cool, or what?"

"Yeah, like we'd never make that much off our crab pots!" His companion added, equally excited, before the patrol officer could even get them to the station to be mirandized and questioned.

At least they were pretty sure now that the suspect *was* on the ferry.

He had thought he was just getting paranoid.

It happened.

But pulling up stakes and moving on had kept him ahead of the law, so far. This time, he thought he'd had a pretty cozy setup and could relax and enjoy the good life a little.

The lush Northwest, with its trees and mountains and saltwater and sailing, beat the hell out of living in the hot desert lands near the southern border. Island life had given him a built in isolation from his more public persona. It had all had that too-good-to-be-true feel about it, which was probably why he'd gotten paranoid.

His woman had gone chilly on him and was asking too damn many questions. If she thought that little game she tried to play on him in Vegas would get him on his knees, she had a surprise coming. Arrogant bitch. He never should have gotten involved with her in the first place, he was here to do a job, that was it.

Hell, he hadn't been able to resist her, though he kept rationalizing that she was a convenient alibi for his repeated trips. A convenient, delicious alibi—until she had become so high maintenance he couldn't concentrate on his job.

His connection in Vegas hadn't liked her showing up one bit. They didn't like eye witnesses, and told him so. If he didn't clear out soon, she would be a major liability.

Personal problems aside, he had been getting that skin prickling feeling on the back of his neck—like he was being watched —much too often lately. Knowing he'd been distracted, and not as alert as usual on the job had him worried. More than worried. Paranoid.

He was constantly looking over his shoulder, scrutinizing everyone walking behind him or jogging by, unable to shake the goose bumps no matter how innocent looking his surroundings.

It was time to deliver his last load and move on. He'd warned his Seattle connection to be prepared to pay for a big shipment, and he had to take it now. The guy had grumbled about ruining his plans for the day, but busy or not, he'd promised to go contact the cut out middleman in Seattle for the cartel. so they could get the cash ready.

He wasn't sure he trusted Red, but it wouldn't matter after tonight.

He just hoped his shipment was still safe. He shouldn't have let himself get spooked by that helicopter that had seemed to shadow him from the San Juans. It was probably just one of those life flights, or a forest fire spotter. He also remembered reading they had helos flying grids over the west coast doing air quality sampling since that Japanese tsunami caused a reactor melt down and radiation release. It was probably something like that but he'd let himself panic. At the time, it made sense to take sudden precautions. Now he felt like a spineless idiot.

Definitely time to relocate.

He lucked out on the ferry, spotting a pickup with a tarp in the back that belonged to a scuba company located down in the port area. Slipping under the tarp, he gotten off the ferry unobserved, and been delivered within blocks of his berth. But he cursed himself for a paranoid, over-cautious fool as he lay in the truck bed crushed by heavy scuba tanks, and suffocated by the oily tarp.

Slipping out, he sucked in the fresh sea air and joined the tourists on the boardwalk that lined the boat slips. Coming around the corner of the restaurant by the guest docks, he scanned the waterside bench tables and froze when he spotted a woman talking into her chest.

Undercover cop!

Shit!

He didn't dare go near his sailboat berth now.

chapter twenty

His most obvious escape route was too risky now, if they had cops watching all along the waterfront, as seemed likely.

He had scoped out the dog park one day, walking south along the chain link fence line that separated the park from the rushing trains. He had found a few places where erosion, or digging paws, had left gaps under the fence line, with flimsy patched repairs made of planks or piled rocks made by pet owners, that would be simple to clear and provide a spot to crawl under—but not in daylight with the park full.

Down at the far end of the fenced area, he had found a gate that lead out to a small open area between the shore and tracks, just where the tracks curved out of sight. He could cross the tracks easily and privately there, to reach the high treed bluff that rose above the water—but that had its own risks—he'd never actually tested that route yet. The area was known for its landslides; composed of glacial till, the unstable hillside had come down across the coast hugging railroad tracks several times, taking a box car of mail into the sound on one occasion. He didn't dare attempt an escape scrambling up there and setting off even smaller rock slides that would attract attention from all the people and their barking dogs below.

Leaning far over the boardwalk rail, head down as if studying the boats tied in the marina below, he tried to calmly consider his options, while nerves flinched along his spine. He forced himself not to check behind him, to focus solely on the boats and water, like any other tourist.

The first reality he had to face was that his boat and his shipment were most likely lost to him. If the cartel wanted to try to swipe the boat and their drugs out from under the cops noses, they were welcome to it. But either way, he was going to be on the run from more than just the law now.

If he could get to Rhonda and get his hands on her car, his escape would be much easier. But she had not returned his calls. He didn't know where to find her. Chances were her place was being watched, anyway. With her connections, she'd probably been the one to mention she expected him this weekend—not realizing her casual comment in that crowd might set up a manhunt.

So his only choice was to head straight into town, try to blend in, lose himself long enough to get into a wooded park and then slip out any of a number of routes. But the Port itself was a bottleneck, intentionally, and aided by fencing to keep people from the path of the constant freight, Amtrak, and local Sounder commuter trains.

Fortunately, he still had on the sweatshirt he'd donned that morning against the chill of the fog and breeze off the water. Flipping up his hoodie, he turned and headed for the crossing over the railroad tracks that was farthest away from the ferry, assuming a swinging fist posture and pace of the fast walkers he saw marching along the waterfront daily. Even in the short distance he'd come so far, he'd seen an unusual number of walkers about, but it was a weekend. He'd find some and stay close.

He'd managed to get across the two most exposed and restricted crossing points undetected—the railroad crossing, and the ferry holding lanes—buried within clusters of walkers. The cops were probably still waiting for him to show up at the waterfront.

He'd just breathed a sigh of relief when he started up the hill into the residential areas, with their clutter of alleys, and hiding places, shadowed and dense with shrubs. But as he passed near the commercial area of the old downtown, he started to see more uniformed police loitering at the main intersections, checking passing faces.

Cutting over mid-block, he walked casually through a parking lot behind a building that had an internal corridor between its businesses. Passing a window where a yoga class was in progress, he tried not to be distracted by all the contorted, sweaty, shrink wrapped female bodies. Reaching the glass door that fronted Fifth, he glanced both ways then took advantage of packed cars stalled for a light, and sprinted across the road between them to the alley beside the old bookstore.

Slipping up the shaded side of the alley, he skirted dumpsters and cars parked haphazardly along the sightless backs of the assorted buildings. Hearing a door slam nearby, he ducked across to the gray concrete block structure behind the American Legion. He waited, catching his breath and watched a patrol car cruise slowly past the upper end of the alley where he was headed. The sight did not help his breathing. He longed for a bottle of water to wash the dry and bitter taste of fear from his throat.

Moving across to an underground parking lot beneath an apartment building, he savored the dark shaded cool as he rested and gave himself a little more time to get his breath back—he would need it. It was literally all up hill from here to get out of town and into some wooded areas.

A patrol car drove down the alley he'd just left.

Escaping the garage, emerging out on the crowded sidewalk, he wove his way ever upward, his breath choppy with exertion and fear, setting his pace to match those beside him.

He noted a few cops, but now everyone looked to him like a plainclothes hunter out to trap him. He felt hunted. He felt the net tightening. Beginning to think he'd never make it into the woods, still many steep blocks away, he spotted a young teen leaning against a picket fence who was panting even harder than he was.

"I give up," he heard the too solid, sweaty teen complain. Spotting him speed walking toward him, the youth asked, "You in that Scramble too?"

"Yeah, but I put my vest down and forgot it. If you're all done, how about you loan me yours so I can finish? It's worth ten bucks."

He'd barely yanked the fluorescent orange nylon vest with the stenciled word "Scramble" on, before he took off running straight uphill. Now he fit right in, with an excuse to be running. But he only made it another steep block before pain sliced his side and his lungs were laboring. He needed another plan.

His shipment was lost, but he had to escape. That was the only way he would have a chance to change his name, appearance, and get the hell out of this country for a while. Slowing to a walk, trying to catch his breath and ease the cramp in his side, he reevaluated his odds on reaching the woods. Slim, very slim, with the town saturated with the law looking for him. And he was getting so paranoid, that every person he saw looked like a cop. Even that white-haired lady in the housecoat out pruning her rose bush.

Inspiration struck—he needed a hostage.

Jordan was cursing himself now for his last instructions to turn off her cell phone, because he desperately needed to get Ronnie right now and warn her they'd lost track of her ex-lover when he arrived in Edmonds.

It was useless to curse and swear over the bumbling that had let him slip by where it should have been an easy grab, trapping him in the glass tunnel where the passengers walked off the ferry, and glancing in each car as it stopped and squeezed between the portals of the ferry as they were released up onto the dock. Unfortunately that had been the extent of the rushed plan. They had never expected a man with a sailboat to take the ferry. And even if they'd had someone on the ferry, they wouldn't have been able to take him there without endangering the passengers. So they had tried to get in place in time and waited at the other end.

Then … lost him.

I instead of an international border, their suspect had run to a place he knew like the back of his hand. A place where he knew people.

Jordan swore to himself as he jogged uphill on Main Street for the Center where Rhonda had decided to go with Sam to her Writer's Conference. She said it was because she'd be bored hiding out otherwise and admired the bestselling author that was giving the keynote speech for the conference. But Jordan suspected it had as much to do with giving Sam her moral support.

He couldn't help but chuckle a little, even as he jogged up the steep hill in his suit and dress shoes, hanging onto his tie so it didn't whip around and slap him in his face, passing people jogging downhill in neon orange vests. There was just something funny about using the word moral and Rhonda in the same sentence, since she delighted so much in openly being just the opposite. But deep down, she was probably the most generous, caring woman he knew.

Except for his Sam, of course.

What a pair those two were! Miss Prim and Ms. Not Even Close!

He stopped laughing as he dodged to keep from bowling a window shopper over. Remembering the seriousness of the current situation, he tried to catch his breath and run uphill faster, his mouth grim.

Maybe Ronnie would know some contact or drinking buddy of her ex-lover that they hadn't had under surveillance. It might be their only hope to catch him before he got out of the county.

He knew they had an agent near the Center, but he had other duties. Jordan's only duty now was to get to his wife and warn her best friend, no one else would be worrying about them today. His wife and his best-friend-in-law, he corrected himself with a little smile.

A hostage! Perfect. But he did not want someone's grandmother.

What he needed was an extremely high-profile hostage. Someone that would freeze the local law enforcement in its tracks, not willing to take any chances because she was close to them. Close to a top authority locally that would and could make a deal for her.

Someone like the Prosecutor's beloved new wife. And she just happened to be close at hand and, his grin was nasty, he knew right where to find little Sam.

Cutting back across the street, he dove into the darkness beneath a concrete bridge that spanned the gap between the library and the Frances Anderson Center, but hearing a whistle he threaded back through the parked cars to exit on the Dayton street side, away from any search on main.

A series of concrete steps climbed from street level up onto the Plaza. He would look just like a contestant trying to find his way back to the playfield finish line on the other side of this complex, confused by its jumble of stairs, ramps, and interconnected buildings. He started trying doors into the back of the former school building. Then saw people passing through a door down a short stairwell and he rushed over following down those steps into the building.

For a moment the dim light disoriented him, then he realized he'd stumbled on one of the old wide school corridors with doors opening on both sides—and convenient signs noting which classrooms were in use for the writer's conference. The doors were closed now; the corridor emptied. Shrugging out of the orange vest, he let it slide from his shoulders to the floor, using his foot to stuff it behind a waste can. Prowling down the hallway, he peered in the glass panel tops of each door, and finally spotted his quarry.

Bett Bone

Samantha Campbell—Mrs. Prosecutor—sat in the middle of a row toward the front of the class. Edging quietly inside, pausing to smile apologetically for being late at the few heads that turned his way, he waited back by the door. His target was not one of the people who had turned to look when he entered, so he tried to decide whether he should just wait until the class filed out past him...

"What the hell are you doing here, asshole?"

Shit! He hadn't spotted his formerly favorite brunette, auditing the class from the opposite back corner near the windows. Damn bitch! Didn't she realize she had interrupted and drawn everyone's attention? Trying to make his plan still work, he smiled charmingly and he moved quickly over to Rhonda.

"Hey, sorry I'm late, sweetheart." Grabbing her elbow like a vise, he turned and apologized nicely, "No need to disrupt all these nice people now, dear. Excuse us, please continue."

His other arm locked around her waist and he buried his lips against her ear like a kiss, but snarled with soft menace.

"I have a knife and a gun, so shut up bitch, or someone is getting hurt. You first, then Sam." She had enough sense to settle down and smile to the crowd, before they turned back to their lecturer.

Seeing Sam still turned in their direction, a look of concern on her face, he ordered, "Now," his face was still pressed to her ear. "I want you to motion your little buddy to come back here. Do it now!" He emphasized his demand with a prick of his knife in her rib cage——one that would draw blood.

Rhonda waved to her friend so he could see her motioning, but frowned an urgent warning to keep her from coming, which Potter couldn't see.

But poor sweet Sam ignored Ronnie's scowl and the warning in her eyes, and slid out of her chair and quietly moved back to join them.

Potter pulled her in front of him, making sure she saw the knife pressing into Rhonda's ribs, before turning her to face the room, like Rhonda, screening him in the corner.

"You two bitches keep your months shut, and when everyone leaves we go last. You two are going to walk me out of here as my hostages, and get me to your car. Behave and everything will be fine."

Rhonda snorted, earning herself another little stab from the knife. All three stood silently in the corner of the room, pretending to watch the lecturer, but each desperately trying to come up with a plan.

While they were looking for him at the ferry, the marina, on the exit route roads south to Seattle, scouring the beaches, and on the streets of the town, their suspect was getting a free lesson from a noted author on how to create memorable characters.

Until the door to the classroom flew wide open again, and the disheveled tie-askew prosecutor, Potter had reason to hate, appeared in the doorframe.

Shifting his knife to Sam's throat, Potter pulled her back against his chest, his forearm wrapped around her waist.

Jordan Campbell immediately blanched and raised his hands out to his sides, palms open, while the classroom erupted in screams and shouts. Everyone shoved to get to the far corner of the room and duck down, out from between the two angry men.

Jordan felt a wave of helpless pain weaken his joints to see his beloved Samantha at Potter's mercy. But he couldn't take any chances with the love of his life in the asshole's grasp. He tried to slow his heartbeat, take a deep breath, but he couldn't calm himself, so he spoke as quietly as he could. He shot a quick glance at Rhonda frozen beside Sam, relieved to see her looking calm and quiet.

"You don't want to do this, Peter. There are a lot of innocents here, pal, don't get them in the middle of this. Just let her go, and I'll let you walk out of here."

"Innocent? Innocent!" His laugh was tinged with desperation. "This isn't any innocent, Campbell, this is your wife! And that sneaky, traitorous bitch's best friend. She's part of this, so shut up! Now! I want you to take that jacket off, very slowly, one arm at a time. Keep the other hand where I can see it. Then turn around and face the wall."

"I'm not armed, this isn't necessary..."

"Just shut your mouth and do it! Now!"

The shrieks in the room had gone dead silent.

As Jordan obeyed, he was able to hear a tiny moan behind him from Sam. His jaw clenched so hard it almost broke like his heart did when he heard the small sound abruptly cut off as Potter moved his forearm to her throat and choked Sam into silence.

What Potter had never reckoned on was the one woman in the room that was overdressed for the occasion. Most of the attendees wore fairly casual clothes to the conference. Any who knew how bad the parking was near the center, with hundreds of attendees, wore comfortable shoes.

But not Ms. Rhonda Sayles.

She had purchased a new pair of massively expensive red designer heels recently and, determined to wear them, told Sam the long hike in heels would just insure she got her money's worth out of the small amount of shoe leather they contained. The sharply pointed toe, and extra high heels would have been called fuck-me shoes by a naughty mouthed person—which Ronnie was, and did. But it turned out she was wrong—slightly.

While her ex-lover was concentrated on Jordan, his back to her, legs widespread and braced to hold Sam immobile, the overdressed woman slipped behind him, swung her leg back, and kicked hard with her pointed toe, getting him square in his cojones.

"Fuck *you*! Let go of my friend, butt wipe!" Rhonda shouted.

And he did, crumpling to the floor where he could better admire her deadly *!#@! rechristened shoes, which were the same crimson color as his face.

As Sam rushed into Jordan's arms, Ronnie dusted her hands together dramatically for the crowd and, with a smug smile, boasted to her friend.

"Don't ever let me hear you complain again that I didn't get my man, Sam."

Laughing helplessly and a little hysterically, Sam turned to congratulate her friend, but her mouth froze open and her eyes went round.

chapter twenty-one

Jordan shouted.
"Look out!"
Potter hadn't stayed down.
But he wasn't up for long.

The undercover agent that had been positioned at the playfields earlier, at the start of the Scramble, had made a few loops around the Center complex, as much from nerves as need, as he heard the chatter from the fruitless search over his ear mike.

The original Edmonds Elementary School built as a wood frame structure in 1891, had been replaced with a brick Spanish Mission style three story L-shaped block building in 1927—though it had not been damaged in the big downtown Edmonds fire of 1909. It had since sprouted a welter of single story additions and wings, and later been attached to the Plaza terrace. It was a fascinating welter of nooks, crannies, staircases and ramps for him to explore, trying to feel useful.

As he was completing a circuit back to the upper playfield, he passed the main lobby entrance that fronted on Main Street. A large sign set in the landscaping proudly proclaimed the Frances E. Anderson, Cultural and Leisure Center, named after, not a politician, but a revered citizen, woman, teacher, principle, and president of the Woman's Improvement Club founded in 1910, and later organizations that created the Art's festival.

He admired strong women.

He was smiling as he passed the entrance, then thought he heard screams from his right. Bending low, he slipped into the shrubbery and worked his way along the wall to a classroom wing that jutted west. He crouched lower beside the waist high block wall beneath the series of paneled windows. In the lowest panel of windows was one of those old fashioned swing out windows that had been opened to provide ventilation to the crowded classroom.

He listened a moment, surprised to hear the prosecutor's voice. Taking a quick peek over the sill, he ducked back down. The perp and the women had their backs to him, but he had seen the knife.

He was able to see the ceiling of the classroom, and the exposed metal pipes that crisscrossed the room. He was determining if he could enter the window quietly enough to leap for a pipe and swing a kick that would temporarily paralyze the man so he would drop the knife, when he popped his head up for one final check of the situation.

Before he could act his favorite woman curled the man forward and down with a high heel attack on his groin, causing him to release his victim—who turned out to be Samantha Campbell.

Jake was already rolling over the open window ledge when he saw Potter rise behind Rhonda. Spinning on the floor he kicked his foot hard against the side of the suspect's kneecap, popping his joint and putting him down fast. He had rolled and pinned the man spread eagle on the floor, checking for weapons, before Rhonda even realized the dark blur that came through the window was someone familiar.

Taking a long look at her rescuer laying at her feet, she asked the DEA agent, in a style unique to Rhonda, "Well, if it isn't Call-me-Jake. I suppose you just dropped by to see if I'm ready yet? I must say I *am* grateful—*very* grateful." She gave him a wicked, promising smile.

But she wasn't very happy with him a few minutes later.

"I can't believe you took my shoe for evidence!"

"Just one," he replied with an amused smile, before shoving her in front of the TV cameras while he dissolved into the background, slipping away unseen, and unheralded—just as it needed to be.

The television news camera broadcast live from the scene.

A tall, flamboyant brunette towered over the fresh faced male reporter holding the microphone to her face—even without her shoes.

She was smiling directly into the camera as she spoke to him, shaking her head slowly saying, "...No, no, please. Don't call me a hero. I'm not a hero. I much prefer the term heroine." And without ceasing her grin into the news camera, and only slightly deepening her voice, added, "And if you don't stop referring to me as a senior citizen, I'm going to cut your b..."

"Ronnie!"

A tiny blonde lady lunged into one side of the frame, gripping the heroine's arm, turning to beam into the camera, also. The newsman's eyes widened suddenly, registering the threat to his anatomy, and edged out the other side of the frame, motioning frantically for the camera man to stop filming.

"My friend is truly a heroine," gushed the blonde. "She saved everyone in the room! Who knows what would have happened if she hadn't...

"Pasted him!" The two women said in unison with delighted grins, just before the camera cut away from the dangerous heroine.

Watching in the conference room at the prosecutor's office, Jordan, Shelley, Detective Mallory, and the undercover DEA agent all howled with laughter until tears came to their eyes.

"That Ms. Sayles sure has a lot of brass."

"Thank God, my wife caught her in time. Don't they look great?"

"Pasted him? Everyone is starting to talk like young Timmy."

"That woman has guts, even if her choice of weapon was a bit bizarre."

Their various comments where tinged not only with humor and pride, but a giddy sense of relief that all had ended well—and they had their man.

Or rather, Rhonda had *her* man.

But hardly in the traditional sense that her best friend, Samantha, had wished!

There had been a closed unpublicized private session later at the prosecutor's offices to honor those whose faces would never grace the news cameras, and to gather taped depositions while memories were fresh and vivid.

Two civilians had been instrumental to the investigation and arrest, their part would remain unknown, their identities disguised on tapes never meant to be part of the public record at trial—except in direst need. They had been quietly thanked and honored by the task force.

One was the young teen girl from Friday Harbor on San Juan Island, that styled herself a modern Nancy Drew and would receive a donation to her college fund to pursue her interest in criminology. When Detective Mallory congratulated her and presented her with a Junior Detective shield with a nameplate that read Drew, N, she was in heaven.

The undercover DEA agent videotaped his deposition with his face disguised. After a lifetime spent undercover, he would be retiring and transitioning to a more public and normal life. After completing his own debriefing, the agent made a point of introducing himself to the young teen who flushed, horribly embarrassed, when he shook her hand and told her, "Just call me Jake."

He grinned at her, amused, and never mentioned he knew she had tailed him all over the island on her bicycle.

She didn't mention it either—but she wasn't aware of how easily he'd spotted her. She thought it might be way cool to grow up to be an undercover agent.

Then, on a more serious note, after the teen and her parents had left, the other citizen taped his statement. He was a former drug user that had done an extremely dangerous service, going back to old contacts, back into a dark underground world of drugs, to find information, routes, whispers, rumors, anything that might give the DEA and police leads they could not find themselves—never having lived the same streets and alleys of Seattle in their youth.

To those on the street suspicious of his reformed life as an anti-drug advocate, with law enforcement connections ...?

"Man, I know all the right people," Kevin had told them, voice desperate, limbs twitching like a junkie's. "And they trust me, you know, and that's gold for you dudes. Gold! I can let you know things, like ... like if a big bust is coming down, whatever man, just give me a hit, I'm shaking for it bad…"

As his deposition continued, Shelley listened, chills traveling her spine, sick with fear over the risks he had taken, and miserable with guilt at ever having doubted. She owed him a huge apology.

The DEA agent had taken up the trails and tidbits, and clues from the citizens and followed up, often they paralleled or added the puzzle piece to his own investigations. His follow-up made it unlikely either citizen would need to ever testify in court, but tapes were made and stored for now, just in case. They would be sealed from discovery by the defense, and destroyed if the other evidence sources proved sufficient.

She'd surprised him, arriving for their date dressed like she was ready to grill a defendant in a court of law, maybe he should be worried. But he couldn't help but be stirred by the different look. She always dressed casual, though classy, for their outings with Timmy. That was what he was used to seeing her wear—except that one time, when he had gotten her beautifully bare.

Her dove gray pinstripe jacket was cut loose, meant to be soft, but professional, and hide her figure; except he could still see where the softness brushed the outer plumpness of her breasts. The tailored labels made a V that his eyes eagerly followed from her creamy throat, lightly gilded with the sun from their day of pool play, delicate as the gold chain that slithered between the open neck of her white silk blouse to where his eyes plunged and probed, more enticed than deterred by the business-like apparel. The pencil slim gray skirt, though loose again, and disguised by the long jacket, just made him think of shimmying it down those sleek misty hose-sheathed legs.

Kevin smiled at his thoughts, determined never to let Shelley know that it was much more arousing to picture undressing her from her business suit, than a bikini, and loose and soft could be more erotic than tight and straining. He had the tight and straining handled himself, he thought ruefully as he shifted uncomfortably, his eyes lifting to capture hers before she ventured on her own visual exploration.

Her thoughts were clearly not where his were, her blue eyes earnest and worried, her face looked much too serious.

"Hey, what is it, lady?" He asked, softly. "I'd think you would be ready to celebrate." He moved closer to wrap his arms around her waist, caught a faint gardenia scent as light and lovely as the woman, but she held her palms out to ward him off, keep him away.

When Shelley was cleared from her legal responsibilities and reports at the office, she sought out Kevin immediately. She was still wearing her business suit, but it gave her confidence, so she hadn't gone home to change before going to Kev's apartment to confess.

Despite his warm welcome, she avoided his arms, needing to face the truth first, get it over with. A man that had acted with such unselfish honor had to know that she'd let him down, lacked faith in him, probably did not deserve his friendship—if not more. It was only fair to let him free himself to find someone he could trust. She couldn't bear to lose him, but she cared too much to keep him falsely.

"I...," Shelley swallowed, squared those business like shoulders, and raised her chin, "Kevin, I'm afraid I have a confession to make, before ... well, before anything else."

Shelley didn't want to remember those niggling doubts, wondering why Kevin had suddenly turned so romantic from an acquaintance/friendship, worrying he wanted to get close to her—or, at least, close to the task force investigation—for some hidden reason.

She did not wish to recall those nasty thoughts that had arisen after she heard the suspect had green eyes.

Heard it after a night of lovemaking that left her emotions vulnerable, when she wondered where he disappeared to for long stretches with no explanation. Had it been easier to think he had been betraying himself and his cause, than it had been to think he had been betraying her with another woman? Or that he was intimate with her just to gain inside secrets? Those were very insecure thoughts, very selfish thoughts, very scary thoughts.

Was it not natural that she would wonder—even for a moment—when she was told of a man, a handsome man with green eyes, a regular guy, not a drug user, that the first man that would come to her mind was the man whose bed she'd just left? Then in the next moments to remember his background, to recall that he had said he would do anything for the money to support his shelter. *Anything?*

And what about her own fears? Was she falling for the old weakness she'd heard blinded females—fought endlessly in her struggle to make a career in law enforcement—that women let their emotions interfere with their judgment? "That's just a cop out," she had laughingly told one annoying old cop, "so you old boys can protect your jobs."

It didn't feel quite so funny when she found herself wondering if *she* might temporarily be suffering from that disease, might be wearing blinders, when it came to Kevin.

So she had ruthlessly tried to correct any problem by overbalancing the scales to the other side. Questioning every word, look, action, intention, shoving trust and intimacy aside to shield her eyes from the warmth and sunlight that were her feelings for the man.

Trying to believe in him, and trying not to, at the same time.

And Jordan had asked her not to share any information on the case with anyone. She wouldn't have, he knew that. All law enforcement personnel knew that perpetrators tried to insert themselves into an investigation, or close to an investigator to find out how much the cops knew. So why? Why had Jordan specifically told her 'not even Kevin'? As a reminder, or as a targeted caution? That had probably reinforced her worries more than anything, as she knew that Jordan and Kevin had some sort of cooperation on an earlier case, though she never knew the details.

Yet Jordan still invited Kevin to all his barbeques, was friendly and casual with him, laughed with him, and knocked the supports out from under her suspicions. But did Jordan do that because he trusted him, or so he could keep a better eye on Kevin?

God, it gave her all such a headache—and heartache. Because her heart was feeling wonder, even love, and her head kept screaming caution, back off. And so she had—or tried to—and mostly failed. And Timmy, god, he was devoted to the man, idolized him, except for a territorial possessiveness of her.

That had been another fiasco warning her to keep her distance and perspective. But Tim and Kevin had had a young man to main man talk that seemed to have resolved that problem—for them, anyway.

And, oh god, she had never really believed it of him anyway. Not really. Had she?

"I can see it all spinning around in your head like a Class 5 tornado."

Kevin's words startled her.

Her heart twisted that she might have hurt him; that he might have seen those doubts in her mind; that even a moment of her doubt would have wounded him after all he had done, the risks he had taken.

"Don't think I didn't know what you thought when you heard about the green-eyed dealer and remembered I used to be heavy in the drug scene." He watched her shake her head.

"Yes," he said, his voice firm, but not angry, as he took hold of her shoulders. "You are a prosecutor, Shel, I understand. It's okay."

"But I..." She couldn't look at him, focused her eyes on his chest. She took a deep breath, opened her mouth to confess and spill it all ...

Then he did the most amazing thing.

He apologized to her!

"I took advantage of your strength. We all did. I'm sorry I couldn't tell you. And I knew that you would not talk to me about the case. I knew that you would start to think the worst, and as cruel as it seems, it was intentional. Partly so you would keep your distance, and partly so you would be just wary enough so that anyone watching your reactions would see that lack of total trust

"And I knew they would watch you. I bragged of being connected to inside information as part of my cover, implying I had a lady that...

"Gawd! This sounds so brutal. I'm so sorry. I used you. We all used you, Shelley."

Her face was stark white, eyes wide and wounded looking, he reached out to brush his fingertips across her cheek, as she just stared at him.

"I didn't do it to hurt you, I did it because I ..." Realizing his guilt and awkward apology was making things worse, he buried his head between his hands, took a few deep breaths, and started again.

"Maybe I better tell you how things happened" He spoke in a quiet voice, not looking up at her.

"It started with you, and me, and Timmy. We became friends. I admired you, had fun with you, got to know you better and respected you more, liked you more. A lot more. You're beautiful, smart, such a great sport," his head came up and he looked right into her pretty blue eyes, as he added, "You had become very special to me."

Turning his head away, staring into the distance, he shook his head, "I was just getting up the nerve to ask you out, just the two of us, when this whole situation came up. I was approached to see if I could maybe help with old contacts. I had to help—.

"But, dammit, I was pissed at the timing! I was just getting close to you and I hoped... well, long short, I wanted to help, but I didn't want to just disappear from your life for months, and give up a chance with you—if I had one. Sooo...

"When we worked out a plan, how I'd claim a law enforcement inside connection to ease back in, I was selfish. I suggested you. We all agreed it was a good cover. You were a logical choice, a girlfriend that might give out inside info without realizing it. In the eyes of the street dudes, I mean.

"All of us knew you, knew that would never happen, and knew you were a strong woman that knew the ropes, and would volunteer if asked. But you could not know. It was too dangerous. All your reactions had to be natural. It wasn't just Potter watching you, there were others, and we didn't know who all then.

"So I was to stay close with you. Exactly what I wanted to do anyway, at least at the start. And I was to hang out with your other law enforcement friends. So I started easing my way in to my cover the weekend of the arts fair..."

"What! Even that? You were *close* to me at the fair because of... not Timmy I guess, but your secret job? Was that what it all was? Even when we..."

"Whoa. Stop! No. Well ...," Oh man, he never should have opened his mouth. But he had to. She deserved this, needed to see it clearly. It would kill him if he tried to keep it secret and she ever heard or guessed herself—and was hurt more later through a misunderstanding.

He held his palms up, seeing the murder in her eyes, before the pain.

"Please, Shel, let me tell you everything first. Please try and stay calm. Wait to kill me later. But my story does have a happy ending, if you let me get that far alive."

"Fine. Speak fast." The look on her face scared him.

"Okay, so," he ran his fingers up her arm. She stepped out of his reach.

"Right, so yes of course. All of it was fake," he tried for humor. "That bracelet I bought you to match your eyes? GPS tracking device with a voice recorder."

He watched those matching blue eyes go big and round and started laughing.

She did not.

"Joke, just a joke, sweetheart."

Her eyes narrowed, lips white.

Foolishly he tried to cajole his way through this rough part, reaching his arms around her, holding tighter when she struggled.

"And the pool? We heard that you were hiding a drug smuggler in your bikini. So, of course, I had to bring you over and strip search you just to check it out. For the job. Nothing personal, of course—

"Shel, laugh, *please*." He covered her face with loud, wet kisses. Nuzzling her ear, he whispered, "Never did find him, even after flipping you over in bed a few times, but I do know where you are ticklish, and if you don't smile . . . expect torture."

She did smile, but against his chest where he couldn't see it, but it tinted her voice when she tried to sound exasperated, demanding, "Just tell me the rest of it!"

"Sorry, sorry. I'm nervous so I'm making asinine jokes."

"Why are you nervous?" Suspicion edged her voice.

"Because I took one of the biggest gambles in my life…"

"Oh, of course, the risk of being back on the streets…"

"No Shel, not that. *You*. Us! That's what's at risk. I need to get this all out in the open with you, before… Hey, just be patient with me, please.

"Then two things happened, about the same time," he continued. "First, I was back into my old Seattle street scene, picking up rumors, little more. Then I connected with an old buddy my age, who is wanting to retire from the life. He had just got me patched in as the link on a phone cut out designed to distance the important guys from the lower levels. He recommended me as a guy that knew the ropes and could be trusted. He's planning on getting out, moving to Idaho, getting a new name, some land to graze a couple horses, spending his winters ice fishing, and dying of natural causes. He said he didn't mind doing the favor cause he was set to disappear. He's tired of seeing young boys strung out and dying. But the point is, I was in, connected. Things would become more dangerous.

"Second, Jordan had just warned me that a tip had come in that would implicate me, and he was going to have to release the information to the task force; meaning you would hear it. I didn't know what the future would hold, but knew the time had come we'd have to be more distant, and I needed… I wanted and needed to be with you.

Just once, if that was all we'd have. But I wanted to imprint that memory in my head—and, hopefully, in yours.

"I know you, Shel, know about you. You don't let men in easily —or ever, according to the scuttlebutt I'd heard. A very dedicated professional woman focused totally on her career and the law, though it is love of justice, not ambition, which feeds that focus. So when you trusted *me*, when you let *me* love you, when you opened your arms so fully and beautifully to me that night . . .

"Well, I fell hard, completely, the search was over before I ever realized it had started. You gave me your trust. First. Before all the rest began. With Timmy, and then with yourself. You gave me your trust first, and I took it. I took it, and flew with it, and it freed me to do what was needed.

"I took that open trust of yours and I used it so cruelly, babe, but *I* trusted *you*. I trusted *your* inner toughness, your resilience, your heart and sense of fairness, to let me depend completely on you to give me a chance someday to explain, to make it right.

"I know it hurt you." Kevin's voice was anguished, earnest. "It hurt me to leave you that morning. But I gambled that what we had was strong enough to survive the hurt and doubt. That is how deeply I knew it was you, and *only* you, for me. Knew it would be me and you always, through anything, no matter how hard. That if we survived this challenge we would *never* lose each other's hearts.

"But it is all over now, and I suspect Jordan, at least, knew I was not romancing you for any job. Ah, good, *now* you are smiling and listening. I really want to just toss you in bed and show you how much I love you... Yes, I love you, Shel, but I have some serious stuff I need to tell you that I'm not done with yet. You need to know this.

"So. I apologize. I beg you to see the love and trust I gave you when I so greedily took your love, your trust, as if I already owned it.

"I beg you," stepping back, he lowered to one knee, smiled at her gasp, gathered her hands, "I beg you to forgive me, and love me, and trust me again so I may start spending my lifetime making up for this.

"Will you, Shel? Will you be my main woman? My beautiful wife? Will you marry me?"

"Oh. My. God."

"Close enough." Kevin stuffed a ring on her finger, jumped up laughing, and spun her around in his arms.

chapter twenty-two

It was a most common wedding, though it was not the *expected* wedding.

At least not the one Sam had expected.

But she certainly hadn't expected her own either. And, honestly, to say she expected was an overstatement. She had hoped, really, hoped that the love, well, lust affair (blush) that had its start at the Arts and Crafts Festival, would bloom to something real and permanent for Ronnie. Sam had hoped to see it come to vows instead of blows and howls. But...

And maybe what was surprising about this wedding was that no one had paid attention to the classic love affair developing right beneath their eyes. Eyes distracted by Ronnie's torrid, and near terminal, affair.

This was not the happy couple Sam thought she would see. But it was just as well—as it turned out.

And *this* romance *had* bloomed at the arts fair.

A young man with his girl at the fair, buying her a bracelet to match her eyes, so sweet, so lovely, so classic, such a normal, common, everyday tale. A young couple meets, they share a common interest and a growing bond. They walk a festival holding hands. He buys her a trinket she admires, then he sends her flowers. They fall in love quietly, completely.

Ahh, so sweet, and here they are now... Except, of course, it hadn't been *that* easy—it never was. But no matter how unnoticed, unexpected, or challenging, it seemed like a very common story.

Yes, it was a very common wedding—with flowers and friends, a blushing bride and nervous groom. Such a lovely couple glowing with love for each other, with smiles and a few tears from those attending. The reception followed with the cutting and sharing of cake, toasts, roasts, best wishes, the bride kissed, the groom's shoulder slapped, then the laughter and dancing—as expected.

Yet, every event has its little surprises.

Sam was listening, yet again, to her friend's grievances at the wedding rehearsal dinner the evening before the wedding.

"I still can not believe they collected my shoe for evidence," Rhonda complained. "Can't you get Jordan to do something, get them to release it? What good is one half of a pair of outrageously expensive designer shoes, I ask?"

Sam wondered if she should suggest Rhonda put a frame around her half, maybe hang it on the wall with a memorial plaque, like the police had framed the one in the evidence locker listed as "the lady's weapon of choice?".

Probably best not to mention that.

"You hardly ever wear your expensive shoes more than a few times anyway, Ronnie. Besides, think how much better it will be to wait until after the trial to wear them again. They'll be famous then."

"I guess," Rhonda grumbled. "I suppose I could go buy another pair in a different color," she mumbled in a suspiciously less than convincing tone.

Sam smiled and patted her hand.

"Why don't you buy a new outfit to go with it? Just to comfort yourself on your loss, of course."

"Yes, maybe I should," Rhonda agreed, distracted, glancing across the table to where Kevin spoke to one of his groomsmen, the undercover agent.

Sam was thinking that Ronnie never needed a justification to shop, knowing that wasn't the real issue here. Ronnie was still furious that she had allowed herself to be played for a fool by someone. And not just someone, but a *man!* An area of Ronnie's life where she was used to being in complete control. It was a crushing defeat for a woman of her nature—despite the fact that she won in the end. But without *the* shoe in her own hands to gloat over, it seemed to be taking longer for Ronnie's spirit and ego to heal.

"And just think," Sam continued to try to cheer her friend, "of the beautiful new dress and shoes you'll be wearing tomorrow, Ronnie."

"Doesn't count." Her friend said stubbornly.

"It should. Shelley let you pick out our attendant dresses after all. I love mine!" Then Sam's cheery smile faded. "I was hoping the next time I dressed up for a wedding it would be for yours, my friend," she sighed.

"Don't be ridiculous, Sam. I'm always the bridesmaid, never the bride, and thank God in her heaven for that!"

"I just thought, well, you'll be retiring soon, it would give you something to do," Sam offered lamely.

"If I feel the need for someone following me around nipping at my high heels, I'll get a dog."

"You're hopeless, Ronnie." Sam laughed..

"No, actually, I am not. I'm hopeful, ever hopeful, that there will always be another, ever better man to...," she paused to dance her eyebrows naughtily, "explore."

And before the night was over, a gallant man volunteered— to be explored, discovered, and mapped in exquisite detail.

When the haughty brunette declined his offer, he blackmailed her, with just one word.

Vegas.

Jordan and Jake had been discussing the closure of the smuggling case off to the side of the reception room, after cadging a second piece each of the wedding cake, when the music changed to a slower beat.

"Well, if you'll excuse me," Jake grinned, "I think I'll see if I can hunt down a tall, sassy brunette. See if I can talk her into a tango with me."

Jordan grinned and nodded, watching the broad shouldered man disappear in the crowd of wedding guests. He suspected Jake probably meant "tangle" rather than "tango; he looked as if he relished the prospect. Jordan was fond of Sam's best friend, but a man never knew what to expect when he tangled with her. She could be one tough woman.

He should know. The first time he'd tangled with her, she'd been busy hiding a crime that wasn't. Now the woman had seen to it that her lover was sent to jail!

Scary woman. Though … she did have a softer side—or maybe just a spot—devoted mostly to Sam and her children. He'd even thought Ronnie might have fallen for the potter, almost thought the next wedding would be hers, instead of Shelley's.

Ha! He should have known better. The man that wanted Rhonda would probably have to hunt her down, render her unconscious, and cuff her to get her to agree to vows.

But, Jake had cuffs. Jordan smiled to himself. And the man clearly looked like he was on the hunt. Jordan liked the guy, raising his glass in a silent toast to wish him luck, he set off to find his own sexy, but sweet, woman.

"May I have this dance?"

Rhonda didn't even turn at the question or soft touch on her arm.

"No, thanks," she brushed him off, "maybe later."

"But the next dance will be faster, not slow, and sultry, and close like this one."

His words, and the husky male voice that delivered them slowly, had Rhonda turning despite herself.

"But I am still angry at you."

"No, you are not," his grin was unconcerned. "You are angry at yourself."

He had her in his arms before she could push him away, where the intense magnetic attraction between their bodies would keep her bonded and close to his heart.

At least for a few moments.

Sam watched Ronnie ease onto the dance floor with Jake, and fold herself into the undercover agent's arms. She hadn't had an opportunity to talk to her friend all day, but Ronnie looked like she was enjoying herself in what could only loosely be called a slow dance. It *was* slow. And it was definitely close. But it looked much too sultry to be called dancing. Sam was feeling a little steamy herself, just watching the couple.

Her own handsome lover swirled her out on the dance floor and pulled her close, noting the direction her eyes had been focused.

"So how do you think your friend Ronnie is doing after the attack and arrest, and all? Think she's okay?"

Sam smiled up at him, "Oh, you know, Ronnie. She'll be fine." Snuggling closer to her husband, with a secretive smile, she added, "In fact, she looks to me like she's thinking of going … undercover."

"Really?" Jordan thought about it, as he tucked his wife under his chin, swaying more than dancing to the music. "She might make a good undercover agent."

Sam laughed softly against his chest, shaking her head. She didn't bother to enlighten her husband. She'd rather drag him home after the party was over, and give him a demonstration of her meaning.

Sam finally caught Ronnie alone, with a laughing challenge.

"Hey, lady, where the heck were you this morning? I called everywhere for you, Ronnie! Wow, you look great! How *do* you survive those heels? If my feet could take them, I should be the one wearing them. That way with those on me and you in these flats, we'd be about the same height. Well, closer. I feel like I'm talking to a skyscraper," the petite Sam laughed. "So where did you run off to this morning?"

Rhonda seemed startled, her smile forced and tense, in the gaiety of the celebration.

"Oh. Hi Sam. I, ah…," her hands fluttered uncharacteristically before she clenched them together. "You were a lovely matron of honor, Sam. Wasn't it a nice wedding?" Ronnie reached up scraping the dark hair that always swung sleekly around her check back behind her ear, ruining the normally sleek and perfect hairstyle. "You know, I thought…"

"Ronnie," Sam grabbed one of her friend's nervous hands to still it, "What on earth is wrong with you? Are you feeling okay?"

"Actually, I am feeling a little… ah… off today, you know? I think I'll make an appointment with the doctor next week. Maybe get my annual physical while I am it, get my shots, you know," her voice dropped to a low mutter, "maybe get spayed."

"What?" Sam choked out a laugh.

"Joke." Ronnie tried to flash her a grin that failed miserably.

"Are you sick? Coming down with something?" Sam asked, worried now, automatically reaching up a hand to check Ronnie's forehead, that her friend managed to swat away.

"Stop that. I'm fine." Rhonda gave up the pretense. "No, oh hell, Sam, I'm a mess."

"What is it? What's wrong?"

"It was *him*!" Her friend stated firmly, cobalt eyes flashing with temper. Jaw rock hard, her hands no longer flitted nervously, but clenched in more Ronnie-like fists at her side, her elegant nostrils flared as if scenting battle. She looked like a raven haired warrior queen in designer label armor, and heels spiked like weapons.

Sam almost laughed at the transformation.

Ronnie never had done confused and helpless well.

Biting her tongue, Sam asked, solicitously, "Him what? Did he hurt you? Is this the him I think you mean? The agent?"

Rhonda's eyes shifted again, turning sly and seductive, as a memory flashed.

"Hurt me? No," she smirked, "fortunately I'm very flexible . . But," abruptly she snapped out of dreamy mode back to sheer anger, "I don't trust him!"

"Why?" Sam asked softly, worried. Surely it wasn't another betrayal, like the potter? Even Ronnie wasn't tough enough to withstand another betrayal so soon, but the agent was a cop, and an honorable man, surely he hadn't...?

"He kept me there all night!" Rhonda snarled, incensed.

Oh, God! Sam thought. Handcuffs? Bondage? No that couldn't be the problem—not a problem for Ronnie, anyway. Sam felt a flush rise at her wicked thoughts, but Ronnie would probably object to not being the one in charge. It appeared her friend had already been doing her undercover work, last night.

"And I mean *all* night," Ronnie growled. "That's why I was missing this morning"

She huffed out a breath, trying to regain some control, her voice turning low and confidential. "You know I never stay over for breakfast, Sam. Never! The damn man probably drugged me, " she complained, but less forcefully."

Sam couldn't believe it. "No! Do you really think so, Ronnie?"

"What else explains it?" Rhonda snapped, hands tugging at her hair again.

"Ah," Sam blanked, "Explains what exactly? You mean spending the whole night *and* morning with him?"

Rhonda folded her arms across her chest, one outrageously expensively clad toe angrily tapped the floor. "And that is not the worst of it!" she snarled.

"Oh, dear!" Sam bit her lip. It wouldn't do to giggle when her friend was clearly supremely piss … agitated, her prim mind automatically corrected.

"Guess where I woke up?" Ronnie asked, her eyes narrowed, voice laced with disgust.

"I'm truly afraid to ask," Sam admitted with all honesty, and mentally braced herself.

"On. His. Chest!" The words ground out hard and evenly spaced as if spelling disaster.

"His . . . chest? Oh. Well. That's not so bad," Sam sighed with relief and unclenched her eyes.

Catching Sam's expression, Rhonda was momentarily distracted. Frowning thoughtfully at her friend, she asked Sam, "What did you think I was going to say?" Seeing the pink tint rise up again in Sam's face, she sighed heavily, "Never mind. Anyway, really Sam, it was horrid. Just horrid. There I was still in his bed and it was . . m-m-morning! And…. worse yet," her voice dropped low, to groan, "I think I was... k-k- cuddling!"

Sam would never know how she managed to keep from laughing outright at the look of absolute rage on her friend's face.

"I do NOT cuddle! Slither…yes, but cuddle? Never!" Rhonda stated firmly, and maybe a little too loudly. She glanced quickly around the crowded room to make sure her secret shame was safe, before leaning close to whisper something even worse.

"No!" Sam gasped, throwing a hand up to cover her mouth. "Are you sure?" she asked, a suspicious gurgle in her voice.

"I'm pretty sure," Rhonda answered solemnly, stepping back to scan the room again, clearly embarrassed.

"But… snug . . . Snuggling?" Sam tried to sound aghast, but giggled helplessly.

"SHHhh!" The angry brunette hissed.

"Keep you voice down! So, now you see why I need to see a doctor right away. I've probably cracked a nerve, or something. I'm obviously coming down with some nasty, weakening disease," she spit out, before whirling to stomp off on six inch heels, as only Ronnie could manage.

Sam jumped as lips descended a moment later on her bare shoulder from behind, then enjoyed the familiar sizzle of nerves, as her husband nuzzled his way to her ear.

"Trouble?" he asked. "I saw Rhonda storm off in a huff. I know she's allergic to weddings, but did you two fight?"

"Oh, no, no," Sam replied, her voice choked, her eyes watering, she turned into him and buried her face against his chest, her shoulders shaking.

"Sam?" He gently eased her back to see if she was crying.

"Just another of her allergies acting up," his wife blurted, unable to hold back, she burst into laughter. He gave her a puzzled look, unable to resist smiling as she laughed until she had to brush tears from her cheeks.

Nothing could break down the prosecutor's stern barriers like his sweet, petite blonde.

"I actually came over to ask the most exquisite lady in the room to dance one last time. Shall we, darling?"

"Oh, Jordan, how sweet, but my feet ache."

"Not a problem, " he leaned over to place a kiss on her forehead, then wrapped her in his arms and lifted her into a slow, sultry dance, her toes nowhere near the floor.

Delighted, she stroked her hands over his cheeks, murmuring what a sweet and considerate man she had found, before wrapping her arms tightly and letting her head rest on his broad, strong shoulder.

"Do you think we will ever dance at Ronnie's wedding?" he murmured into her soft, scented hair a few moments later.

Sam's lips were at his throat when she answered. So distracted by her sweet nibbling on his neck, Jordan was sure he must have heard wrong!

Something about Ronnie getting spayed?

No matter.

Who knew if Ms. Rhonda Sayles would *ever* marry.

It would probably be a miracle and front page headline if she did. But that was a problem for Ronnie, and for another time, and another man. Jordan had his own priorities.

"Did I ever tell you that you are my miracle, Sam?" he whispered to his wife. "Why don't I take you home and show you, love. We've barely started on our own happily ever afters."

Samantha was more than ready to play honeymoon again, with her own special man.

As they headed home for their own private celebration, Sam recalled one of the most touching moments of the wedding that had come later on in the evening at the reception.

Everyone had kissed the bride and groom, toasted their health and happiness, and danced and drank to their own joyful state, when the music stopped and a request was made to clear the dance floor.

The bride had looked puzzled, especially when asked to return to the center. Everyone turned to watch, anticipating some private dance requested by the absent groom. Then that young rascal Timmy had stepped onto the floor, looking serious, or scared to death, or both.

Still dressed in his tuxedo from the ceremony, Timmy's 'manly' gelled hair was rapidly collapsing into the floppy, sandy chaos of a boy that had run, strutted, and bounced in celebration, but never, until now, walked so soberly and ceremonially. For this special moment he had even had his 'sissy' bow tie redone. Kevin, just as serious, followed him to the center of the floor and stood at Tim's back, facing his new wife.

Shelley's mouth opened to question what was up, when Timmy dropped to one knee before her. Her eyes widened with a startled glance up at Kevin to catch a quickly suppressed grin, and a very solemn nod, before she looked back down.

Tim's face earnest, blue eyes slightly wary, the young gent reached up and took Shelley's right hand in his. He swallowed, choked, put a finger up to yank his tied collar out of the way, and gulped again, his eyes steady on hers, before his voice came out in a croak.

"See, it's like this...," Timmy closed his eyes and grimaced when Kevin cleared his throat. Gazing back up at Shelley, the young lad started over with another gulp.

"You are like really special to me . . . um ... and I um ... like..," his voice dropped to a hoarse whisper, "love you, you know?" He peered up, warily.

Bravely keeping eye contact, Tim's voice strengthened.

"I am asking you to honor me and be my foster mother."

When Shelley just stared at him, speechless, he added quickly and a little desperately, "I mean. *Will* you be my foster mother?"

Shelley pressed her lips tight, blinking rapidly.

You could almost see her heart melt as soft sighs from the guests filled the silence.

"It's okay with Kev," the boy added desperately.

Dabbing her eyes, she gave Tim's hand an encouraging squeeze and trying to smile, asked her young suitor a sober question.

"Well, Timmy, does this mean you will mow my lawn for me? And bring all your friends over and let me feed them cookies and lemonade?" Her voice had became higher and tighter as she tried to hold her composure, and give Tim's request the serious consideration and respect that it deserved.

"Oh yeah, cool!" He grinned, then dropped her hand, bounced up, stuffed his hands in his pants pocket, then his jacket, pulled something out, dropped back on a knee, and grabbed her hand again.

His face was suddenly deeply serious again as he pleaded, "Please say yes. See, I even got a ring!"

"Oh!" Shelley clapped her other hand over her mouth. "It matches my bracelet."

Squinting up at her, he said, "Well, it's supposed to match your eyes." He shrugged, adding, "When they're not all watery like."

Impatient, he shoved the ring on the third finger of her right hand. "I got the ring last summer at the art fair. I knew I'd ask you sometime. And, Kev gave me credit." Another shrug, eyes flickering down.

"So? Whadda ya think? I'll be really good, and ..."

"Oh, Timmy! Yes! Yes, yes. I love you too! I'd be so honored!"

They nearly cracked heads as Tim bounced up into her arms.

Kevin had to clear his throat, before wrapping his new family in his embrace.

The guys pretended that all those happy tears rolling over their smiling faces all fell from Shelley's wet jeweled eyes.

epilogue

He caught the angry brunette by the arm outside, before she could escape, and spun her around.

"Just where do you think you are going, lady?"

"Home. Alone. Take your hand off me. And don't ever threaten to tell my best friends about that stupid weekend in Vegas, again. Or. You. Will. Regret it! There is no reason for them to know about that undercover sham. Besides, it was some Danny-boy guy with some ridiculous name, that I *fake* married," she tossed back over her shoulder as she twisted free and stomped off across the parking lot at a dangerous pace in high heels crunching over gravel.

He shook his head wearily, watching her. He needed to get the woman some sensible shoes.

He noted that she slowed down and added some sway to her hips, probably just to taunt him with what he was missing, if he knew Ronnie. Leaning back against the door post, he folded his arms and smiled at her antics, enjoying the show. He just let her go.

For now.

Ridiculous? Fake? Afraid not, sweetheart.

Daniel Jackson Hunter, the Third, to be precise. Good ole southern name. They called his father Daniel, he had a cousin Jack, so as a kid they had just called him Jake.

When he saw that she had safely reached her car and driven off in a spurt of gravel, he turned and went back inside humming the wedding march to himself, and smiling.

Too bad the legal Mrs. Jake wasn't there to appreciate it.

She would—eventually.

First he had to plan a way to inform her she really *was* married.

Without getting himself instantly divorced.

He should probably wear his bulletproof vest when he told her.

Author's Note

In this fictional work, I have taken very little literary license with the charms and locales of the town of Edmonds—a place truly dedicated to the arts throughout its history. Most notable, I have continually referred to the City of Edmonds as a town without apology because it still retains the warmth and cozy spirit of a town for all its size. To learn more about the early pioneer days of Edmonds, a 1950s era book—The Gem of Puget Sound—is fascinating in detail, including a 1910 politician campaigning with the promise to work for a breakwater for the harbor. The Port breakwater was not built until the 1960s, so ... some things clearly have not changed all that much.

I intentionally did not seek input on security or Port procedures from Port officials or local law enforcement for my fictional crimes, as I believe anyone inclined to attempt them as presented deserves a big surprise—especially when they try to land at the non-existent Z dock!

I have also moved a few events to fictional timelines and promise the only weapons ever brandished at the writer's conference are via the pen.

But if you come to Edmonds, you will see all its other charms are there to welcome you.

Enjoy. Bett

About the Author

Bett lives in the beautiful Pacific Northwest near what is now known locally as the Salish Sea and just an hour—or so, depending on the ferry lines—from the Olympic National Rainforest. Just a short drive in any direction brings plenty of scenic inspiration. In addition to reading every chance she gets, Bett loves to visit the national parks of the Northwest U.S.

Bett has written two books of her National Park Roads Series—*Buffalo Road* and *Going to the Sun Road*, about Montana's Parks, Yellowstone and Glacier, and is working on a third book in that National Parks series.

An Arts and Crafts AfFair is the second book in her "Beware of Boomer" romance trilogy, a trip down memory lane for the Boomer Generation.

Contact her by email : Bett@bettboneauthor.com

further reading

re:history

Cloud, R. V. (1953,1983). *The Gem of Puget Sound. Snohomish County Historical Society.*

re: Geology of the Area

Alt, D. &. Hyndman D (1984). *Roadside Geology of Washington. Missoula,MT: Mountain Press.*

Alt, D. & Hyndman D. (1995). *Northwest Exposures: A Geologic Story of the Northwest. Missoula: Mountain Press Publishing.*

Babcock, S. &.Carson, B (2000). *Hiking Washington's Geology. Seattle: Mountaineers.*

Williams, H. (2000). *The Restless Northwest: A Geologic Story. Pullman, WA: WSU Press .*

re: our teen's favorite series

Keene, C. (1965). *The Secret of Shadow Ranch - Nancy Drew Mysteries. NY,NY: Grosset & Dunlap.*

re: the real non-fiction Edmonds & the ARTS

The City Of Edmonds home page with Government Departments including the parks & rec dept/ Frances Anderson Center/ and the Arts Council & Commision/and its writer's conference can be found at: http://www.edmondswa.gov/

The annual arts festival—62yrs strong in June 2019— is thanks to a non-profit, all volunteer community group known as the EAFF-Edmonds Arts Festival Foundation. An amazing organization you will want to learn about at:https://www.edmondsartsfestival.com/

Other Stories by Bett

Can't get out to a National Park lately?

Hitch a ride with the National Park Road Series by Bett Bone

Enjoy amazing scenery, ancient stories, travel, romance and laughter.

**Visit Yellowstone in <u>Buffalo Road</u>
then travel on to NW Montana to
Glacier Park in <u>Going to the Sun Road</u>**

both available at Amazon

beware of boomer romances

Guilty Plot

Samantha Wilson is a boomer with an empty nest, an unfulfilled lifelong dream, and a determination to finally pursue it - no matter *what* it takes! Because if not now ... When?

Life has only embittered Jordan Campbell, though after shifting his career path he has become a successful prosecutor. And—— most unfortunately——a handsome bachelor. One without any respect or trust in, or time for beautiful women.

What will happen when these two boomers cross paths?

An ARTS and CRAFTS AfFAIR

Samantha, the new Mrs. Jordan Campbell is taking her best friend, Rhonda Sayles - *femme fatale* - to the Annual Arts Festival to help her with promoting her charity. She should have known that when she asked her pal to "Man the booth" she would take it *much* too literally!

There must be something in the festival air, or the charming, waterfront town that has couples thinking of romance - but surely there is another term to describe what Rhonda has a case of...?

But trouble is brewing under all the gaiety, events, and charming seaside scenery that has Sam's prosecutor husband extremely distracted and uneasy.

What *are* the odds that a guy named Peter Potter would actually become a ... Potter? Rhonda plans to do a thorough, in depth, and very personal investigation to check him out. If that "Call me Jake" guy will get out of her face.

coming next........> I DO KNOT

Coming Next

I Do Knot

Rhonda Sayles—*femme fatale*—has a few challenges on her hands, though her friend Samantha Campbell says the correct word would be 'battles' the way Ronnie approaches them.

Ms. Sayles has a lonely shoe, it's mate is locked in an evidence locker awaiting the trial of her former lover, Peter Potter, the potter. Which it turns out is not the real name of the drug smuggler.

It seems to be a problem with the lady and her lovers.

Her other challenge is that "Call me Jake" man, former undercover agent, and forever in her face!. He is claiming that Rhonda is . . . well, you'll see.

I DO KNOT is the third and final book in the Beware of Boomer Romance Series trilogy due out in 2020.